BY
ALEXANDER GORDON SMITH

ESCAPE FROM FURNACE

LOCKDOWN

SOLITARY

DEATH SENTENCE

FUGITIVES

EXECUTION

THE NIGHT CHILDREN:
AN ESCAPE FROM FURNACE STORY

EXECUTION

ESCAPE FROM FURNACE

5

ALEXANDER GORDON SMITH

EXECUTION
ESCAPE FROM FURNACE 5

FARRAR STRAUS GIROUX
NEW YORK

Farrar Straus Giroux Books for Young Readers
175 Fifth Avenue, New York 10010

Copyright © 2011 by Alexander Gordon Smith
First published in Great Britain by Faber and Faber Limited, 2011
Printed in the United States of America
Designed by Jay Colvin
First American edition, 2012
1   3   5   7   9   10   8   6   4   2

macteenbooks.com

Library of Congress Cataloging-in-Publication Data

Smith, Alexander Gordon, 1979–
    Execution / Alexander Gordon Smith. — 1st American ed.
        p.   cm. — (Escape from Furnace ; 5)
    Summary: Alex Sawyer has escaped his underground nightmare
to discover that the whole world has become a horrible prison run
by his nemesis, Alfred Furnace, and only Alex can stop him, even
if that makes him the executioner.
    ISBN 978-0-374-36224-9 (hardcover)
    ISBN 978-0-374-32239-7 (e-book)
    [1. Prisons—Fiction.   2. Fugitives from justice—Fiction.
3. Science fiction.   4. Horror stories.]   I. Title.

PZ7.S6423Exe 2012
[Fic]—dc23

                                                                    2012004870

THIS ONE'S FOR MY "CELLMATES"–

thanks for breaking out of Furnace with me.
There are too many of you to mention here,
but extra special thanks go to:

Sophie Hicks, for making the deal,
Julia Heydon-Wells and Wesley Adams, for making it real,
and Trevor Horwood and Karla Reganold, for making it readable.

See you on the other side!

EXECUTION

BENEATH HEAVEN IS HELL.
BENEATH HELL IS FURNACE.

ESCAPE FROM FURNACE 5

THE BOY

I ONCE KNEW A BOY. HIS NAME WAS ALEX SAWYER.

He was the boy who stared back at me from the mirror, a kid like any other. Not bad-looking, a little scrawny. You wouldn't have looked twice if you'd seen him on the street.

That boy, he's dead now. I let him die. But I want to tell you his story. I *need* to tell you his story.

I don't remember much of Alex's—of *my*—life before Furnace. It's a blur of faceless people and half-formed places. He had a family once, I think, a mom and a dad. And friends too. But he wasn't a good kid, I remember that much at least. He was a bully, and a thief. He took from the ones he loved and all he gave in return was grief. I can't even remember how it all started, only that he wanted things like shoes, a bike, a computer.

That's what I find hardest to believe about all this—not the truth about Furnace, or the monsters spawned inside the prison, but that Alex's life was destroyed because he was so desperate to get a new pair of sneakers.

Bullying in the playground, stealing the odd fiver at lunchtime, it wasn't enough. Alex and his best friend, Toby, started burgling houses, stealing cash and valuables every chance they could. One day they broke into a place they thought was empty. It wasn't. They were caught by silver-eyed giants in black suits and a shriveled figure with a gas mask stitched into its face. Toby was shot and Alex was framed for his murder—sentenced to life without possibility of parole in Furnace Penitentiary.

Furnace. The prison. I've been out for less than twenty-four hours but already my memories from inside are fading. Buried a mile beneath the ground, nothing but rock in every direction, it was a place that society put children they no longer wanted, where even their parents would forget them. It was a place where kids like Alex were buried alive.

But it was something so much worse than that too. The gas-masked wheezers stalked the cells, dragging inmates into the blood-drenched tunnels beneath the prison. Deformed creatures emerged in the dead of night, tearing their victims to pieces. And watching over it all was Warden Cross, a man as cruel and as dangerous as the devil himself, a man whose eyes were so full of madness, of hatred, of rancid glee, that meeting them was like watching yourself die a million times over.

Together with friends—Donovan and Zee—Alex made a plan to get out, smuggling gas-filled gloves from the kitchen and blowing a hole in the floor, jumping into an underground river. They did what nobody else had ever managed, they found a way out of Furnace. But that river only carried them as far as the tunnels below, and the unthinkable horrors of solitary confinement.

It was here that I—no, not me, that *Alex*—discovered the truth about Furnace. The prisoners were being turned into monsters, their minds and bodies broken and stitched back together into something new, something awful. Under the ever-watchful gaze of the warden those kids were pumped full of a dark, gold-flecked fluid known as nectar. It primed their bodies, made them stronger than they ever could have become naturally, able to withstand any injury. Then the wheezers opened them up, packing them full of muscle, giving them eyes of silver and setting them loose upon the world.

The lucky ones died on the operating table. Others became blacksuits—the hulking guards who remembered nothing of the children they once were, who craved only more and more power. Some found themselves broken beyond repair, losing their minds completely to become rats—feral killing machines that roamed the tunnels beneath Furnace butchering anyone they encountered.

And some became something worse still. Their genes evolved, making them bigger, faster, stronger than nature ever intended, beasts of unimaginable fury that looked more alien than human. The berserkers.

Alex and Zee were rescued from solitary by a boy called Simon—a kid who had been half turned by the warden's surgery, his torso and one arm now that of a blacksuit, his eyes silver. And they—we—had made a break for freedom, trying to climb the shaft of the prison incinerator. But they were found, they were recaptured, and this time the warden wasted no time putting Alex under the knife.

I don't remember the pain, only the strength it brought. My body, it was cut apart and put back together. It was *improved*. I was no longer Alex, I was something better, something more. The warden filled my head with promises of power, told me of the war that was about to come between the strong and the weak, between the monsters and the humans, spoke of the new Fatherland that would rise from the ashes of the old world. I almost forgot who I was, I almost became one of the warden's children, a Soldier of Furnace.

And it was then that I first heard Alfred Furnace himself, the mysterious force behind all of this madness. Furnace didn't live within the prison, but his dark presence filled every single one of the creatures who dwelled here; it gripped their every thought, determined their actions. He was their commander, their god, and his power was absolute.

But some part of me resisted him, remembering my name, remembering my old life. Zee, Simon, and I, we fought our way back to general population, to the main body of the prison, and together with the inmates we cracked the gates, we busted out of Furnace.

We thought we'd made it. We thought we were free. But the prison break was just what Alfred Furnace wanted. His forces were waiting in the shadows—an army of blacksuits and berserkers. And with the city distracted by the escaping prisoners he made his move. He began his war on humanity.

He had a secret weapon too, a new strain of nectar, a red-flecked poison that spread like a plague. Any child who was bitten, who was filled with this improved nectar, became a super-rat, driven by fury and intent on nothing but slaughter. Within hours of the break the city fell as the new breed of rats ran riot. The army was called in, a state of emergency was declared, but it was too late: Furnace's nightmare force was unstoppable.

And my role in this?

I'm not sure I know. I was bitten by a berserker shortly after we escaped, my blood tainted by the new nectar. But it was a small bite, not enough to turn me into one of them. After that I had visions in my head, visions that came from Furnace himself, channeled into my mind through the nectar. He showed me a tower, a skyscraper, on which a creature sat and howled at the world below. I thought it was him, thought that beast was Furnace, and I knew

I had to try to kill him. I made a plan with Simon, Zee, and Lucy—a girl we'd met in the city. Zee and Lucy went off to find the army, to tell them to destroy the tower. Simon and I went after Furnace.

I didn't find him there. I found the warden. He filled himself with new nectar, becoming more powerful than any human had the right to be. Then we fought, both of us almost dying. The only way I survived was by drinking the blood from his veins, draining him of the new nectar. It saved my life, but it cost me the last of my sanity. I killed the warden—fed him to his own ghastly creations—but in doing so I became something worse. Because that's what Furnace wanted too—the warden had failed him, and he needed a new general. He wanted *me* to become his right-hand man.

Warden Cross may have lost, but Alfred Furnace had won.

I climbed to the roof of the tower—now engulfed with flames as military jets bombarded it with missiles—I perched on the spire, and saw the city crumbling beneath me. Then I screamed, realizing that the creature I had seen in my vision wasn't Furnace at all.

It was me.

It's no wonder I didn't recognize myself. I had lost both of my hands—my right arm turned into a blade of obsidian flesh, my left blown off at the elbow by a grenade. My body had been changed by the new nectar. I was taller than ever before, stronger too. But it was more than that. Furnace's poison surged through my mind as well, stripping away the last of my memories, the last scraps of the boy I used to be.

I made a promise, right there on that tower: I would find Alfred Furnace, and I would kill him. And if the world stood in my way then God help it, because I would tear it apart, I would watch it burn.

Nothing would stop me from having my revenge.

That boy, that kid called Alex Sawyer, he wouldn't have wanted this. But he no longer has a say. He's dead.

I need to tell you his story, though. I need to tell you how it ends.

Because it's the only chance I have of bringing him back.

HOOKED

THE GATES OF HELL had opened. Monsters stalked the streets, beasts of unimaginable fury who turned life to death.

And I was their new prince.

I sat on my burning throne and watched as anger devoured the world. Perched on the spire of that tower I saw the horror spill across the smoking ground, gripping the city in a fist of molten rage. Ranks of blacksuits trod the bones of soldiers into the tarmac, too fast and too powerful for those poor mortals in camouflage. I saw their victims flee into the alleyways only to find far worse things there, nightmares made flesh. Beasts that had once been children but which now stalked the shadows with hatred in their blood and murder in their eyes.

And more creatures howled from the rooftops, beasts of impossible size and strength, their bodies warped and their minds broken. The berserkers earned their name well, pouncing on those terrified humans like demons greeting the damned at the gates of the underworld—rending, tearing, devouring.

It was an army the likes of which the world had never seen, and commanding it was a man whose laughter rang in my ears, a man whose dark presence drove every single one of the freaks below, a man whose vision of the world was nothing but fury.

Alfred Furnace.

He was the person I had come here to kill, the creature I thought I had seen in my visions—a beast who sat on the peak of his kingdom and watched the old world purged by the new dawn. But that creature hadn't been Furnace, it had been *me*—changed beyond recognition by the battles that had torn me apart, and the nectar that patched me back together. I understood now why I'd had to come here, why I'd had to fight the warden, why I'd had to change.

Because it was the only way I could ever hope to beat Furnace.

Far below, something exploded, the detonation causing the entire roof of the building to shake. The enormous radio antenna fixed to the peak of the tower snapped free with a whip crack, slicing through the air as it cartwheeled earthward, vanishing into a pillar of smoke. There was a second blast, followed by a third, louder than the first two put together, and this time a section of the spire caved inward, swallowed up by an inferno that raged just under the roof. I backed off to the edge, trying to snatch in clean air, trying to work out a way to escape.

But there was none. The spire was circled by a wall of fire, hot enough to melt the reinforced steel skeleton of the tower. The skyscrapers around me were too far away to reach, even with my newfound strength and speed. There was only one way out, and although I had the nectar inside me—the new nectar, a million times more powerful than the old—I wouldn't survive a fifty-story fall, no way.

Panic was beginning to claw its way through the rush, the sting of the fire on my warped skin making it all too clear how painful it would be to die up here. I used what remained of my left arm—the short blade that jutted from my elbow still growing as the nectar worked on it—to wave the smoke away from my face, the sword-like right to feel my way along the sloped side of the spire.

The jets that had attacked the tower were long gone, their job done. There were other things in the sky, though: black helicopters that hovered like falcons, shaded windshields all facing this way, watching as I was condemned to the flames. It brought back a distant memory of standing in front of a jury, being judged guilty of a crime I didn't commit, and sentenced to a living death. It was another life, another *person's* life. I wasn't that boy any longer. I was something so much more.

I stood, ignoring the vertigo that made the city spin beneath me, and I held up the blade of my right hand, spitting out another choked roar of hatred.

"You can't kill me!" I screamed when my breath had recovered, knowing that nobody in the helicopters would be able to hear me. "I won't let you!"

Another explosion, this time out in the city. Black smoke churned upward from a gas station, so dark and so dense that it looked like a granite mountain pushing its way out of the earth. Two of the choppers broke away, banking gracefully. I caught a glimpse of shadowed faces behind the tinted glass, and through the open door of one of the birds was a cannon. They continued to rise, heading this way, heading for me.

I backed off, using the smoke from the tower to shield myself. But as I did so I heard that voice in my mind, a whisper that was at the same time a shout, louder even than the howl of the wind and the thunder of the flames.

Let them take you, said Alfred Furnace, speaking through the nectar. I slapped my ruined left arm against my head, trying to knock his tainted voice away. He'd had his filthy fingers inside my skull right from the start, from the moment we first made our break from the tunnels beneath the prison, taunting me, manipulating me, controlling me with the ease of a puppet master pulling the strings of a marionette.

I still didn't know why he had taken such an interest in me, why he had led me to the tower just to fight the warden, why he had given me those last, vital words of encouragement that had enabled me to defeat his general, and why he wanted me to stand at his right hand as he ushered in his new kingdom. It didn't make any sense.

"No," I growled, speaking to him this time. "I won't listen to you. I'm going to find you, and end you."

You're going to die, the voice replied, a bone-rattling hiss. *And all our work will be for nothing. Let them take you, and I promise you will find answers to the last of your questions.*

The two choppers were approaching fast. They reached the level of the tower and held their position twenty meters or so away from me, their blades causing the smoke to dance in sweeping, majestic plumes. I wondered what I looked like to the people inside—more nightmare than human, two asymmetric jagged blades for arms and eyes like churning vortexes. I knew the terror that my new body must have inspired, and it made me feel good, made me feel powerful, made me feel like I could crush those soldiers, all of them, and take control of the world.

I could hear Furnace's laughter, but even the knowledge that I was acting the way he wanted me to didn't dull the sharp edge of excitement that wormed through my thoughts.

One of the choppers swung around, the open side hatch facing me. Through the burning air it took on a shimmering, surreal quality, but I could still make out the machine gun inside, pointing right this way.

"Come on," I bellowed. I'd been shot before and survived. There was nothing they could do that could kill me. Let them try, and I'd show them what true power was. "Come on!"

By the time the cannon opened fire I was already on the move, throwing myself farther up the spire, a cloak of smoke draped over me. I waited for the hammer of bullets against the roof, the storm of shrapnel, but all I heard was a dull clank. I turned as the chopper was rising again, using its rotors to blow away my cover. And I was just in time to see the gunner cut loose a rope and load in another.

It wasn't a cannon at all, it was a grappling gun.

He fired, catching me off guard. I tried to jump out of the way but a sliver of steel punched through my gut, dragging a black rope after it. It pinged off the concrete spire, opening like an umbrella. I grabbed at the rope, but with blades for hands I couldn't get purchase. The grappling hook that had sliced through me slammed into my back, the prongs holding it there, and before I even knew what was happening I was wrenched off the tower.

The universe came apart, the sky and the ground becoming one endless blur as I spun through the air, my stomach lurching so hard that for a second I thought it had left my body completely. I realized I was screaming, or at least as much of a scream as my air-starved lungs could manage. Then the line went taut, the grappling claw fixed into my flesh, and I swung beneath that chopper like a fish on a hook.

They began to reel me in and I was powerless to stop them. The only thing I could do was try to cut the line, but that would mean falling to my death. The other chopper was too far away to reach, arcing away as I watched, heading for the ground. The bird above me did the same, the world tilting sickeningly once again as we plummeted earthward. The tower flashed by beside me, every window hemorrhaging smoke, massive craters in its side where the missiles had hit, the entire building groaning like a mythical beast brought down by spears and arrows.

I'd wait, bide my time until they pulled me close enough. Then I'd strike, too fast and too strong for them to stop. I ran my eyes up the black cord that rose from my stomach, then focused on the bottom of the chopper, the bird getting bigger as I drew close. I'd be there in seconds.

A shape appeared from the hatch, a soldier leaning out over me, a harness holding him in place. He had a gun in his hands, and he aimed down the sights for no more than a second before pulling the trigger.

Something thudded into my arm, no more painful than a nettle sting. I glanced at it, a growl already spilling from between my lips. It wasn't a bullet. It looked more like a feather, a red plume sticking out just below my shoulder. The soldier fired again, and again, and again, a crimson forest sprouting over my torso and my neck.

Smoke began to cloud my vision. Except I knew it wasn't smoke. It wasn't nectar either. It was something else, a creeping darkness that cut off the relentless glow of the sun, that blotted out the city, that left only the grinning face of the soldier as he was pulled back inside the helicopter.

Let them take you, Furnace's voice again, and even this was muted by the unbelievable, inescapable tiredness that had settled into my thoughts, into my bones. *You will have your chance for revenge, I promise you that.*

Then the last scraps of daylight sputtered out like candles, and the world was no more.

WATCHING

MY DREAMS LED ME TO A PLACE OF INFINITE QUIET.

I stood in a forest, nothing but trees in every direction. Their gnarled trunks grew into fingerlike branches that twisted and entwined overhead, so many of them that they almost blotted out the twilight sky above. Only a sliver of cold moonlight made it through, and by its silver touch I saw piles of rotting fruit on the damp ground. Apples, thousands, black-eyed crows picking at them as if they were corpses, worms wriggling through the decomposing flesh.

Not a forest, then. An orchard.

I knew this place. I had seen it before; not like this, but carved from stone. It was the orchard that had been replicated at the top of Furnace's tower block, the one I had just been pulled from. Except back in that penthouse there had been a sculpture of a boy nailed to a trunk, the young Alfred Furnace, his stomach cut open. I scanned the trees before me—stretching off like an army of skeletons—but could see no sign of him.

I tried to turn around but my head was locked, my body paralyzed, as so often happens in dreams. Panic rose from my stomach like vomit, but I forced myself to swallow it back down. *It's only a dream,* I told myself, even though I knew it was something more than that.

The blanket of silence that cradled the orchard was so immense that it was almost a sound in its own right, a mute roar that I could feel against my ears as though I were deep underwater. The leafless branches swayed in the breeze, the birds fought and flapped between their feastings, but they made no noise. I couldn't even hear my own breath, or feel my pulse.

It was the fire that alerted me to their presence. The deep velvet shadows between the trees began to flicker gently, a ghostly dance of light and dark against the bark. Those forms gradually solidified into shapes that marched through the orchard, a procession of men and women, all holding flaming torches. Their clothes were like something from an old movie, the sort of thing peasants might have worn hundreds of years ago. Their faces were contorted with emotion—maybe fear, maybe anger, maybe both. And they held those torches against the encroaching night as if they were the only thing that stood between them and the devil.

They marched before me, from right to left, and it was only when they were directly in front of me that I noticed two other figures in the crowd. Both were being carried—one on a wooden board, a wreath on his motionless stomach, the other struggling and screaming between two hulking men, his hands and feet bound. I recognized the second kid immediately, even though his grief-filled face was the exact opposite of the calm expression worn by the carving in the penthouse.

It was Alfred Furnace, and he was no older than me.

Several of the mob seemed to scour the area before settling on a large tree to my left. They ran toward it, planting their torches in the wet soil and ushering the rest of the group forward. The two men threw Furnace down and the boy tried to squirm away, burrowing into the ground as if he could tunnel his way to safety. One of the women used a knife to cut open the twine around his wrists and ankles, but before he could make a run for it the men had hoisted him up again. They spun him around and one of them lashed out, slapping him across the cheek. There was still no sound, but my imagination was happy to provide one.

I wanted to step out, to try to stop what was happening. I knew the boy was Furnace, but the way he cried for help, tears streaming down his filthy cheeks, his skinny arms held out toward a nonexistent savior—those weren't the actions of a crazed psychopath, they were those of a terrified child. My body was still locked tight, however. I might as well have been one of the trees in the orchard, rooted to the ground and held fast by the branches of my brothers.

The biggest of the men lifted the boy against the tree, pinning him there while more of the crowd surged forward. Two women grabbed one of Furnace's arms, bending it back around the trunk, while another put a huge iron nail against his palm. All I could do as they struck the first blow was close my eyes.

When I dared look again I saw the crowd step back, leaving Furnace suspended from the bark, crucified. He hung there in agony, his legs scrabbling for purchase, unable to find the ground, blood streaming down his arms, pattering on the crushed fruit of the orchard ground.

The men and women gently laid the corpse of the other boy down between them and the tree. The dead boy was younger than Furnace, maybe nine or ten, but their faces were similar enough for me to know that they must have been brothers. One woman knelt by his side, howling into the boy's chest, and when she looked up at Alfred Furnace her expression was so warped it was almost inhuman. She hissed at him, the way a cat hisses at an enemy, and even though I couldn't hear her, or understand the word her lips formed, the dream interpreted it for me.

Murderer.

The emotion in the crowd swelled, two dozen people all shouting the same accusation. Somebody threw something at Furnace, the missile bouncing off his shoulder and leaving a mushy stain there. Seconds later the air was full of rotten fruit, a storm of apples that pelted the boy across every inch of his body. He sobbed, sniveled, begged, but his words were as silent to the crowd as they were to me.

I don't know how long the assault went on. Time has no meaning in dreams. But when the men and women grew tired the mountain of fruit was piled almost as high as the boy's feet. It had knocked the last of the fight from him, and he slumped motionlessly against the tree, his skin darkening with bruises, only the lazy blinks of his eyes letting me know he was still conscious.

A man stepped forward, dressed in black and holding a leather-bound book. He placed a comforting hand on the woman's head as he addressed the young Alfred Furnace.

You have committed a crime of unthinkable hatred and malice, he said, the words playing voicelessly in my head. *The slaying of thine own flesh and blood is the gravest sin, and you have been found guilty.* The man opened up the book—the Bible, I realized—and began to read. *"Where is Abel, thy brother?" And he said, "I know not: am I my brother's keeper?" And he said, "What hast thou done? The voice of thy brother's blood crieth unto me from the ground."* The priest, if that's what he was, snapped the book shut. *And now art thou cursed from the earth, which hath opened her mouth to receive thy brother's blood from thy hand.*

I could see the crowd murmuring, nodding their heads, some spitting onto the soil. The priest walked slowly to the tree, placing a finger under the boy's chin and lifting his head until their eyes met.

The Lord placed a mark on Cain to ensure he would not die. For his punishment was to wander the world tormented by the knowledge of his sin. But you shall not be allowed to wander. Your fate lies here, in this wood. Your punishment shall be death. Do you have anything more to say?

Alfred Furnace opened his mouth, a worm of blood slithering over his chin. His face was swelling, his eyes watery blue pools in his head. Even in the time I had spent in Furnace, among those kids who cried and wailed and groaned every hour of every day, I had never seen somebody look so weak, or so scared. His lips shaped a word, maybe two or three, but I couldn't make them out. The priest let the boy's head drop and stepped away, holding his hands out to the crowd.

He makes no protest, he said. *Justice has been done, let us leave him to the wolves.*

Seemingly satisfied, the crowd began to shuffle away, retreating into the woods with their torches. The last few to go carefully lifted the dead boy back onto their shoulders, disappearing between the trees until the only people to remain were Furnace and the woman. She stood before him, her shoulders lurching up and down as she mourned. The boy somehow found the strength to look up at her, and once again he shaped those same words, words I could make no sense of.

Her reaction was as shocking as it was brutal. She pulled a knife from the hem of her skirt, a wicked blade that caught the moonlight, and in a flash of silver and red she dragged it across the boy's stomach, side to side. The boy looked down at the wound, more in shock than in pain, and when he spoke I heard the word all too clearly.

Mother?

The woman threw the knife to the ground, staggering back as though she couldn't believe what she had done. She crossed her fingers over her chest, then turned and bolted.

As impossible as it was, the orchard seemed even quieter than it had been to begin with, as still and as silent as if it were a photograph. Except I could see the blood gushing to the ground, the steam rising into the cold air, could see the pulse in the boy's neck grow weaker. I don't know how he found the strength to do it, but he managed to lift his head once again, and this time he looked right at me.

I didn't do it, he said, the words crystal clear even though I knew it wasn't my language he spoke. Those pale blue eyes caught the light from the remaining torches, burning with a raging fire despite the fact he must have been right on the edge of death. I wanted to go to him, to hold out my hand to him, to cradle him, but it was hopeless. The only thing I could do was listen to his voiceless denials, to believe him. I could do that, I *would* do that.

"I know," I said, the words only in my head. And I *did* know. The kid, Alfred Furnace, was telling the truth. He seemed to manage a smile, nothing more than a tremor of his thin, blue lips, two final words tumbling out alongside his dying breaths.

Thank you.

THE HOSPITAL

FOR A SECOND—A SINGLE, TERRIFYING SECOND—I thought I had woken up in Furnace Penitentiary.

I was lying in a cell, walls of white-painted concrete and a door of solid iron barricaded shut. A single bulb hung from the ceiling, filling the room with blinding light. My body had been wrapped in black wire from neck to toe, so much of it that I felt as though I had been cocooned. I tried moving, but just like in my dream I was powerless, my binds fixed to a bed or table beneath me. Cables slid out from various parts of my body, connected to half a dozen machines along the left-hand wall of the cell, all beeping gently as if discussing the news of my waking.

It took me a moment to work out that I wasn't in the prison infirmary, a moment that seemed endless. I looked up and back, seeing a window in the wall behind my head. It was barred, but the dust-specked glow that streamed through came from the sun dangling right outside. Its golden touch filled me with relief, my heart calming and my muscles relaxing. I was aboveground, I wasn't in Furnace, I was safe.

There was a camera mounted in the corner of the room and it must have been switched on because a series of thunderclaps echoed out from the door, bolts being slid back and locks being opened. It swung inward, and I expected to see blacksuits enter, or soldiers, armed to the teeth and ready to attack. Instead, the person who stepped cautiously into the room was a woman in her forties, dressed like a doctor, a delicate silver chain swinging from her neck. Her graying blond hair was cropped short, and her crinkled blue gaze was the kind that instantly makes you feel welcome. She was carrying a canvas chair, unfolding it beside my bed then perching on the edge, never taking her eyes off me.

She opened her mouth to speak, then hesitated, her arms reaching up to the necklace. She unclasped it, leaning forward, and I saw the small pendant attached to it, a man carrying another man over a river. *I should know what this is,* I thought to myself, but the memories just wouldn't come. The woman deftly clipped the chain around my neck, slipping it under the wire so that the cool silver lay against my chest.

"We found this in your pocket," she said, and I noticed that her accent was the same as somebody else's I once knew, a boy called Zee. I tried to pull an arm free but the wire gripped me like a million fingers, refusing to grant me an inch. The frustration boiled up my throat and I heard myself growling, a throbbing snarl that filled the room like liquid. The woman didn't flinch.

"It's okay," she went on, resting her hand on my shoulder. "Please just relax, there's nothing to be afraid of. I wanted to give it back to you myself, a sign of good faith. I wanted you to know that you're safe here."

I was too confused and too angry to take in what she was saying. What right did she have to keep me here? Didn't she know who I was, what I was capable of? The nectar was a growing storm inside me, I could feel it in my veins, giving me more power than this woman could ever comprehend. And yet when I tried to move, I couldn't. I thrashed my head back and forth, dirty spittle streaming from between my lips. The woman shook her head, frowning, as if my pain was her pain. It had been so long since anybody had looked at me like that, with kindness, that it confounded me.

"Your name is Sawyer, isn't it?" the woman asked.

Sawyer didn't sound right. I delved into the chaos inside my head, pulling something loose from the nectar.

"Alex," I whispered, coughing. The word felt alien, sitting uncomfortably on my tongue.

The woman took something from her pocket, a small canteen. She unscrewed the cap and held it to my lips, letting a trickle into my mouth. I swallowed, the sensation blissful.

"My name is Colonel Alice Panettierre," she said as she replaced the cap on the canteen and sat down. "I'm in the army, as you can probably guess, but I'm also a doctor. I'm here to help you."

Her voice was warm, soothing, almost hypnotic.

"You're lucky to be alive, Alex. The air force had orders to destroy that tower and everything in it. Everything. It was only when we saw you screaming at us—screaming *words* at us—from the spire that we issued a capture order. We were lucky to get you before the building collapsed."

I tugged at my binds again, tired of hearing her speak. I had a job to do. I had to find Furnace and kill him, and she was just another obstacle in my way. Another expendable obstacle. She rested a hand on my arm, wrapped tight, and shook her head.

"Don't struggle," she said. "This is shipping wire. It's the stuff that holds up transporter crates when they're being hauled off the boats. It can withstand tension of over a hundred tons, and we've wrapped you pretty tight. But it's there for your own safety.

Those poor limbs of yours, they're pretty dangerous weapons. We tied you up so you wouldn't accidentally hurt yourself." I tried again to move and she looked at me like a mother looks at a naughty child. "Although if you keep struggling like that, then I can't guarantee it."

She stood, walking around the bed to one of the machines and staring at the readout.

"Your health is good," she reported. "Which is incredible, really, when you think about it. You had a massive hole in your chest, another through your stomach, and an X-ray showed no fewer than fourteen bullets in your body. Every single one of your major organs has taken a pummeling, and yet they're all still functioning. In fact, they're operating at a higher level than anything we've ever seen."

She turned back to me, sitting on the edge of my bed with her hands in her lap.

"I guess what we'd like you to do for us is explain how that's possible."

It took me a while to dredge up the right words, the simple sentence seemingly the most difficult thing I'd ever had to string together.

"I'm just lucky, I guess."

Panettierre smiled with her eyes, but I could sense something else there. A flicker of impatience, maybe.

"It's good to know you've still got your sense of humor," she said after a moment. "God knows we all need one, especially at the moment." She leaned forward, putting her hand against my brow. Her skin was cool, her touch calming. "We've spoken to your friends; they've told us quite a bit already."

"Friends?" I asked, searching for memories. But they were lost beneath the nectar like photographs submerged in tar.

"Zee Hatcher," she explained. "And the girl, Lucy Wells. They were the ones who found us, who told us about the tower. We picked up another one too, Simon Rojo-Flores. They all told us the same story, and I'm wondering whether you will too."

"Furnace," I said, spitting the word out like a mouthful of rancid meat. "This is all his doing."

"Alfred Furnace?" the woman replied. "The man the prison was named after, right?" I nodded again, watching her cross the room. She checked a machine as she spoke. "Well, this is what we're finding hard to take in. Because there *is* no Alfred Furnace, not in any of our records. Sure, there's the Furnace Foundation, the people who set up the penitentiary, who owned the tower—owned buildings all over the place, actually. But the man? He can't be alive, Alex. As far as we can tell, Alfred Furnace was born centuries ago."

"He's still alive," I said. "I've spoken to him." I didn't even try to explain how.

"No, you've spoken to somebody who claims to be Alfred Furnace," Panettierre said. "And that's who we're trying to find."

"That makes two of us," I said. "I don't care what you think, you don't know the truth. I was there, in the prison. This is what they did to me, the warden and his freaks." My body was covered up but I knew what it looked like—too big to be mistaken for human anymore, puncture wounds all over it from my fight with the warden, and my arms two blades that were sharper than scalpels. "Alfred Furnace was behind it all. He was never there but he was in charge, he called the shots. It's his army in the city, and they won't stop. *He* won't stop, not until the world surrenders itself to him." Fury flared, and this time when I flexed my muscles the bindings around my chest creaked. "But he didn't count on me, he didn't plan on me coming to kill him."

I gave up, taking a deep breath to drain away the frustration. "And I am going to kill him," I said, softer this time. "Just as soon as I find him."

"You know where to look?" asked Panettierre.

I shook my head.

"Okay, it's good to know we're on the same side," she said after a pause. "And right now that side is the losing one. Around a third of the Home Battalion is KIA, dead, and we can't pull in reserves quickly enough. Hell, sixty percent of our troops are overseas. The emergency services are screwed, and it's spreading, faster than we can keep track of. It's already passed the county line, west and north. We're lucky we've got the coast to the east, otherwise it would be totally out of our hands. If we don't find a way of stopping this . . . this plague, then I give the whole country days, maybe a week, before it's overwhelmed."

She returned her attention to the machines, to one in particular—a large, empty bell jar connected to me with a thick, transparent plastic tube.

"We need to find whoever's responsible for this," she said. "And at the moment the person at the top of our hit list is Warden Cross. You know where he is?"

"Dead," I said, remembering his ravaged face, one eye blinking at me as the wheezers overwhelmed him. "I killed him."

Panettierre didn't say anything, just ran a hand over the jar.

"That gives us one less lead to follow," she said after a moment's pause. "Okay, then tell me about the liquid, the black blood that's inside you, inside the creatures. What do you call it? Nectar?"

"That's what Furnace calls it," I said, taking it slow, trying to remember what I knew. "They never told us what it was, only what it does. It messes with your genes, making you stronger and bigger. And it keeps you alive when you've been injured; it can patch up wounds, heal broken bones. It can make you immortal too. That's how he's still alive, Furnace." The poison in my blood seemed to know I was talking about it, my pulse quickening as it blasted through my system, an animal waiting to be unleashed. "But it's more than that. It alters your mind too. Strips away all the weakness. And most people, when it comes down to it, that's all that's there underneath—weakness. When that's gone, when all the pathetic emotions are gone, all that's left is anger, hatred. That's what those creatures are—they're what's left when you take away everything human."

"But you're different," Panettierre said. "You can talk, you know what's happened to you. How is that?"

I tried and failed to shrug my shoulders.

"I refused to forget my name," I said. And there was no other way of explaining it.

Neither of us spoke again for what could have been a full minute, and I was the one to break the silence, if only to reassure myself that time hadn't stopped.

"Let me out of here," I said. "I can help you. We both want the same thing. I'll find Alfred Furnace, and I'll kill him. It's the only chance there is to end this."

The colonel's shoulders seemed to sink and I heard her sigh. She lifted a hand toward the machine, hesitated for a second, then flicked a switch. I heard a motor start up inside it, the bell jar chattering like joke false teeth. Something tugged in the skin of my arm, the discomfort of a needle buried deep in my flesh. I struggled, but I might as well have been paralyzed from the neck down—it was just like in my dream.

"I'm afraid I can't do that," she said over the din. "It's just too dangerous for you to be released right now. We're here to look after you, Alex. That's my priority, to make sure you're okay." That uncomfortable smile appeared on her face again. It showed too many teeth. She patted me on the top of the head as if I were a dog. "And at the moment the best place for you is right here, in bed."

There was a sucking sound, and suddenly the tube leading to the bell jar turned black, piping nectar out of me. It spurted into it, clinging to the sides, steaming, filling it fast.

"What are you doing?" I asked, struggling pathetically.

"You don't need to worry about it," Panettierre replied, stroking my hair. "We're just taking a sample of the nectar from you. We only want to run a few tests on it, try to find the best way for us to help you, to cure you."

"Losing the nectar will kill me," I growled. The woman's smile widened for a moment, and I wondered if it was meant to comfort me. It didn't. It made her look like a shark, those teeth, and the glint in her eyes, imprinted on my retinas.

"It will make you better," she whispered as she walked to the door. "Hush now, sleep for a while, get your strength back. Remember, we're here to watch over you. You're safe now, I promise. We won't let anything bad happen to you."

Even as the threads of reality began to come loose, the room growing dark as if being buried beneath a mountain of sand, I could sense how difficult those last words were for her.

She was lying.

DRAINED

I DIED IN THAT ORCHARD.

Furnace's voice rang in my ears as the nectar drained from my arteries. All I could do was watch as the black fluid cascaded into that jar, my racing pulse emptying my body of the life force that fueled it.

The edges of the room began to crowd with shadows. My head thrashed back and forth as I tried to stay awake. I knew that if I let the darkness take me now, then I'd never see the light again. But the more nectar that spilled from me, the more the world began to fade. I tried to talk, to plead, but Panettierre had already gone.

I died, but it wasn't the end, he continued, his words seeming to push the last of the light away. The room flickered, the nightmare orchard flashing over reality for a fraction of a second, leaving skeletal trees imprinted like veins over my retinas.

I blinked and the scene reappeared, every leaf, every decomposing apple, every feather on every bird picked out in perfect detail, so much so that it seemed more real than the room I was in. I could even feel the breeze on my face, a cold zephyr like a dead man's breath, and it was this sensation that finally made me surrender. I blinked again and I was back in the hospital. I turned, saw the jar almost full, then I closed my eyes, Furnace's words ringing through me as though my whole body was now hollow, his whisper carrying me into unconsciousness.

Death is never the end.

IT WAS AS IF I had woken from a deep sleep—the cell, the bed, the woman called Panettierre nothing but a blurred memory that faded away after a couple of blinks.

Only I knew that *this* was the dream world, the nightmare.

The orchard around me was impossibly clear, focusing a little more every time I visited. There was sound now too, the creak and crack of distant branches, the rustle of the leaves in the breeze and the coarse caws of the crows as they abandoned their feast of apples and crowded greedily around the boy on the tree.

No time had passed since I had last been here. Heavy night suffocated the moonlit orchard as before. Furnace's eyes were open but only just, looking at me as if I'd never gone away. The flow of blood had all but stopped, leaving his skin as pale as bone. His chest fluttered, as weak as a newborn bird, fighting for every breath.

I didn't expect to be able to move, but when I tried to turn my head I found that I was no longer completely paralyzed. My legs were still rooted to the ground, my torso as stiff as wood, but my hands were now free, and when I lifted them in front of my face I saw that the nectar-grown blades had gone. My hands looked like they had before I'd gone to prison—the normal hands of a normal kid. I stretched my arms out toward Alfred Furnace, but he was too far away to reach. His eyes swam in and out of focus as he fought to see me.

"Where are we?" I asked, my voice startling the birds, causing some to take flight into the safety of the branches. The braver ones ignored me, looking around briefly before dipping their beaks back into the blood-soaked soil. But when I clapped my hands, the noise like a gunshot, even those scattered in a flurry of raucous cawing.

"This is a dream, right?" I said, as much to myself as to Furnace.

The boy shook his head, the effort seeming to drain him of the last of his energy. His lips opened, words tumbling out in that strange guttural language that I could somehow understand.

To you, it is a dream, he said. *To me, it is a memory.*

Even here I could feel my body grow weak, and I remembered that back in the world, the *real* world, I was being drained of the nectar that kept me alive. But almost as soon as I sensed it, the dream numbed my panic. The real world didn't matter here. There was only the orchard, and Alfred Furnace.

"A memory?" I said. "You mean this actually happened? When?"

A long, long time ago. The boy spat out a bullet of crimson phlegm, his entire body spasming. *They thought I killed my brother. But I didn't.* He *did it—the stranger who lives in the orchard.*

"The stranger?" I looked around nervously. "Who do you mean? Is he still here?"

Quiet, hissed Furnace. *He'll hear you. And you don't want that. This may only be a dream for you, but he still has power here.*

"So the orchard is real?" I tried again.

It was once real. This is a bad place, it always has been. Battles were fought here many centuries ago, countless lives taken, countless souls crushed. The soil here is tainted, the fruit of these trees nourished on blood. That is why he is here. He paused, his eyes swiveling as his thoughts took him somewhere else. *We were told never to come to the orchard, that it was cursed. But we dared each other, we came, and my brother paid the price. Now it is my turn. They have left me here for the wolves but the stranger will get me first. I do not have long.*

"Tell me what to do," I said. "I can help."

It is too late, Furnace replied. *The boy I once was died a long, long time ago. These events have already happened, they cannot be changed. But it is important that you see for yourself.*

"It's not too late—"

Furnace shot me a look of white-eyed terror, and the rest of the sentence dried up in my throat.

Hush, he hissed. *He is here.*

The temperature in the orchard dipped, as though the forest had been submerged in ice water. Even in the dream the cold clawed into my bones, making me feel like I had never in my life experienced warmth. The air grew thin, stripped of oxygen, yet at the same time the darkness seemed to gain weight, an invisible fist grinding me into the dirt. As I gasped for air I felt something swell inside my chest, a feeling a million times worse than death, so awful that I would have chosen to leave the world right here and now, forever, rather than suffer it any longer.

It was terror, I realized, the kind reserved for nightmares, when your mind has no defense against the dark. It was the most primitive, most powerful emotion of all, and I had never, ever felt it like this. This wasn't just a fear of losing my life, but a fear of losing my soul.

I scanned the orchard, frantically searching for the source of my panic. The gnarled trunks of the apple trees circled us like the bars of a cage. Between them were pockets of night, so utterly black that it was as if nothing existed beyond, as though to step out of this clearing would be to step right out of life itself, into the abyss.

My eyes fell on the void that separated the two trees closest to where Furnace had been crucified. There was nothing there, at least nothing that I could see. And yet I knew that something stood in that spot, shrouded in shadow, watching us. I could feel it, radiating coldness and darkness like an inverse sun, dead eyes scouring the orchard.

My heart lurched, my mind screaming, every fiber of my body railing against the thing in the woods. *It's a dream,* my mind howled, but there was no fooling myself. It was real, completely and utterly real. Nothing in my entire life had been more certain. Whatever stood there was real, and it was evil.

More than that, I realized that this thing was trapped here, among the blood and the filth of this orchard. Don't ask me how I knew that, I just did. Some truths are instinctive, absolute. They have to be, because your survival depends upon getting as far away from them as possible.

I ordered myself to wake up. I just needed to be away from this thing, this unspeakable terror that made the end of life seem so welcome. I yelled at myself, trying to pump adrenaline into my system, trying to shunt myself out of the nightmare.

It was working. The tops of the trees were splintering, dissolving into fragments that soared up into the night. The orchard began to flex and bulge, breaking apart, pieces of dream world scattering like scraps of burning paper.

Don't leave me, said the boy, Alfred Furnace. *Please don't leave me with him.*

But nothing on earth could keep me there, not with that soulless entity between the trees, watching us with eyes as black as pitch—a force so malevolent that it made Warden Cross and Alfred Furnace both look like angels. I put the boy's pleas out of my head, pushed up from the dream like a diver breaking from deep water, desperate to reach the surface.

I had almost made it when the stranger stepped from between the trees, bringing the darkness with him—a silhouette of flickering shadow who reached out for Furnace with one impossibly long arm, and for me with the other; who fixed me with an invisible grin as I rose from the dream; who watched me go with an expression of wicked delight, and whose silent, deafening laughter followed me all the way back to the waking world.

TESTS

I OPENED MY EYES with the echo of that insane howling still reverberating among my shattered thoughts.

I blinked away the last few scraps of sleep to see that I was inside a large, noisy room, the walls and floor covered in pristine white tiles, so bright that it could have been built that day. It looked like a hospital operating room, only much bigger. I was still lying down, wires and sensors strapped to almost every inch of me, countless needles taped beneath my skin. Tight coils of shipping wire pinned my legs and my chest to some sort of metal table. Even before I attempted to struggle free I knew I wouldn't be able to.

My arms were exposed, held in viselike clamps on either side of the table. I looked at my right hand, the blade of the nectar-blackened limb longer and sharper than ever. I glanced at my left, seeing that the nectar was still at work there. The stump of my left arm had split into three stublike protrusions. They weren't fingers, not recognizably, anyway. They looked more like the shoots of a plant jutting from the charred flesh. Each was no longer than a big toe, but when I wiggled them they all moved.

It didn't make any sense. Had the nectar been trying to grow me a new hand? Could it do that? Why hadn't it happened with my right arm? There were too many questions and none of them had answers. The transformation must have started when I was unconscious, before they drained the nectar from me. Maybe the nectar behaved differently when you were asleep, when you weren't in the middle of a fight for your life.

I tried to get a better look, but it was hopeless. I felt like the boy from my dream, Alfred Furnace, trussed up and left to bleed out. It was as though my body had been drained almost to the point of death and I was now running on fumes. The blackened, nectar-filled veins beneath my skin were nowhere to be seen, and my flesh had paled to a sickly gray color. There was only a trickle of blood left inside me, just enough to keep my heart pumping. Every beat of my pulse felt like it might be the last.

I turned my head, trying to make sense of the room I was in. All around me was chaos. Rows of tables like the one I was on extended in every direction. There must have been a hundred or more. Half were occupied, mostly by rats dressed in the tattered remains of their prison overalls. There was nothing left in them of the children they had once been—before they had been contaminated with Furnace's new nectar. They thrashed against their restraints, their blackshot eyes full of hatred, hunger, so hungry for blood that their teeth gnawed at their own lips and tongues, pools of poison spilling beneath them.

I heard a guttural bark and swung my head around to look at the far side of the room. Chained to the wall was a berserker. It stood head and shoulders over the soldiers around it, its rage radiating from it in waves of heat but its face that of a child. Like me, like all of us, it was bound tight, mummified in a cocoon of shipping wire. The only thing it had to defend itself with was its voice.

On the table next to me was another figure, a blacksuit, although he was no longer wearing the uniform of his master. Scalpel handles rose up from his bare chest, dozens of them, like a miniature graveyard. He looked as though he was out cold, maybe dead, his unblinking silver eyes staring at the skylights above him through which sunlight dripped like honey.

I turned my attention away from the freaks to the other people in the room, the ones who weren't tied up. There must have been thirty of them. A few were dressed in black combat suits and armed with machine guns, but most were wearing long white coats or surgeons' gowns. And it was these men and women, not the monsters, who filled me with fear, who made me want to rip away my restraints and run.

Because they all had gas masks on.

A few of the scientists were monitoring machines whose blinking displays painted the walls with light. Others walked among the forklift trucks lined up against one side of the room or supervised transparent vats of bubbling black fluid, burning red stars sparkling in their depths. Tubes stretched out from these vats, connected to several of the rats, pumping them dry, leaving nothing but husks. Most of the gas-masked scientists, though, moved between the tables, surgical equipment gripped in their gloved hands, their eyes bright behind misted visors.

I sensed movement above me and I realized the room had an observation balcony, a narrow, glass-walled walkway that ran around all four sides. There were more people up there watching, wearing a mix of suits and military uniforms—not camouflage, but dress gear that bristled with medals and insignias. The phrase "top brass" popped into my head from nowhere, although I didn't really know what it meant. I managed to open my mouth and call to them.

"Hey," less a word than a grunt, but it obviously did the trick because an intercom crackled, a faint voice hissing out of it.

"Fourteen is awake," it said. There was a pause, indistinct voices, then, "Begin the procedure."

I felt like a puppet whose strings have been cut. The only parts of my body that still seemed to function were my eyes, which turned in their sockets as the mob in the room approached. I could hear their wheezing breaths, heavy with excitement, and their movements were staggered and anxious. A sense of déjà vu sat like a boulder of ice in my stomach.

The closest one reached me, and through the mask I realized it wasn't a wheezer but Colonel Panettierre. She reached out with a white-gloved hand and rested it on my chest.

"Don't panic," she said, her voice muffled. "The masks are for your protection, not ours. We've drained you of about ninety percent of your blood supply, and we're worried that without the nectar you'll have almost no immunity against infection. This room is part of the hospital. It's where we're going to try to make you better."

I knew exactly what kind of room this was. The infirmary back in the prison had been a hospital too.

"Zee," Panettierre said, giving a thumbs-up to the balcony overhead. "You want to have a word?"

The intercom flicked on again, nothing but static for a second. Then I heard a voice.

"Alex?" it said. "Just do what they say, don't fight them. I think they're trying to help. Don't fight them, or they'll kill—"

There was a clatter, a squeal, then the intercom cut off. I tried to look up, peering through blurred vision to see a shape behind the glass above me, a boy among the soldiers. I blinked, my eyelids so heavy they almost wouldn't open again, and for a second I saw a kid that I recognized. The kid Panettierre had called Zee. There were memories connected with him, too deep for me to make any sense of. But they existed, I was sure of it.

He banged on the soundproof glass, screaming silently at me, and by the time my head had dropped again he was already being hauled away.

"He knows what's best for you, Alex; what's best for you and your friend Simon."

I scanned the room, looking for the face that matched Simon's name, but I could barely remember what he looked like. Panettierre removed her hand from my chest, holding it out to somebody beside her. One of the other gas masks passed her something, metal glinting in the sunlight.

In the silence that followed I almost fell back into sleep, dark trees seeming to sprout from the bodies in front of me, spreading like a web of cancerous arteries across the ceiling. I had a flash of the young Alfred Furnace, and of the dark figure who was still mid-step from his pocket of shadow, and that pumped enough adrenaline into my heart to shove the dream away. Better here than there. Better anywhere than in that orchard.

"This will be painful, Alex," Panettierre said. "And for that I apologize. But a cure can often be more painful than the disease; that's simply the way of things."

The scientists moved in, staring at me like I was the main course at a banquet. I felt like it too, like a spit-roasted pig, trussed up and ready to be carved. I wanted to howl at them, to lash out, to show them I wasn't some carnival freak show, but the simple act of moving seemed as impossible as leaping over an ocean.

"Are you ready?" Panettierre asked, placing the object in her hand against my shoulder. It was a scalpel. I shook my head, opened my mouth to protest, but before I could answer she pushed the surgical knife deep into my flesh. It didn't hurt, no more than a mosquito bite, anyway. I'd experienced far greater pain, far more severe injuries. But at least most of the time I'd been able to fight back. Tied up here, unable to defend myself, felt infinitely worse—it was just like being back in the tunnels beneath Furnace.

"Keep your eye on his heart rate," Panettierre said to one of the other scientists as she drew the blade in a tight semicircle over my shoulder. I could just about twist my head around far enough to see the wound, wide open but bloodless. The woman smiled down at me, although through the visor it looked more like a leer, her lips pulled back too far. "You're doing great, Alex. It won't be much longer." She turned to the group of scientists who were all eagerly monitoring the machines beside me. "Any change?"

Somebody muttered something back to her and she nodded, obviously pleased. She pushed the knife deeper, so deep that I felt it grind against my shoulder joint. I winced, more at the thought than at the pain. She placed her other hand on my chest, making shushing noises.

"Does it hurt?" she asked.

"Yes," I spat back. "Couldn't you have done this while I was asleep?"

"We need to gauge your reaction," she said. "Physiological and psychological. Besides, I don't think it does hurt that much. Be brave, it's going to be fine."

She pulled the scalpel free, handing it to somebody else. The scientists clustered around me, all staring at the wound, their piggy eyes greedy and unblinking. They weren't looking at a boy, at a human. All I was to them was a science experiment. A *specimen*.

Across the room, something screamed, the noise of a rabbit caught in a snare. I tilted my head back as far as it would go, everything upside down, and saw another group of scientists surrounding a rat six or seven tables away. The creature writhed wildly, nectar spilling from between its lips. It was no longer human. It wasn't even an animal anymore—it had no desire to eat, or to sleep. It would live a short life of violence before the nectar deserted it, and then it would simply stop existing. If anything, the rat was like a virus, living only to spread to another host.

And yet it still wore those overalls, torn and bloodied but recognizable. Just days ago this rat had been a prisoner inside Furnace Penitentiary, a kid like me wanting nothing more than to survive, to find a way out.

Be careful what you wish for, I thought.

The scientists around the rat turned and nodded at each other, then called for a soldier. One of the camouflaged figures strolled over, spoke briefly with one of them, then without hesitating placed his pistol against the rat's temple and pulled the trigger. There was an eruption of dark liquid, mist spraying against their visors, the creature's movements growing less frenzied, settling into sporadic twitches.

"Don't worry about that," said Panettierre, forcing my head forward until the image was out of sight. "Some things are broken past the point of fixing." She muttered an order and somebody passed her an instrument. It caught the light, leaving a fragment of sunshine in my eye, and for a moment I thought it was another blade. "Right, I'm giving him two milliliters directly into the wound. Pay attention to BP and A-T counts. Everything set?"

Not a blade, then—a syringe.

There were murmurs of assent, and Panettierre slid the needle into my skin. As soon as the liquid entered my body I knew what it was. Nectar. Not much—a thimbleful—but enough to turn my thoughts to thunder. I watched that trickle of red-flecked poison vanish into the hole Panettierre had carved into my shoulder, a single black bubble bursting from my flesh.

And then it hit me: my thoughts turned to fire, every cell of my body reawakened. I roared, the noise rocking the room, sending the scientists flying back like bowling pins. Only Panettierre stood her ground, her eyes burning as if they were reflecting the flames inside me.

"Keep watching those readings," she barked. "I don't want to miss anything."

My roar subsided into a growl, a throbbing purr that settled in my throat. I tugged at my hand, knowing how easily I could slice through the woman in front of me, through all of them, with my bladed fingers. And I would have too. If I'd been free, I'd have killed them all where they stood.

"There, there," Panettierre said to me. "Hush now; be brave. There's no reason to get upset. This will all be over very soon." Then, to somebody else. "Oh my God, it's working, look."

I pushed against her fingers, seeing the scalpel wound already clotting with hardening nectar. I didn't see what the big deal was, I'd recovered from far worse injuries than that. But the scientists were obviously impressed as they were practically fighting each other to get a closer look.

"Fairhurst, get a sample of that," Panettierre said, prodding the scab with her gloved finger. I tried another growl, but what little nectar had been pumped into my system was already used up. Somebody shoved his way to the front, using another scalpel to slice off a section of the clotted wound before scampering off with his prize. "You seeing that?" Panettierre went on. "Readings are off the chart. His temperature is going on for fifty-eight degrees *centigrade*."

They busied themselves around me for what seemed like forever, measuring, gauging, prodding. All I could do was lie there, hoping that they were telling me the truth, that they were looking for a cure. I don't know how much later it was that Panettierre lifted the scalpel again, holding it a few centimeters away from the first hole she'd made.

"Just a few more of these," she said. "We need to do this because we have to understand how you work, we have to unlock the truth of your genetic mutations. You must realize that if we can't, if we fail, then the country will fall."

I protested, but even as the words tumbled from my mouth her blade was slicing into my skin, parting it as if it were paper.

"Don't be a baby, Alex," she said. "I know you're braver than this. Just grit your teeth and it will be over in a minute."

But it wasn't. I don't know how long it went on, my consciousness flowing in and out like the tide on a moonless night. It could have been hours, it felt like days. The scientists came and went, anonymous behind their masks. Only Panettierre stayed, cutting hole after hole then fixing them up with a droplet of nectar. Each time she'd whisper comforting words into my ear, stroking my brow. But her eyes never met mine. They never left the canvas of ravaged skin laid out in front of her.

At some point I lost the strength to keep my head up and it fell to the side. Past the churning ocean of gas masks I made out the blacksuit on the table beside me. He hadn't been dead after all, because he stared back, his eyes more lead than silver, a trail of black blood leaking from his lips down over his cheek.

I didn't look away, and neither did he. We just lay there, watching each other. We were enemies, yes, but right now we were bound by the same horror, the same powerlessness, the same fear. We all were, everything in this room—the blacksuits, the rats, the berserkers, and me. We were enemies, but I had never felt closer to them. We were enemies, but we were brothers with a common goal.

We had to get out of here.

INTO THE PIT

IT WAS NIGHT by the time they finished with me. The skylights had darkened into eyes that peered inside like observers at an autopsy.

I had been drifting in and out of consciousness for hours now, each tiny dose of nectar rebooting my system for just a few seconds. Every time I fell into sleep the orchard rose up around me, trees sprouting from the ground, branches coiling up over my bed like the tentacles of some sea monster. Then I'd blink and be back in the hospital, Panettierre slicing away while her doctors stared goggle-eyed. But I knew the dream was still there, awaiting my return. I couldn't hide from it forever.

At some point the blacksuit next to me died. I watched it happen, saw the spark in his eyes sputter, flare brightly for a fraction of a second, and then fade. A while later some soldiers cut his body loose from the table and dragged it away, I guessed to an incinerator somewhere. It was shortly afterward that Panettierre threw her scalpel into a dish and wiped her nectar-encrusted hands on her white overalls.

"I think we're done here," she wheezed through her gas mask. "Send the results to my quarters, I need to double-check them."

The scientists began to drift away until only the colonel remained. She rested a hand on the table and wiped her other arm over her mask, feigning mopping the sweat from her brow. "Phew," she said to me. "That was tough. But you've done well, Alex. We've learned a great deal today, about you and the disease inside you. Are you feeling okay?"

I didn't need to see my body to know what it looked like—pockmarked with fresh wounds, craters in my skin, like the surface of the moon. When she saw I wasn't going to answer she carried on.

"The nectar, it's astonishing," she said. "It's unlike anything we've ever seen before. It's almost—I don't know—intelligent, the way it targets wounds. Like a supercharged clotting agent, only more than that too. It functions so much more efficiently than blood, carrying twenty, maybe thirty times as much oxygen. And it makes your physiology go haywire, seems to act like a neurological drug, numbing emotional transmissions, fear, any kind of reason." She shook her head, as if she couldn't believe the words coming out of her own mouth. "It's no wonder we're getting hammered out there. An army filled with this stuff could win any war, full stop."

She paused, lost somewhere in her own imagination, and the way her eyes lit up made my skin crawl. It was a while before she remembered I was there.

"But there's so much left to do before we truly understand what this liquid is. It's quite unpredictable. For instance, why does it affect different people differently, turning some into psychotic, mindless killers, the ones you call rats, and others into monsters? I mean, those berserkers have completely changed, there's nothing human in them anymore. And how come some of you can talk, the ones in suits?"

She looked at me as if expecting to be enlightened, only waiting for a second or two before continuing her barrage of questions.

"And what about you? You seem to be somewhere in between. You have the body of a monster, a berserker, and yet you seem to have the mind of a normal teenager. It really doesn't make much sense. Do you remember anything about this? Did the warden explain it?"

My life in the prison seemed so long ago now that even if the warden had told me the full truth about the nectar I doubt I could have remembered it.

"Well, no matter," she said. "I can understand why you're too tired to speak. It's been a long day. But it's not quite over yet, I'm afraid. There's a little something we need you to do for us. It won't take long, and then you can sleep, I promise."

She nodded to somebody behind me and I heard an engine start up, the sound of gears crunching, the whine of an approaching vehicle. Panettierre stood to one side as a small forklift truck wheeled into view, its prongs sliding under my table. There was a jolt as the table was lifted off the floor, the room spinning like a fairground ride.

"Don't worry, Alex," came Panettierre's voice. She walked along beside me as the truck carted me across the room, heading for a large loading door. Dozens of creatures watched us pass from the operating tables, their constant motion as they thrashed and bucked making me feel like I was on a boat sailing across an ocean of wounded flesh. "It shouldn't be dangerous, not for you. We just need to see how the nectar works in a . . . I guess you'd call it a combat situation."

I didn't have time to ask her what she meant. A couple of soldiers pulled open the loading door and the truck passed through it into a canvas tunnel that concealed the night sky for the fifty-meter journey across a concrete yard to a second brick building. We crawled toward it, entering through a wide door.

At first I thought it was another white-tiled operating theater, like the one I'd been in moments ago. Then I noticed the massive pit in the floor. No, not a pit, a *pool*. It was a swimming pool, only all of the water had been drained away. It was surrounded by a metal cage, its sides parallel with the edges of the pool. I peered through those shining bars as the forklift carried me closer, almost expecting to see a pair of cage fighters, as if this were some bizarre TV game show. But all I saw was a sloped floor rising out of a crimson swamp, as if somebody had been trying to fill the pool with blood. There were soldiers and scientists surrounding the cage, all in gas masks, too many of them to count.

My guts began to twist, and I wondered if I should be trying to get loose, trying to escape. But I stayed quiet and I stayed still. Instinct told me that I'd need to save what little strength I had for whatever was about to happen.

"Put him straight in," Panettierre shouted. "Prep the others."

A door in the side of the cage slid open and the forklift eased me forward until I was dangling over the deep end. To either side of me there was a roar as two chain saws started up in stereo. I heard somebody barking out a countdown and then I was bathed in sparks, the whole room lighting up. Before I could make sense of what was going on, the coils of shipping wire around me loosened, the forklift lurched, and I found myself falling. I landed in a pile of something soft and wet, my operating table striking the floor next to me, splintering the tiles. There was a crunch overhead as the cage door grated shut and I looked up in time to see the doctors crowd around it, Panettierre pushing to the front.

I managed to lift myself onto my haunches, but that was as far as I could go. When I attempted to stand up the whole room cartwheeled, my legs too weak to hold me. I crouched, trying to haul in a breath, my whole body trembling with the effort. I realized that I was dressed in a flimsy hospital gown, needles and sensor pads still plastered all over my skin.

"Can you hear me down there, Alex?" said Panettierre. "Those pads on you, they'll tell us all we need to know, you don't have to worry about any of that. All we're asking you to do is help us out a little. Will you do that?"

Something howled, a banshee's cry that echoed off the tiled walls, scraping down my spine.

"Stand well away," I heard somebody say. "Dump it straight in."

Another forklift truck rolled into view on the lip of the pool. This one held a cage, and cramped inside it was a berserker. It wasn't like any I had seen to date, its body made up of yellow-white skin that was knotted and warped as though carved from solid bone. Its skull was huge and cone shaped, arching back like a cycling helmet. I'd seen pictures of African tribes who bound their skulls to make them long and pointy, and this reminded me of them. The creature's forehead jutted so far forward that its face was cast into shadow, and only when it arched its back did I get a good look at it.

Its eyes, nose, and mouth were clustered right in the middle of its head, squished together like the punched-in features of a cartoon figure hit with a frying pan. I didn't see how a face like that could still function, but it must have because the berserker turned its eyes in my direction, sniffing the air, a tiny tongue poking from the pencil-sharpener hole of its mouth, licking at nonexistent lips.

The berserker's cage was pushed right up against the door

above me, and in a single motion both hatches were slid open. The creature leaped down into the pool, causing a crimson tsunami. I scrabbled back, adrenaline making the most of what little nectar was left in my system. The berserker didn't attack, just cocked its head as if trying to get a good look at me with its underdeveloped eyes. This close I could see they were lumpy and off-white, like fried eggs with their yolks broken.

The forklift truck wheeled back, beeping, but as soon as it had gone another appeared, also holding a cage. This one contained something else, smaller but wilder. A rat. I thought for a moment that the clothes it wore—drenched in a bib of black blood—were prison overalls. But I was wrong. It was wearing beige combats, and when it moved something glittered around its neck.

Dog tags.

The rat hacked and slashed at the bars, so hard that its fingers were torn and bloody, its nails long gone. But it didn't care. Of course it didn't. It was mindless, emotionless, just a vehicle of flesh controlled by the nectar inside, nectar that gushed from its distended jaws.

Once more the cage was pushed up against the metal fence around the pool, the two hatches sliding open as one. In the blink of an eye the rat was out, swinging onto the inside of the pool cage like a monkey at the zoo. The scientists fell away, but one was too slow. The rat reached through a gap and grabbed his mask, wrenching him forward so hard that his head bounced off the metal. A dozen arms wrapped themselves around the injured scientist, pulling him away before the rat could inflict further damage.

I was still retreating, shuffling on my knees toward the far side of the pool, my gown drenched in blood. The berserker was studying me, not showing any sign of movement. I'd fought creatures like it before—back in the prison—and I'd won. But right now, drained of nectar, I didn't stand a chance. Especially with a rat in here as well. The smaller creature turned to me now, its eyes like lumps of coal in its head, a cry of animal rage bubbling from its lips.

I felt cold tiles against my back, realized there was nowhere to run. Above me the scientists had returned to the bars, their desire to watch obviously overpowering any thoughts of personal safety. I held up my left hand to them—even this seeming like an impossible act—silently begging them for mercy. But there was no compassion in their eyes, only greed.

With another gargled howl the rat dropped into the pool, its bare feet slapping in the mush as it charged at me. Its broken hands were held out toward my throat, its teeth gnashing at the air. It was possible that it only wanted to bite me, infect me with the nectar. If that was the case then I could let it—it would give me strength, help me survive. But it could just as easily open up my throat, finish me off. It was a chance I didn't really want to take.

Sheer terror got me to my feet, the side of the pool the only thing stopping me from toppling over. The rat was almost on me, launching itself into the air so fast it was just a blur against the tiles. I did the only thing I could think of, sticking out the blade of my right hand, hoping that the freak would impale itself. I closed my eyes, waited for the impact, but it never came.

There was a choked squeak, the snap of a bone breaking. I looked past the extended blade of my hand to see the rat in a pile on the floor, one leg sticking out at a bizarre angle. Towering over it was the berserker. The rat screeched, no emotion registering on its twisted face. It didn't pay any attention to the creature next to it, just hurled itself at me again. This time I saw what happened, the berserker lashing out with one of its arms, catching the rat in the ribs and sending it flying. Its flailing form hit the side of the pool hard enough to crack the tiles before falling into the muck.

Despite its injuries, the rat looked as if it was about to try again, but before it could move the berserker was on it. It hefted the squirming creature up in its two giant fists, then, with a grunt of effort, bent it in half, snapping its spine. I stared at the berserker, unable to believe what I had just seen. It looked back at me, beads of oil-black blood dripping from its ivory skin.

Then, incredibly, it walked over to me and laid the dead rat at my feet. It shuffled back, never taking those egg-yolk eyes away from mine. I stared into them, wondering what thoughts were going through its head—and whether they were its thoughts at all. Was it a berserker who stared at me, who nodded expectantly toward the corpse, or was it Alfred Furnace?

"What is it doing, Alex?" I heard Panettierre shout. The berserker turned in the direction of her voice, uttering a bark like a gorilla's: a warning. I didn't answer, I didn't move, my confusion too great. The hulking beast pushed the corpse toward me the way a mother lion might offer a dead gazelle to her cubs, a high-pitched whine escaping its tiny mouth. I understood what it meant—it wanted me to eat.

I struggled to move, eventually managing to crouch over the rat. Somebody was banging on the bars above me.

"Hey," one of the scientists yelled. "This isn't part of the experiment. Leave it alone!" But no sooner had he spoken than I heard Panettierre countermand the order:

"Leave them, let's see what happens."

I ignored them all, lowering my mouth toward the rat. I could see the nectar still pumping out of it, the crimson specks inside glowing like molten lava. My strength faltered, but the berserker scooped the corpse up, pushing it against my lips.

"Stop this," the man's voice said. "Take them down, right now."

"No!" screamed Panettierre, but as she did so there was a shot, something thudding into the berserker hard enough to rock it on its heels. It grunted, but still it didn't move, holding the rat in front of me. I glanced once more at Panettierre, her delight visible even behind her mask, then I opened my mouth and let the nectar flood inside. That familiar disgusting taste gushed over my tongue, unbearably rancid, but it was forgotten as soon as the poison hit my system. It burned through me, strength raging into every muscle like a flash fire. I gulped down as much as I could, even as another shot punched through the berserker's chest, then a third, finally driving the creature back.

It didn't matter. I had no need of outside assistance now. I was up and moving before I was even aware of it, tossing away the corpse as I propelled myself up the side of the pool and grabbed hold of the bars with the mutated fingers at the end of my left arm. Everybody staggered away, all except for Panettierre, who didn't even flinch. I thrust the blade of my hand through, trying to stab her, to end her, but she was just out of reach. She studied me for a moment as I tried to smash my way through, then she turned and gave another order.

"That's enough. Sedate him; dice the other one."

Half a dozen soldiers pushed through the scientists, rifles aimed at my chest. I dropped from the bars but I was too late, a flurry of red-feathered darts whispering between them and into my skin. I fought the drowsiness, running to the far side of the pit and trying my luck there. I didn't even make it up the wall, my feet slipping, depositing me into the filth.

The pool was filling, not with liquid but with darkness—those same nightmare trees pushing up from the tiles, growing to full height in the blink of an eye. My thoughts were crushed into dust beneath the nectar and the tranquilizer darts. There was nothing left inside my mind, a black void of utter stillness. I scanned the pool, my gaze falling on the berserker. It was tripping backward, bullet holes erupting across its torso like bulging red eyes. It collapsed to its knees, its mouth opening, a single cry dropping out.

I don't know why, but I used the very last of my strength to crawl through the muck of the pool toward the berserker. It's not as if I wanted to save it—it was too late for that anyway, not with at least twenty armor-piercing rounds inside it. No, it was something else. I guess when you're trapped inside a cage, hundreds of eyes watching you teeter on the edge of death, you just want to know you're not alone.

The berserker was on its side now, a lake of nectar spilling out from its belly and chest. It blinked its pus-yellow eyes at me, and it might have been my imagination but I swear it lifted a hand, letting me crawl closer before wrapping it protectively around my shoulders. It was the last thing it would ever do, because with a bone-breaking judder its body stalled, then lay still.

I looked up past its knotted limb, realized that Panettierre was watching me from the edge of the pool. She was smiling, the searing lights of the room reflected in the glass of her visor looking like a grin that seemed to stretch off the sides of her face, making her eyes gleam.

And the last thought I had before falling out of time was that she looked just like the warden.

THE STRANGER

THE NIGHTMARE WAS WAITING FOR ME, AS IF I HAD NEVER LEFT.

And it was more real than ever.

My vision was blurred, the way it is when you wake from a deep sleep, but even though I couldn't see the orchard I knew I was back there. I could feel the mush of flyblown fruit between my bare toes, worms squirming beneath me. That cold wind still brushed across my scalp like fingers, only now it carried with it the smell of the place—the stench of rotting wood, of rancid blood and bird crap, and, past that, something else, something worse.

I gagged, doubling over, my body able to move but my feet once again rooted in place as though the hands of dead men rose from the soil to claim me. Tears streamed down my face as I fought for breath. I was coughing so hard that something clawed up my windpipe, scuttling from my mouth and over my cheek, disappearing into my hair. I moaned, a noise of utter desperation. It was just too much—the real world and the dream world opposite corners of the same hell.

And I hadn't even opened my eyes yet. I couldn't, because I knew that *he* was there. The stranger. Maybe if I couldn't see him then he wouldn't be able to see me.

It was the sobs that finally made me look, pitiful cries that could have been my own but which came from the other side of the clearing. I wiped my eyes, seeing that the kid, Alfred Furnace, was still nailed to the tree, his body hanging like a broken branch. At first I thought he was alone, and then I saw the stranger. He stood right in front of the boy, his body nothing more than a silhouette, a pit that sucked in the sickly light of the orchard and returned only cold waves of darkness. It was as if the view before me was a photograph, and the shape of the man had been burned out of it—he wasn't human, he was the absence of humanity.

He was tall, towering over the kid by a good meter. Tall and skeletally thin, his arms and legs too long, too many joints there, his fingers like distended shadows. His spine was crooked like an old man's, and yet this thing, whatever it was, reeked of power. It looked down at the boy, not moving, just staring. And even though Furnace's cries tore at my heart, I was glad of them, because it meant the stranger wasn't looking at me.

Something fell from a branch overhead, a soft, feathered body that struck the ground, flapping its wings a couple of times before lying still. Another followed, then a third—this one so close it almost hit me. I watched the crow's wild eyes fade. Seven, maybe eight more birds dropped dead from the trees, and where they landed the grass and weeds turned brown, shriveling back into the soil. Even the movement of the worms grew more urgent, their bodies writhing as they fought to escape the putrefaction that gripped the orchard.

Furnace's cries reached a crescendo, a symphony of terror as he tried to wriggle his way free from the tree. The stranger walked around him, studying him, and even though I could make out neither eyes nor a mouth in the pool of darkness that served as his face, I knew he was smiling. There seemed to be no end to the torment, and I wondered whether Furnace's misery would go on forever, whether I would be stuck with him in this loop of broken time.

But eventually the boy grew weak, his cries drying up, his body trembling like a dead leaf. His head lolled to his chest, and I thought for a moment he had finally died. Then his mouth opened and he spoke in a whisper.

What do you want?

The stranger didn't reply. Instead, he reached down toward the pool of blood that had formed beneath Furnace. He didn't bend; it was as if his arm extended, stretched out like licorice. One finger uncurled from his loose fist, the nail as long as my palm, and he used it to scoop up a nugget of crimson soil. The arm swept back up in a lazy arc, contracting to its former length. A crack opened up in his head and he popped the nugget into it, his entire body shivering with perverse delight.

And then the stranger spoke. Or, rather, communicated, the outline of his face-that-wasn't-a-face unfolding and refolding like an origami mask. There were no words, but there was meaning. It pulsed out of him in waves, making the trees and the wind whisper, making the ground rumble and the air above us thunder—the whole orchard becoming a voice that shifted in pitch and volume, the effect making me seasick.

DEATH IS NEARLY UPON YOU, ALFRED. BUT DEATH DOESN'T HAVE TO BE THE END.

The boy didn't reply, just hung there, and I knew that he was willing his own passing, that he was praying for the end to come. Because better that death took him than this thing. I understood it because the same thoughts were racing through my own mind.

The stranger reached out again, a dark shadow that unfolded beneath Furnace's chin, lifting his head. His fingers were so long that it looked as though a huge spider was resting on the boy's face.

WAS YOUR CRIME WORTH IT, BOY?

This time Furnace responded.

You know I didn't do it. You killed József; you are my brother's murderer.

The stranger's hand retreated, reminding me of the way a snail's horns shrink into its head when they are touched. His not-face opened and closed, a myriad of dark corners weaving in and out of each other, and once again his wordless message was clear.

I KILLED YOUR BROTHER IN ORDER TO SAVE YOU.

I knew that was a lie, and Furnace did too because he shot the man a look of undiluted hatred. The stranger's face moved relentlessly, reminding me of the cogs and blades inside an engine, and yet somehow I could still see the smile there. A noise rose from him, a wet purr that thrummed across the clearing, and once again he reached out, fingers pushing the hair back from Furnace's face then resting over his brow.

As soon as the contact was made, shadow against flesh, an image flashed up in my mind—Furnace, free of the tree, his eyes burning black, radiating strength. Another followed, the same boy crouched over the bodies of his accusers, the people who had crucified him, his mother included, steam rising from their corpses. Him again, older now, at the head of an army, the soldiers behind him half man and half beast. Berserkers. The visions blinked on and off, each brighter than the last. Past them I could see Furnace thrashing against the man's touch, and I knew that he was seeing the same things, he was witnessing his future.

"Don't listen to him!" I shouted, my fear overcoming my paralysis. "It doesn't have to be like that."

Without looking at me the stranger stretched out his other hand, the shadow sweeping over the clearing, impossibly far, clamping across my face. It was as if my head had been dunked in ice water, the sensation taking my breath away. Before I could recover, more images pummeled their way into my brain—this time showing Furnace and me, together, beating our enemies into the dirt, riding high over the world.

I fought to block out the images, the same way I'd fought a lifetime ago back in the warden's screening room, the same way I'd fought every time the nectar raged inside me, but it was impossible to deny that rush of excitement. When you're powerless, what greater temptation can there be than a promise of omnipotence?

YOUR TIME WILL COME TOO, ALEX.

Furnace was struggling as hard as I was, but I could see that his resolve was weakening. He'd been shown an alternative to death, he'd been shown a world in which he was more than just a kid, more than just a victim of injustice. He'd been shown a future where he could take his revenge. I'd been there, I knew exactly how that felt.

The stranger's hand dropped away from me. He stepped toward Furnace, cradling the boy's head against his chest almost tenderly.

DO YOU ACCEPT MY GIFT, ALFRED?

Furnace's head lolled against the stranger's body. He was almost gone. Another minute maybe and death would claim him. I was amazed that he had lasted as long as he had, his body sliced open by his own mother's blade.

You killed my brother, Furnace whispered. *I'll kill you for that.*

THE ONLY WAY TO KILL ME IS TO ACCEPT MY OFFER.

Furnace lifted his head as best he could, his eyes glinting at the thought of retribution. The stranger continued to stroke his hair with his branchlike fingers, the same cooing purr vibrating from his throat.

JÓZSEF DIED FOR YOU, ALFRED. HE GAVE HIS LIFE SO THAT YOU MIGHT LIVE FOREVER. IF YOU DO NOT ACCEPT, HE WILL HAVE BEEN LOST FOR NOTHING. IF YOU DO NOT ACCEPT, I LIVE ON TO KILL AGAIN.

The boy's eyes were now closed. He could sense death there, we both could. And I guess that's why he made the decision he did—not because of his brother, not so that he might live forever, but because when you're standing on the edge of the void, when you feel yourself about to tumble into the unfathomable, unthinkable darkness of death, you'll do anything to stop it. I willed for him to pass, but it was pointless. I already knew Furnace's story, after all. I already knew what his answer would be. He gave a single, almost imperceptible nod.

I accept.

The stranger's face unfolded, shadowed petals blossoming, contracting, blossoming again. Then he threw back his head and laughed—not a sound but a sonic pulse that exploded through the orchard, splitting trees, bringing branches crashing to the earth. He stepped away, holding his left arm in front of Alfred Furnace, his hand tilted back. Then he dragged the nails of his other hand across his wrist.

Black blood began to fall to the earth, slowly at first, then gushing like an oil well. My heart recognized what it was before my brain did, my pulse beating furiously. Nectar. The stranger pulled the boy's head back with his free hand and brought the severed vein to Furnace's mouth. The boy choked as the liquid flowed into him, disappearing down his throat. Nectar gushed from between his lips, but not for long—soon he was swallowing it eagerly, his body demanding more, like a starving man at a banquet.

Furnace's face was changing, his cheeks bulging as the tainted blood poured into him, surging down his gullet. He spat out a cry, tugging his right hand until it tore free from the nail, clamping his fingers around the stranger's arm and holding it there. He did the same with his left, the effort cleaving his palm in two and sending him crashing onto his knees. But he didn't seem to notice the pain. All he cared about was the creature's blood, the nectar.

My mind reeled, unable to believe what I was seeing. I knew this was a dream, taking place only in my head, but if Furnace was right, if this was a memory for him, it meant this had actually happened.

The stranger was growing weak, the dense cloud of shadow that hung around him becoming less opaque. His right arm began to crumple, folding in on itself like the tendril of a burning plant. One of his legs buckled, then the other, and he staggered to his knees. It was as if he was sinking into a vast sea trench, the pressure of the water compressing his body. With an almighty crack his head began to shrink, deflating, crushed by an invisible force, pulled down into his neck.

Furnace kept drinking, consuming every last drop of the stranger's blood, until all that remained was a desiccated husk on the orchard ground.

The kid was crouching on his haunches, more animal than human. He shook himself, tar-colored blood spraying from his lips, and when he opened his mouth a growl fell out of it, one that pulsed around the orchard with the same ground-shaking force as the stranger's laughter. He cocked his head toward me, and when he opened his eyes they were vortexes of shadow, so deep and so furious that they threatened to pull me in.

We are all puppets hanging over an ocean of madness, the boy said, and it was no longer the whine of a child but the voice I knew so well, that thunderous whisper of Alfred Furnace. *All it takes is one simple snip and we fall.*

He held his ruined hands up to his face and I could see the flesh there knitting back together, the stranger's blood healing him. When he turned back to me his mouth had flopped open into a cruel imitation of a smile.

Now you know.

He threw himself across the clearing, running on all fours, his black eyes seeming to pump out their own impossible light that corrupted everything it touched. I saw trees crack, the bark splitting, apples disappearing beneath growing tides of mold, dead birds decomposing into tattered skeletons, all in a blink of the boy's nightmare gaze.

With a laugh he vanished among the trees, but his voice floated back to me on the breeze, as clear as if he was standing right next to me, whispering in my ear.

Now you know how it all began.

HISTORY

I WOKE TO THE SOUND OF MY NAME.

At least, I think I woke. Almost completely drained of blood and nectar, teetering between insanity and death, I could no longer say for sure what was real and what was a dream. I was sitting in a chair in a small cell, almost identical to the one I'd first woken up in. My torso was bound once more with wire, but my body felt numb—except for the memory of the orchard ground against my feet, the stranger's touch on my forehead.

It was almost as if this world was slowly losing itself, dissolving into my imagination, becoming a dream.

There was something else too, a muted pain in my head. I shook it from side to side, and that dull throb seemed to shift, sliding back and forth over my brain like there was something trapped in there.

My name again, spoken with an accent. I opened my eyes to see a blurred shape by my side. Was it Panettierre? Something had happened, hadn't it, before I slept? Something about a pit, and a berserker. Had it been another test, like the one the warden had given me back in the prison? I couldn't for the life of me remember.

"Alex, are you in there?"

I blinked, focused, realized that the person in my room wasn't Panettierre at all. It was a boy. More memories, but there was so little nectar left in me that they were like fish dying in the bottom of a leaking barrel. One managed to leap up above the rest, hanging there just long enough for me to grasp it.

"Zee?"

The boy's face opened up, his smile almost dazzling. He looked different from the last time I'd seen him—a time that seemed like aeons ago—cleaner, his hair washed and brushed. He was wearing a set of overalls, and for a second I thought they were Furnace stripes. But they were green rather than dirty white. Army fatigues. I felt his hand on my shoulder, a reassuring squeeze. It was only then that I realized my arms were laid out on a table, secured in place. I wiggled the strange protrusions on my left hand. The blackened stumps hadn't changed. I guess there wasn't enough nectar to work with.

"Good to have you back, Alex," he said. "I was getting worried. You looked like you were about to die in your sleep."

"I was dreaming," I muttered, shaking my head, trying to wake up, to work out what was going on. "What are you doing here?"

Zee's smile wavered.

"Is that any way to speak to your best buddy?" he asked, and then the smile fell away completely. He glanced over his shoulder, the cell door shut, then he looked up at a camera on the wall, pointing right at us. "Let's see if I can make you a bit more comfortable." He stood and bent over me, straightening my gown, his back to the camera. When he spoke next it was in a whisper. "They're listening, so don't say anything that they won't—you know, won't like." I started to protest but he cut me off. "This place is messed up, big-time. It's almost as bad as Furnace, only these guys don't know what they're doing. The only reason you're alive is because you can still talk. But that won't save you for long."

He sat back, his voice returning to normal.

"There, that's better. I told them that you'd listen to me, that you'd tell us how to find the people behind the invasion."

"But I don't—"

"You don't remember, I know," Zee interrupted. "But it will come back to you, right?" He winked at me, nodding furiously. "If they're patient for a few more days, then it will come back to you."

I took the hint, returning his nod with one of my own. Zee seemed to relax, crashing back in his chair. There was a moment of quiet, filled only by the growl of a truck's engine from outside the window and the distant whump of helicopter blades. He flicked another look at the door, leaning in and lowering his voice again.

"I told them everything, all about the prison, what was going on there. They believed me. Not that they had a choice. I mean, they're losing this war, getting torn to pieces. The only thing they won't accept is the stuff about Alfred Furnace. They think who- ever built the prison is somebody else, somebody using his name."

I told Zee about the nightmare, the words falling from me in clumps like rotten fruit dropping from a branch, sounding even more insane than they had in my dream. Zee sat there patiently, his head cocked.

"It *is* Furnace," I said when I'd finished. They say the child is father to the man, and if anyone could have spawned the monster behind the prison, the creature whose dark thoughts blossomed in my head, it was that kid.

"I know," Zee said. "I heard him too, remember. The phone in the warden's office." He shuddered so hard his chair rattled. "But there's a problem. They've looked into it and the only Alfred Furnace they can find was born, like, in the eighteenth century or something. In Hungary."

"What?" I asked, thinking of the orchard, wondering if that's where it was. I couldn't even picture where Hungary was on a map. "Seriously? Hungary?"

"No thanks, I've just eaten," Zee replied, that contagious smile back on his face, seeming to make the room twice as big. "Sorry, I couldn't resist it. Anyway, I tell you he was born over three hundred years ago and it's the *Hungary* bit you don't believe?"

I could see what he meant, but it made perfect sense to me. I mean, if the warden had fought in the Second World War he had to have been about a hundred, and it made sense that his boss was even older. What was a century or two when you had nectar in your veins? I shrugged as best I could and Zee carried on.

"Impostor or not, Alfred Furnace is the only lead they have. They've dug up loads of stuff about him—this is military intelligence we're talking about, and not just ours either, the whole world is joining in. There's not much about his early life, but apparently by the turn of the century—the nineteenth, that is—he had come into a vast amount of money, set himself up as a duke or something. He was famous for his army, led them in the November Uprising against the Russian Empire in 1830, the Hungarian Revolution of 1848, and in the January Uprising fifteen years later too." He paused, swallowing, his eyes flitting up to the window over my head. "Y'know, I've heard about all this stuff. We did it in history. It's real."

"He got about a bit, didn't he?" I said. "How come he wasn't made a king or anything?"

"Hungary was still part of the Austrian Empire then. They

didn't have their own king. Besides, Alfred Furnace was a peasant. As far as we can tell, anyway. But he was certainly as powerful as a king. His soldiers were feared across Europe, across the world."

"Let me guess: super fast, super strong, more animal than human."

"You got it," Zee said. "And famous for wearing black on the battlefield. But they were an elite group, never more than a handful of them."

"I don't remember hearing his name at school, though," I said.

"That's because he wasn't called Furnace, not back then. Alfred Furnace is a translation of his Hungarian name, Alfréd Kazán."

"Kazán? Sounds like a magician."

"Yeah, and people thought he was, too. Black magic and stuff. Anyway, he had this terrible reputation for bloodshed and murder on the battlefield all the way through the 1800s, and then he just disappears, vanishes into thin air. The records, what few there are, assume he died."

"But he didn't."

"No, he didn't. He just moved."

"Where?" I asked, trying to stretch the cramped muscles of my legs, the wire holding me tight. "Here?"

"No, to Austria, Vienna. Except he told the authorities he was his own grandson, Heinrich."

"Tricky," I said.

"Yeah, you could say that." Zee grinned. "Anyway, he had connections with the university, built his own college up there. Any of this sounding familiar?"

"Should it?" I asked.

Zee's smile flashed back for a second, uncertain. "It's like the plot of *Frankenstein*," he said. "Furnace got into trouble, was accused of meddling with stuff that shouldn't be meddled with. Some sort of eugenics, they thought; selective breeding. Only it wasn't that, it was nectar. There's nothing specific in any of the papers or anything, just that he was pretty much forced out of the city. If you ask me, Vienna's when he started trying to reproduce the nectar artificially, rather than just letting people drink his blood or whatever. I guess he couldn't make many soldiers by just feeding them his own nectar so he wanted to replicate it, find a way to generate it, maybe make it even more powerful."

I imagined how much of his own supply it would have taken to build an army. It must have been a constant drain on him.

"I think that's why he went there in the first place," Zee continued. "Because it was like the scientific capital of the world."

"So what happened next?"

Zee shook his head.

"That's where the trail runs cold. There are dispatches that mention a Kazán during the First World War, in Germany, but they're too vague to confirm anything. He must have been in Germany during the rise of the Nazis, though. He's not mentioned by name in any history books, but I think Hitler and those other creeps gave Furnace the chance to work on the nectar. I think they recruited him, charged him with creating the ultimate super-soldier."

"Yeah, that makes sense," I said, remembering what the warden had told me, what he had shown me. "And when they lost the war Furnace came here, changed his name from Kazán, set himself up as a businessman, opened the prison, built his tower, and carried on perfecting the nectar."

"Bingo," said Zee. "Except, of course, they don't believe he's three hundred years old. They're working on the theory that the man who built the prison, the man behind the attacks, is a distant relative of Alfréd Kazán. There's enough of a paper trail to link the Furnace estate with funds deposited in Kazán family accounts around the world. But apparently the actual company records are so messed up and complicated that they don't think they'll ever know for sure. In short, they've no idea who they're looking for; the only thing they're sure of is that it's *not* Alfred Furnace—I mean Kazán—the original one. Ironic, don't you think?"

There was a moment of quiet while I tried to digest what I'd heard.

"They managed to find all that out in a few hours?" I asked. "That's pretty good going."

Zee glanced up at the window again, then over his shoulder at the camera, all the time chewing on something.

"What?" I asked.

"It's not been a few hours, Alex," he said. "You've been drifting in and out for four days now."

"Four days?" I said. "How's that possible?"

"They've drained you of almost all the nectar. It's part of their plan to try to find out what this stuff is, and how your body copes without it. You've only got a trickle left in you." He pointed to the side of the room, to an IV bag filled with crimson liquid. "Plus plenty of that."

"Blood?"

"Yeah. They're seeing what happens when you replace the nectar with normal blood."

"It'll kill me," I said. I didn't know that for sure but I felt it. My body was used to the nectar, putting blood in my veins would be like putting water in a car's gas tank. Eventually the engine would just splutter and die.

"I know," Zee said, nodding slowly. His voice lowered to a whisper again. "They've already killed off dozens of rats, berserkers too, by doing the same thing. They're butchers in here, and that Panettierre is the worst of them. They've dissected them, boiled them, burned them alive, shot them full of acid, hacked off their limbs. I've seen it, Alex. They made me watch because I was in the prison, because I saw for myself what the warden was doing."

He shot a look back at the camera, then turned his sad, tired eyes to me.

"But it won't be long before they try to cut me to pieces too. I made the mistake of telling them I was immune to the nectar." I remembered, back in the tunnels beneath the prison, the warden had been about to throw Zee in the incinerator because his system didn't respond to the nectar. "You should have seen their eyes light up, like it was Christmas. They told me I was safe, because I was human, but I know bull when I hear it."

Zee swore, crashing back on his chair, staring at the wall.

"They've got Simon too," he said softly. "He's in the same ward as me, in a cell. They don't call it a cell, they call it our quarters, but they keep the doors locked. Panettierre's keeping him alive for the same reason she's keeping you alive, because he can talk and everything, because he's still, y'know, human. But he's on her list, I've seen it."

"List?" I asked, trying to put a face to the name Simon, pulling vague strands of memory loose from the confusion in my head—a boy with silver eyes and one overgrown arm, a boy who saved my life back in the tower when I was fighting the warden. Zee nodded.

"Yeah, they've got this list of test subjects, mainly rats and berserkers, but you're on it too, and Simon. You're both marked as expendable. They don't care if they kill you."

"Tell me something I don't know," I muttered.

"Okay," Zee said, leaning forward again. "I bet you don't know why they're trying to harness the power of the nectar."

"So they can stop Furnace," I replied. "So they can find a cure, save the world."

"After everything we've been through, everything we've seen, you honestly think that's why?"

I frowned, shrugging imperceptibly beneath my restraints. The ache in my head was growing. There was a clatter from outside, the door squeaking as it opened to admit two armed guards and a wiry, redheaded man in a suit.

"That's your time up," said the man. Zee looked from him to me, reaching out and squeezing my arm as he got to his feet.

"But they're still looking for Furnace, right?" I said.

"I think they've given it up as a dead end," he said. "I told you, they only care about the nectar. And they care about the nectar because they want it for themselves."

"For themselves?" I asked. "What do you mean? Why do they want it?"

Zee shook his head sadly.

"Because they're going to create an army of their own."

HOLDING ON

THE DOOR SLAMMED SHUT, the lock mechanisms sliding into place, leaving me more alone than I'd ever felt in my life.

It was worse than when I'd been in solitary confinement, miles of rock in every direction except one and a massive steel hatch over that. Even though there was a shaft of pure sunlight blazing into the room, even though I could hear birdsong from somewhere outside, even though I knew there were people all around me, I felt truly and utterly isolated.

At least back in the prison, buried beneath the ground with the blacksuits and rats and wheezers, it had been a clear case of us and them. We were the good guys; the warden and his freaks were the villains. But here I had no idea what was going on. These soldiers, these scientists, they were supposed to be on our side. We should have been working together to try to find Furnace and bring down his army.

Instead, I was a prisoner again, bound in chains and locked in a cell. Not only that, I was a specimen too, just a hunk of meat for them to cut open and study. The warden had butchered me, but the truth was he had wanted to patch me up again, make me better than I had been before. Here they would murder me and call it science. And if Zee was right, then they weren't going to kill me in order to find a cure. They weren't even going to kill me to work out a way of stopping Furnace's freaks.

No, they were going to kill me so that they could create monsters of their own.

I pictured what would happen if the world's militaries got hold of the nectar, if they started to use it on the youngest of their soldiers. All those kids pumped full of poison, driven insane, turned into killing machines. It would be like hell on earth, tens of thousands of rats unleashed on the battlefield, tearing each other—and everyone else—to shreds. The generals, the politicians, they'd think they could control it, harness its power, but they'd be wrong. They'd bring about the destruction of the world far more quickly than Alfred Furnace ever could.

Maybe that was Furnace's plan all along. Maybe he knew the army would capture some of his rats, his berserkers, that they'd discover the nectar. And it didn't take an evil genius to work out that they'd try to use it. Human nature was human nature. If that happened, if the nectar became an official weapon of war, then Furnace could sit back and watch the world's superpowers do his work for him.

I tugged at my restraints, frustration bubbling through my veins, every muscle silently screaming. The chair rattled, but the shipping wire didn't budge. I studied the IV bag that was feeding blood into me. If it was having any effect I couldn't feel it, other than the aching sense of weakness that sat over my whole body. Blood wouldn't keep me alive. Quite the opposite.

Death wasn't an option, though. Not now, not yet. Even though the thought of falling into an endless, dreamless sleep was almost too wonderful to resist. There was too much to do. If the army didn't believe Furnace was alive, if they weren't going after him, then I had to do it myself. I'd made a promise. I would find him, and I would kill him. Then I would have the rest of eternity to sleep.

I flexed the stubs of my left hand, those charred fingers opening and closing. It looked monstrous, but at least the nectar was trying to repair me, studying the blueprint of my genes and building me a new limb. Why was I growing fingers this time when before I'd grown a blade? Perhaps the nectar possessed some intelligence, giving me what would be of most use to me. Before, when I'd lost my right arm on the parking-lot roof, I'd been mid-combat—fighting tooth and nail with the blacksuits and the helicopters that rained fire from overhead. Back then a blade was exactly what I needed, a weapon when I was defenseless.

Now, though, I wasn't in immediate danger—not the same life-and-death kind, anyway. Maybe the nectar sensed that what I needed most now wasn't a weapon but a tool, a hand. True, it wasn't exactly perfect; I'd never play the piano again, but I'd never been able to play the piano, anyway. Still, I might just be able to hold a cup of tea.

If I ever got out of here alive.

I heard an engine start up outside the window, accelerating out of earshot. I wondered where exactly I was. It was a hospital that was being used as a military base, or a military base that was being used as a hospital, that was as much as I knew. Either way, that meant hundreds of soldiers, all armed with machine guns, plus helicopters, trucks, probably even tanks. But compared to Furnace Penitentiary this place might as well have been a nursing home for the elderly with walls made of polystyrene and fences woven from silk. I was aboveground, after all, and those soldiers were only

human—nine pints of blood wrapped in paper-thin skin, so fragile and so breakable that it was almost a joke.

I took a deep breath, tried to relax my cramped muscles. Then
I looked at the camera, its red light blinking, and thought about
the men and women watching me, thought about how easily I could
tear through them. All I needed to do was get out of these restraints
and find another dose of nectar, then not even the elite forces of
the world could stand in my way.

In the quiet of the room I wasn't sure whether it was my own
imagination or the voice of Alfred Furnace that whispered to
me—a breath that seemed to reverberate around my mind like the
echoes of an explosion, making that shifting pain beat ever harder:

I can help you do that, Alex.

I SAT in that room like a statue, the minutes grinding past, each
hour a vast gulf of time in which I drowned in boredom. There
was no clock in here, but the shadows of the bars on the window
drifted lazily across the wall in front of me, trekking from left to
right in what felt like a week. I couldn't even talk to Zee by banging on my toilet—the way I had back in solitary. All I could do was
watch those shadows while the anger smoldered inside me.

Only without the nectar those flames wouldn't take; I might as
well have tried to start a campfire with wet wood.

With nobody to talk to, even Furnace's voice would have been
welcome, but after that brief message he seemed to have faded
as well. I guess with hardly any nectar in my system it was harder
for him to communicate with me. Or maybe he wasn't interested
in me anymore. Panettierre had told me that I would die here,
sooner or later, so why would he bother with me? I still didn't truly

know why he was interested in me, whether he wanted me dead, or as his right-hand man—but either way I was useless to him right now.

The thought of Furnace woke the memory of my dreams, the orchard bulging to the surface of my thoughts like a whale breaching the ocean. Had he really shown me that, or had it just been a hallucination caused by the lack of nectar? It had seemed so real. But if it was real, then what was that thing, the stranger? And why did he have nectar for blood? Images and explanations churned in my head, too fast and too muddled to make any sense of. I watched the shadow moving imperceptibly but inexorably, the passage of the sun the only certainty in my life.

At some point—it must have been toward the end of the day because the shadow had grown, pooling in the corners of the room—Panettierre came to talk to me. She looked tired, her skin like gray wax, massive bags under her eyes. She didn't look at me, just walked to the machines by my chair, studying readouts, tapping buttons. It was only after ten minutes or more that she turned around.

"Any luck with those memories?" she asked, and even though she spoke through a smile her eyes were carved from stone. "We're running out of time here."

She watched me shake my head, her gaze dropping to my hands.

"We thought reintroducing human blood into your system might counter, maybe even reverse, the effects of the nectar, but that was a dead end. Your immune system has improved, but otherwise the readings are exactly the same as before. Do you feel any different?"

"Weaker," I managed.

"Did Warden Cross ever tell you what was in the nectar?" she went on.

"He said it came from the war," I replied, trying to remember what the warden had told me back in the prison. There were only scraps, half-thoughts that didn't make sense. "The Second World War. From men, people who were scared. He told me it came from them."

"That was a lie," Panettierre said. "Either he was trying to deceive you or he didn't know the truth himself."

"What do you mean?" I asked.

She looked at the monitors beside my chair, then back at me. It took a while for her to respond. "What I mean is that whatever the nectar is, it isn't human. It has never been human."

"How can it not—"

She cut me off by raising her hand, taking a few steps toward my chair. "It doesn't matter."

"Doesn't matter?" I spat back.

"Not to you."

She rested the same hand on my forehead, stroking my hair with her thumb.

"Alex, we're going to need to take a look inside you," she said softly. Panic surged up my throat like vomit and I tried to move my hands, my legs, my body, anything. She held my head firmly but gently, hushing me the way a mother would an upset child.

"I'll tell you who's behind this," I said. "I remember now, I can tell you everything, where to find them, honestly I can."

She stared at me, seeing right through my lies. Her other hand appeared, holding a syringe gun, and my heart dropped into my stomach.

"We appreciate everything you've done, we really do," she said. "When this is over, when we win this thing, the world will honor you, it will know your name. You'll be a hero. But for now, we really don't have a choice. I'm so sorry."

"Wait!" I shouted, then the syringe gun was against my throat. There was a soft hiss and a sharp pain, and once again I was falling into that ocean of darkness, velvet waves washing over me, pulling me under. "Please, don't . . ."

"You're going to a good place," she said, her words like stale candy. I realized that hers was the last voice I would ever hear, the last face I would ever see, and for reasons I couldn't explain, that seemed a million times worse than dying in Furnace with the warden watching over me. "A place for brave boys, boys like you who have saved us all."

I fought it, but her hand—that thumb still stroking back and forth, back and forth—pushed me under the waters of unconsciousness, holding me there until my vision began to fade, until I felt I couldn't breathe.

"We all love you, Alex," words spoken from the other side of time. "Now there will be no more nightmares, no more pain. And I need you to understand something, something very important." She smiled, but there was genuine sadness in her eyes. "I need you to understand that you helped us win this war. I need you to understand that you won't have died for nothing."

She lifted her hand, but I could still feel the weight of her fingers there as she spoke one final, terrifying word:

"Good night."

MY BODY GAVE WAY to the tranquilizer straightaway, but my mind fought it for as long as it could.

Hundreds, maybe thousands, of images and memories thundered through my head, a stampede that was so jumbled and so fast I could barely make any sense of it. It was as if my brain knew that death was waiting for me, that it wanted one last chance to help me remember my life before the darkness came to claim me—the same way a candle will often flare up in a final gasp before guttering out completely.

I saw the boy I once was, on the field at school kicking a soccer ball, not a single worry in his head; saw him again, stealing twenty quid from a kid's wallet, a kid called Daniel Richards. This time I screamed for him not to do it, but memories aren't like life, you've already made your choices, they're set in stone. There is absolutely nothing on earth you can do to change them.

More visions: all the times I broke the law, all the times I hurt people, dozens of them, each one like a slap in the face, until there I was in the elevator traveling down to Furnace Penitentiary. That was the day the boy called Alex Sawyer truly died.

My senses must still have been alert, because even buried beneath those memories I was aware of movement, the rattle of my chair as I was wheeled somewhere. I could hear voices too, Panettierre speaking with others. I couldn't follow what they were saying, but I could make out the odd scrap—*spinal fluid . . . cell count . . . start with his heart*. And was that laughter that echoed around me?

The flood of memories pushed the sound away, sluicing through my head with so much force I thought my mind would break. My life inside the prison, every day seemingly played out in full— the beatings, the despair, the terror. But it wasn't all bad. I saw Donovan, my old cellmate, his smile burning through the terror like sunrise. Zee too, the three of us inside our cell giggling like madmen.

It vanished as quickly as it appeared, swamped by everything else that had happened since: blowing up the floor of the chipping room back in the prison, being thrown inside solitary, meeting

Simon, trying to scale the steeple and then the incinerator, the operations to turn me into a blacksuit, the warden's soulless smile, taking revenge on the people who had left me to die in the orchard . . .

Even in my unconscious state, so close to death, I knew that wasn't quite right. Surely that wasn't one of my memories . . . And yet I could see it as clearly as if it were happening to me right now. I ran through the trees, faster than the animals that fought to get out of my way, faster even than the crows that soared overhead. I tore over fields, through rivers, crops wilting in my shadow, the ground splitting, the earth vomiting out the remains of dead things, a trail of rot and decay in my wake.

Then I was entering a village, the houses little more than wooden huts, smoke rising from crude chimneys. There were animals here, cows and pigs, all of which tried to tear loose from their ropes, white-eyed with terror, when they saw me coming. The people too ran from me as if their nightmares had come to life. And they were right. I was a nightmare made flesh. I pounced among them like a fox among chickens, ripping, rending, biting, punching, breaking, feasting until the air was heavy with scarlet mist and not a single man, woman, or child remained alive.

In my memory I studied my reflection in a puddle of steaming blood, trying to remember if that was my face, if this had been real, if it had been part of my life. The boy there was my age, he had been accused of a crime he didn't commit, sentenced to death. And now he was full of rage and full of nectar. Yes, that was my story, wasn't it? That was me. It had to be.

Past the visions I felt myself lifted onto a bed, straps tightening around my arms, legs, and chest. There was the sting of another needle and for an instant my heart lifted, expecting the rush of nectar. But the shot just pulled me closer to death, dragging me deeper into the void. There were more voices, sounding urgent, but I wasn't sure if they were from real life or my dream.

Even the rush of memories was fading now, the images losing their color and their brightness. I fought to keep hold of them, trying to focus on one—any one—because I realized it would be my last.

It took me a while to identify it: back inside Furnace, Donovan in front of me, dead, and a pillow in my hands. No, wait, I was crouched in the village, bodies cooling all around me, cradling the corpse of my brother, József. The two memories flicked back and forth, merging, blending, weaving together into a scene that I had never witnessed before yet which felt so utterly familiar.

Somewhere close by I heard the whine of an electric saw, then the words *Crack him open*. There were protests, shouts maybe, something else going on, but it didn't make any difference to me. I buried myself in the memory, or the illusion, whatever it was. I tried to sink deep inside it, as if by doing so I could fall right out of this life into that one.

The person who was Donovan, and yet who was also my brother, opened his eyes. Then he spoke to me.

Hold on, he said. *Just hold on for a little while longer.*

"I can't," I said, or didn't say.

Try.

It was no good. I felt something running down my chest, the sensation like ice cubes on my skin. And this last memory began to strobe on and off, fragmenting a little each time, drifting apart.

Please, said the boy, no longer visible in the maelstrom. *Just hold on.*

But it was all too much. I inhaled, the air thick with the scent of my own blood. And it was with relief rather than sadness that I finally let myself die.

DEATH

IT WAS JUST AS I expected it to be, only somehow different. I could feel my brain shutting down, turning off the various pieces of my mind the way a pilot flicks switches in a plane after landing. First to go were my senses, what little was left of them. The memories were next, every last one, as if somebody was holding a giant eraser to my past, rubbing it into dust, stripping away everything that had ever made me who I was. Eventually, all that remained was a single thought—a billion actions and dreams and emotions all leading up to this final cluster of unspoken words:

It doesn't hurt.

Then death was there. More than anything else it felt as though I was on a beach at night, a vast black tidal wave blasting toward me, unseen and unheard, but felt in every single fiber of my being. It seemed to make the whole universe groan as it towered overhead, so powerful it could shake the stars from the sky.

It fell, slamming down, pulling me into its churning heart. A moment of terror, followed by an eternity of peace.

No, NOT AN ETERNITY. The peace didn't last. There was a flash of fire in that dark ocean, an underwater explosion. It lit up the world around me for a second and I realized I was sinking. I could feel the pressure growing, making my ears pop. I tried to take a breath and couldn't.

Death wasn't supposed to be like this, was it? I didn't know exactly what I had expected, but more than anything I'd hoped it would be the end of everything—the end of the fear, of the pain, of the anger. But this . . .

There was another rippling blast, fire trapped inside bubbles of air, painting the ocean shades of gold and blue. It seemed to emanate from me, the flames bursting from my chest, making me feel like I'd been punched. I was still sinking, weights around my ankles, unable to breathe. The panic was causing my brain to reboot, words and thoughts lighting up.

I wondered whether I was going to hell. I didn't deserve peace. How could I? I'd committed terrible crimes, against my family, against my friends. I'd *killed* people. That's what was happening, I was going to hell. Maybe this was my eternity—forever sinking into the depths, fire all around me, unable to breathe, unable to switch off, a never-ending descent into madness.

The world exploded again, the flames so bright that they lit up something above me—had those been faces up there? A mix of monsters and men? The light was crushed before I could make sense of the view, but I thought I had seen berserkers, obsidian eyes set into mangled faces. Or maybe they were demons, watching me fall.

I sank into the airless depths, the entire universe squatting on my chest, pushing me down. I squirmed, fighting it, trying to rise to the surface, but those dark waters were as solid as the binds that had held me in the world of the living.

Another blast, and this time it brought something else with

it—pain. I could feel it in my chest, in my arm, like I was having a heart attack. I couldn't be, though, surely, because I was already dead. Something rushed into my arm, as cold as ice water, and when I looked down there was enough light left from the explosion to see a tube fixed into my skin. It seemed to be funneling the dark waters inside me, a pump that sucked the ocean into my veins, filling me with death.

Except it didn't feel like death. If anything it felt like life, as though the darkness was kick-starting my system. I wasn't sinking anymore, I realized. I was rising, and the ocean was brightening, as if all the stagnant water was being pulled into me, leaving only freshness, only light. I rose faster, toward the blinding brilliance of the surface, like the sun was hovering right overhead. I surged upward, ready to burst from the depths into the glorious day. I didn't know what was up there, but I could guess. Maybe I wasn't destined for hell after all. Maybe destiny had taken pity on me, granted me mercy.

All that mattered was that I was leaving the darkness behind me, and heading into the light. I didn't care where I was going, so long as it was somewhere good.

IT WASN'T.

I breached the surface of death like I was being reborn into the world, gasping for breath as though I'd never taken one before; screaming like a baby. For the first few seconds there was only that blinding brilliance, so bright it felt as though my eyes were on fire. I bucked, fought to move, felt hands on me holding me down, heard words that made no sense.

There was a roar, like thunder, more voices, shouts. The brightness snapped off, then returned, then went, strobing on and off. I blinked, tried to focus, seeing a bulb above my head swinging back and forth. There was dust drifting down from a cracked ceiling, and I followed those spiraling flecks through the swinging glow, my eyes falling onto the figures standing in the room, surrounding the table on which I lay.

There were two berserkers here, the ones I had thought were demons. Both were huge, fat and fleshy like the one I'd killed back in the prison. They stood so tall that they had to stoop to keep their disfigured heads away from the ceiling. Between the creatures was a blacksuit, only he wasn't wearing black. He wasn't wearing much at all, just a surgical gown identical to mine, his scarred arms and legs jutting out from the flimsy material. It was almost laughable, except he was holding a scalpel, the blade held against the throat of the last person in the room.

This one was still human, a scientist by the look of things, or a doctor. He was wearing his white overalls, his face bruised, one eye swollen shut. He was sobbing, his tears stained with blood. In his hands were two paddles, both smoking, and it took me a moment to realize they were the electric ones used by doctors to resuscitate somebody whose heart has failed. I put my left hand to my chest, felt the heat there, realized that's why the ocean had felt as if it was exploding.

They'd brought me back to life.

Not only that, they'd given me nectar. I saw the IV needle in my arm, the bag above it almost empty; could feel the strength returning to my muscles. I looked at the scientist and he must have seen the poison at work inside me because he staggered back until he hit the fleshy torso of one of the berserkers. The paddles clattered to the floor, the noise dwarfed by another massive explosion from somewhere nearby, this one hard enough to shake the entire room.

I opened my mouth, tried to ask what was going on, but all that came out of it was saliva. The blacksuit stepped up to me, grabbed my face in his hand, tilting it one way, then the other.

"You'll feel like crap for a while," he growled, his silver eyes flashing. "You were dead a good five minutes. Didn't think you were coming back."

There was a flurry of gunshots from outside and the blacksuit grimaced.

"We don't have much time," he said. "You can walk, we need to go."

Too confused to argue, I swung my legs over the side of the operating table, realizing that the tiled floor of the room was drenched in blood. There were three corpses there, all doctors in gas masks and white overalls. I did my best to jump over them, almost losing my balance when I landed. The blacksuit steadied me with a hand. It took me a while to realize that I was taller than him, by half a meter, my own head close to the ceiling. He turned to the remaining scientist who was squirming in the corner of the room between the corpses of his colleagues.

"Please," the man sniveled. "I did what you asked."

"Then I don't need you anymore, do I?" replied the blacksuit, advancing with the scalpel. The nectar inside me wanted to watch what happened next but I denied it, looking away, trying to put my thoughts in order. It didn't make sense that these freaks had brought me back to life—no more sense than a berserker acting as my bodyguard in the swimming pool. Furnace knew I wanted to kill him, so why didn't he want me dead?

"Stay close to me," the blacksuit ordered as he walked to the door, opening it a crack and peering outside. The reek of smoke and gunpowder filtered past him, clawing at my nose, and there were more shots, louder now. One of the berserkers stood behind him, its flesh hanging down in pink folds, its arms the size of tree trunks. The other was watching me, blinking its black piggy eyes. I peered into those twin inkwells, so deep it was like the creature had gaping sockets in its head, and for an instant I sensed him there: Alfred Furnace.

I realized the pain was still there, that same dull ache in my brain that shifted every time I moved my head, always seeming to point in the same direction. I don't know how, or why, but I knew the pain had something to do with Furnace.

"What do you want from me?" I asked, rubbing my temple with my deformed fingers, the words so deep they could have been distant thunder. The berserker just cocked its head, its expression utterly alien and yet still so childlike. Its fists were bunched, as big as anvils. But I knew it wouldn't try to hurt me. If anything, the monster would sacrifice itself to keep me alive.

"You ready?" the blacksuit asked. It wasn't an order this time, it was an inquiry. Just like the berserker, the blacksuit was here to help me.

"We're getting out of here, right?" I said. The blacksuit nodded, his attention switching from me to the door and back again. I could still hear gunshots, hundreds of them, like a fireworks show. "This is a rescue mission?"

"We should go," he said, and I could sense the anxiety in his voice.

There was nectar in my system, but not enough to blot out all of my memories. Through the raging vortex of my thoughts I saw Zee, Simon, the girl Lucy too.

"I'm not going without my friends," I said. The suit opened his mouth to protest, but nothing came out of it. He shook his head, gazing at the floor in resignation. It seemed to take him forever before he finally spoke, and the words nearly stopped my heart again.

"Whatever you say, *sir*," he said, swinging open the door. "You're in charge."

ORDERS

"I'M IN CHARGE?" I shouted, unable to believe what I was hearing. "What do you mean?"

But the blacksuit was already out the door, the first berserker hot on his heels. The second gave me a gentle shove and I ran after them, hearing the thud of its feet behind me. Outside was a long, windowless corridor, a thin gauze of smoke suspended below the ceiling. There were a dozen or so doors here, half of them open, but the blacksuit ignored them all, jogging past them toward a junction ahead.

"This place was a hospital," the blacksuit said as we reached the end of the corridor. It stretched out to the right and left, both sides identical, still no sign of any windows. The floor shook with another explosion and the strip lights in the ceiling cut out, my eyes painting the passageways in cold silver for the few seconds it took them to spark back on. "St. Margaret's. The army set up here after the war began. It's this way."

He bolted to the left, the doors flashing by. I glanced inside, saw glimpses of red and dirty white, and something pink that appeared to be moving. I didn't stop for a closer look. I felt like I had to keep moving or the chaos and confusion would catch up with me, consume me. There was a door at the end of the corridor, bigger than the others, hanging off its hinges. I stooped through it, saw the blacksuit running along another corridor. The sound of gunfire was clearer. I could hear screaming too. Not just one person but a whole chorus.

The suit crouched to a halt beside a door. It was half-open, and through the gap it looked as if the whole world was on fire. I reached out my good hand, stopped him before he could take off again.

"Tell me what's going on," I said, narrowing my eyes at him, glaring, until he broke contact and looked away.

"I'm not a hundred percent sure," he said. "All I know is that I was a prisoner here, like you. Furnace must have sent reinforcements because all this kicked off, and the next thing I know there were two berserkers pulling me out of my cell. Furnace has ordered me to watch over you. You're his new right-hand man." There was no mistaking the bitterness there, the hatred that boiled just beneath the surface. The blacksuit looked up at me, spitting out the words like he had a mouthful of acid. "I'm surprised he's not told you anything, seeing how you're his general now."

"I'm not his general," I hissed, clutching the blacksuit's gown with my truncated left hand, my right poised by my side, ready to skewer him. "I don't know what he thinks he's doing, but I'm not on his side, I'm not on *your* side. You got that?"

There was a growl in stereo behind me, the two berserkers crowding in on us. I thought they were coming after me, but the nervous way the blacksuit looked at them made it clear who they'd protect if it came to a fight.

"Whatever you say, Sawyer," he replied, shrugging my hand away and focusing his attention on the door. I swallowed my anger, the sensation like gulping down a spiked ball. I could worry about what was going on later. Right now the important thing was to find Zee and Simon and Lucy and get the hell away from this madhouse.

"They're being kept in cells somewhere," I said, remembering what Zee had told me.

"I know," the blacksuit said. "The main hospital building is through this door. It's swarming, our guys and theirs. At least it was when I passed through here a few minutes ago. If we're lucky there will be enough of a distraction to get us across the courtyard to the atrium and the psych ward. That's where they're being held, your friends—if they're still alive." He reached out, peeled open the door a fraction more to reveal an entrance hall. There was an inferno raging out there, but it seemed to be concentrated on the walls to the left, firelight merging with the red glow of the setting sun. "If I were you I'd send out one of the berserkers first, make sure the coast is clear."

I looked at him, one eyebrow raised, and he stared back impatiently.

"I can't—" was as far as I got before he interrupted. Not the blacksuit, but the voice in my head.

You can.

The berserkers were behind me, shoulder to shoulder, practically taking up the whole of the stairwell. They looked like twins, some horrific parody of Tweedledum and Tweedledee. Just the sight of them made my stomach churn, my heart pound, every instinct in my body telling me to run, to get away from them before they turned on me. But they were just standing there, like soldiers, waiting for a command.

"Okay," I said to them, pretty sure nothing would happen. "Off you go."

They didn't move, frozen like golems carved from pink clay. I tried again with the same result.

Don't just say it, said Furnace, his whisper louder than the flames, louder than the gunfire. *Believe it.*

"Better hurry," said the blacksuit. "Something's coming."

He was right. There were footsteps, lots of them, getting closer. I looked back at the berserkers, but this time I didn't speak. I cleared my head, pictured the door, the room on the other side. I imagined one of the berserkers charging into the flames, finding us a safe passage through.

It was on the move so quickly I almost didn't manage to get out of its way, the beast barging through the door hard enough to rip it from its hinges. It arched its back and howled, a war cry if ever I'd heard one. There was the crack of a rifle, a fleshy thud as the bullet struck the creature in its leg. Then it charged, vanishing so fast that it caused tornadoes of smoke to spiral outside the door.

"Nice," purred the suit, that leering grin back on his face. "Maybe you weren't such a bad call after all."

Another crack rose above the flames, not a gun but something else—wood snapping, maybe, or a bone breaking. Something flew past the door, a bundle of wet rags that was engulfed by the fire before I could identify it. Had I really given that berserker an order? It didn't seem possible, and yet there was so much that was impossible but somehow real. The rules that had once governed the universe simply didn't seem to exist anymore.

"Come on," said the blacksuit, propelling himself through the door. I followed, a fist of heat striking me from the raging fires to my left. The room was bigger than I'd thought, a massive hall that stretched a good fifty meters from end to end. The berserker had already reached the right-hand side where a dozen uniformed soldiers were doing their best to scramble out of its way. It had one headlocked in its huge arm. There was a sickening crunch before it discarded the lifeless body, moving on to the next.

I had a flashback to my last day inside the prison, the day we escaped, when Furnace had unleashed his berserkers—the way they had bounded from inmate to inmate, rending flesh and spilling blood. Back then I'd risked everything, my life and my sanity, to kill the freaks. And now I was the one who had unleashed hell, who had set the nightmares loose.

But I was doing it to escape. I had to get out of here so I could find Furnace, so I could kill him. That made it all right. Didn't it?

One of the soldiers glanced across the room, doing a double take when he saw us. He swung his machine gun around and pulled the trigger, the air suddenly alive with the sound of angry hornets. I ducked, but the berserker was quicker. It pounced on the soldier, tearing the gun away from him as we started running again.

"This way," yelled the blacksuit, vaulting a reception desk and sending a computer monitor crashing to the floor. He sprinted to the left, toward what looked like a solid sheet of fire. Covering his face with his hands, he threw himself into the blaze, vanishing with a crash of broken glass. Someone else was taking pot shots at us, and without looking to see who I leaped at the burning wall.

I was out the other side before the fire even noticed I was there, hitting the ground and rolling once before finding my feet. There was a grunt as the remaining berserker followed, patting at its skin with one giant fist in order to put out the flames that had taken hold.

We were outside, the setting sun dazzling. I squinted, seeing a courtyard the size of a gymnasium. Two burned shells that had once been trucks occupied the square, and blackened shapes littered the ground between them like spilled dominoes, still smoldering. Overhead, some distance away, two choppers waltzed together, but other than that there was no sign of life.

The blacksuit was on the move again, just a smudge against the yard. There was a two-story brick building dead ahead, every single window blown out, and without pausing to look inside he bounded into the dark interior. I was halfway after him when I heard the roar of an engine, a Humvee skidding around the side of the building. It hit the remains of one of the trucks, sending burned metal clattering over the courtyard, then accelerated toward us.

I pictured the berserker running at it, willing it to happen, and sure enough a pink shape blasted past me, heading right for the Hummer. I don't know how fast they were both going by the time they reached each other—a combined speed of fifty, sixty miles an hour—but the sound of the collision made my ears ring. The berserker held its ground, its fleshy folds rippling so hard I thought they were going to slough right off. It twisted its body, its huge arms wrapped around the hood, and with a howl of effort it launched the vehicle into the air.

Three tons of metal spun my way, the faces inside frozen in shock. It hit the ground right in front of me, momentum causing it to bounce, whistling over my head close enough to touch before cartwheeling into the burning building behind. A ball of heat and noise struck my back as the ruptured fuel tank exploded, pushing me onward. I shot a look at the berserker as I passed it and the expression it wore seemed to be almost apologetic.

Then we were through the window, swamped in the cool darkness of the atrium. The room we were in was small, classroom-sized, and there was no sign of the suit until he pushed his head through the door in front of us.

"Come on, there's no time," he hissed. I caught up, chasing him down another corridor and through a double door, the berserker close behind. There was still no sign of its brother, the one that had been fighting the soldiers. We must have been in some kind of secure ward, as the rooms here had barred doors like back in the prison, each cell equipped with a bed and a toilet. It was almost like being back at home. One of the cage doors had been ripped clean away, lying on the floor like a metal skeleton.

"This where Zee is?" I asked. The blacksuit was moving between the cells, peering through the bars, talking as he walked.

"I don't know. Probably. This is where they were keeping me."

He stopped outside a cell, his fists wrapped around the bars. I hurried over, expecting—praying—to see a familiar face inside. But there was just another blacksuit there, stripped to his underwear, slumped on a bench. He was covered in fresh wounds, his skin a patchwork of scars and dried nectar. And he was dead.

"Bastards," said the blacksuit by my side, and I think there was genuine emotion there. He blinked his silver eyes, mouthing something that I couldn't quite hear, then he set off again.

"Zee?" I shouted as I followed. "Simon, you here?"

More cells, most empty, some not. Rats thrashed and howled at us from behind a couple, the sound of their teeth crunching against the bars making my stomach churn. We had rounded two corners, and were on the verge of giving up, when somebody responded to my calls, a voice so faint it almost went unheard.

"Zee?" I yelled, running in the direction of the sound. "That you?"

He called again, and by the time the echoes had faded I was looking in through the bars of a cell. There was a boy there, but he wasn't Zee, and the surge of relief I felt was bittersweet.

"Simon," I said, gripping the bars with my good hand. His smile lasted for the second or two until the blacksuit appeared by my side, the berserker taking position behind us, then he was pushing himself back against the far wall of his cell.

"Alex?" he said, eyeing us nervously. "What's going on?"

"It'll take too long to explain," I replied, tugging at the cell door with my left hand. "And I'm not even sure I know. Let's just get out of here, we can talk about it then."

"I'm not going anywhere with those two," he said, raising his own mutated arm in defense. It had once looked so monstrous, that limb, but compared to mine it was utterly human. I looked at it, jealous, trying not to see the scalpel-sharp blade of my right hand by my side.

"You've got a choice," I said, echoing the words he had once said to me. "I don't know how, or why, but for now these two are on our side. They'll keep us safe." Simon spat out a reply but I didn't let him finish. "You either come with us, or we leave you here so they can cut you open, study your insides. Your choice, make it now."

He was silent, and I swore I could see the cogs working behind those silver eyes of his. Then he nodded, straightening up. Once again I cleared my head, saw the berserker ripping the bars away. Sure enough the creature strode forward, grabbing the door and pulling it from the wall in a maelstrom of dust and shrapnel. It cast it to one side, the clang of metal loud enough to wake the dead. Simon scurried from the cell, keeping as far from the berserker as possible, taking shelter beside me.

"That thing better not come any closer," he said, peeking out past my elbow. He seemed to have shrunk since the last time I'd seen him, back in Furnace's tower. He looked thin too, his emaciated body making his swollen arm seem bigger than ever. He must have been thinking something similar because he glanced up at me, frowning. "They been feeding you Muscle Milk?"

"Something like that," I said, feeling a smile tug at the corners of my mouth. It seemed to relax him. He stepped away, straightening the front of his black hoodie—the same one he'd gotten back in the mall, a million years ago.

"So, what's the plan?" he asked. "You guys know a way out?"

"He does," I replied, nodding at the blacksuit. "But first things first, we get Zee. He's here too, somewhere. I'm not leaving him."

Simon's face fell.

"What?" I asked. "Have you seen him?"

He looked at me, then at the blacksuit, then finally over his shoulder at a cell across the hall. It was deserted, the door open.

"He was right there," Simon said. "He's been there since we got here."

"So where is he now?" I asked, tempted to pick the boy up and shake the answers out of him. I managed to bite my tongue, hold my temper.

"I don't know," he said eventually. "They came about twenty minutes ago, just as all the fighting started. Soldiers, and that woman, Panettierre." He shrugged, studying his feet as though Zee's location was printed there. "They came and they took him. He's gone."

FACE-OFF

WE HEADED BACK the way we'd come, hoping we'd think of a plan as we went. I was expecting the blacksuit to try to get me to leave without Zee, to abandon him so we could make our break, but to my surprise he was the one firing off ideas.

"My guess," he said as we left the secure unit, jogging down the corridor beyond, "is that all military personnel will be evacuating."

"How?" I asked, trying to ignore the throb that slid around the outside of my brain as we turned a corner. "On foot?"

"Too dangerous," he said. "There are too many of us in the city. Most of the soldiers will be going by truck, but the people in charge will escape by air, I'm sure of it."

"Helicopters," I said, remembering the ones I'd seen circling the hospital, praying that we weren't too late. "There must be a landing pad here."

"Yeah," said the suit. "There is, out back by the parking lot. I saw it when they brought me in. I'm betting that if they've got Zee, they're taking him with them."

"Why Zee?" Simon asked, his shoulder brushing the wall as he glanced nervously at the berserker behind us. The blacksuit shrugged, slowing down as we reached a large double fire door. I realized that we were heading back toward the main hospital building.

"Because he's immune to the nectar," I said, the truth suddenly dawning on me.

"He's immune?" said the blacksuit. "Then he's not worth risking your life for. Sooner or later, he'll be eradicated. There's no place for people like him—"

"In the new world," I finished for him. "Yeah, I've heard it all before. Now shut up and keep moving."

I could feel the rage building inside the blacksuit, the heat radiating from him, but he held his tongue. He shook his head, then turned away. I snuck a look back at Simon to see that his jaw was almost on the floor. He mouthed something at me—*WTF?*—and I felt another twitch of a smile appear on my face.

The blacksuit led the way through the doors, the maze of passageways continuing ahead of us. I could hear the roar of the fires close by, and past that somebody shouting. We were as silent as we could be as we hurried along the corridor, turning right at the junction at the end. It was lighter here, one half of the hallway made up of windows. I glanced through and at first I assumed there was a meadow out there, grass rippling in the breeze. It took me a moment to understand that it was actually a parking lot, packed from end to end with soldiers and army trucks in green camouflage. There was a tank out there as well.

And behind them all was a giant Chinook transport helicopter, its two rotors spinning lazily.

We all ducked, keeping below the glass. All except for the berserker, that is, which hovered in the shadows waiting for its orders. For a while none of us said anything, we just listened to the grumble of engines and the endless torrent of yelling from out-side. Eventually the blacksuit began to climb through one of the windows.

"Wait here," he said. "I'll take a look outside."

"So," said Simon when we were alone. "What now?"

I didn't answer.

"Because the way I see it," he went on, "we're actually going to fight the soldiers that were meant to *save* us, right? We're now on the same side as a blacksuit and a berserker—on the same side as *Furnace*?"

"We're not on his side," I spat back. "We just want Zee."

"That's just messed up," he said, banging his head against the wall. "We should be killing *these* freaks," he gestured to the ber-serker by our side, "not the ones out there. The soldiers, they're the good guys, Alex. They're the ones trying to save the world."

"But they're not," I replied, remembering what Zee had told me. "At least, their generals aren't. They're going to use the nectar, make berserkers of their own. You saw what Panettierre was doing. She'd sacrifice the whole world if it meant unlocking the secrets of the nectar—I could see that, Simon, in her eyes. She was as crazy as the warden."

"Are you absolutely sure about that?" he asked. "You ever think that maybe Zee's safer with them than with us?" But I could see he already knew the answer. They'd take Zee to pieces, limb by limb, cell by cell, killing him slowly, to find out why the nectar had no effect on him. It would be worse than death, worse than torture. "And you ever think that maybe this is the only chance that some-one will find a cure—a way to make us all normal again?"

This I didn't have an answer for. What if Simon was right? What if Zee was the key to discovering some kind of antidote to the nectar? What if killing him meant curing every other kid in the world? Would I seriously sacrifice the future of humankind just to save one kid—a kid I hadn't even known for that long, when it came down to it? Would I trade a billion lives for one?

The answer was as inevitable as it was illogical: yes, of course I would.

"Yes, but it's *Zee*," I said.

Simon sighed, shaking his head. Then he chanced a tired smile.

"Fine. But when we get him out of here, I'm gonna kill him myself, okay?"

"Okay," I said. I held out my mutated left hand and Simon placed his gently on top of it. I wasn't quite sure why we did it, but the contact felt good and we both seemed reluctant to part. It was only when we heard a hiss of laughter from the blacksuit as he tumbled in through the window that we let go.

"You sissies finished?" he growled. "If we're going to do this, we have to do it now." He gestured toward the parking lot. "There are too many out there for us to take on by ourselves. I'll flank them, get their attention, pull them off to the side. Alex, you need to try to get the berserkers here, as many as you can. It's the only way you're going to get through this alive."

He began to crawl away down the corridor, looking absurd in his hospital gown. He looked back only once, saying, "Just don't let that helicopter take off." Then he was through the door at the far end, heading into the roaring inferno of the main hospital building.

I pushed myself up, peering through the glass to see that the number of troops outside had increased. They seemed to be pouring in from every direction, retreating from the chaos inside the hospital. Several of them climbed into the chopper, none of them dragging Zee. The bird's blades were still wheeling but it didn't show any sign of taking off yet. I sat back down, trying to get my thoughts in order.

"What did that suit mean?" Simon asked. "Get the berserkers here?"

I didn't reply, just closed my eyes and tried to focus. I wasn't sure how many berserkers there were in and around the hospital, whether I could somehow communicate with them all, but I did my best to visualize our location, picturing Furnace's war machines charging this way, converging outside the window, on the rooftops, watching our backs. The beast beside us growled, the floor trembling as it stamped into the corridor.

"Alex," said Simon, his voice shaking. "If you're doing this, stop it now."

It was too late. I opened my eyes in time to see the berserker throw itself through the glass, an explosion of splinters catching the sun like droplets of water. It roared, the noise reminding me of a tiger, and then it began to run, its folds of flesh tensing until it looked like a boulder of solid stone rolling toward the crowd.

The reaction from the soldiers was instantaneous, the remaining windows in the hallway detonating as a hail of bullets tore our way. I crashed to the floor, taking Simon down with me, ricochets burning through the air, molten shells dropping all around us. It was like being in the middle of a tornado, the noise deafening, the world turned upside down. I pressed my face against the tiles so hard it hurt, waiting for the branding-iron pain of a bullet in my flesh.

It didn't come. The storm died out—the thunder of gunshots still audible but directed elsewhere as the berserker moved. I held my breath, my heart thumping too hard as I looked up, past the ravaged brickwork, saw the creature in the midst of the troops. It was pockmarked with bullet holes but it showed no sign of slowing as it went to work.

"Tell me you didn't make it do that," Simon asked, his face next to mine, staring wide-eyed at the carnage.

There was a gargled howl, a blur of pink and black dropping from a window above us and running to join its twin. I recognized the other berserker, the one I'd last seen fighting the troops back in the main hospital building, throwing itself onto a pack of soldiers with a noise that couldn't have been anything else but childish laughter.

"What choice have we got?" I snapped back. "The only way to end this is to find Alfred Furnace and kill him. If the army won't help us do that, then we have to do it by ourselves. If they won't help us, then they're the enemy too, the hell with them."

I felt the nectar inside me taking control. I don't know how much of it there was—I'd been drained and refilled more times than I could count—but there was enough to finish this.

It didn't have to end in bloodshed, though.

I sent out another clarion call, a silent war cry to Furnace's berserkers, one that would hopefully lead them here. Then the nectar drove me to my feet, making me step out of the window onto the flower bed beyond.

"Alex!" Simon yelled at me. "Are you crazy? Get back in here!"

I *was* crazy, there was no doubt about that. But when you've been through everything I have then you've got a pretty good excuse. With the berserkers still carving a swath through their ranks the soldiers had been too busy to notice me. I walked toward them, my pace casual, the nectar keeping the fear at bay. When I was close enough to smell the blood I stopped, lifted my hands in the air, drew in the biggest breath I could, then un-leashed a single word that was loud enough to carry across the battlefield.

"ENOUGH!"

I commanded the berserkers to stop and they obeyed. Of course, they did: I was their general, after all. One threw the corpse of a soldier to the ground, shaking the blood from its mas-sive fingers. The other leaped onto the roof of a truck, snorting like a gorilla. Startled, the soldiers continued shooting, some at the berserkers, some at me. I heard a bullet snap past my ear, humming like a bee's wings and leaving a scar of heat on the air. Another one kicked up a chunk of concrete by my feet, showering me in dust.

"I said, enough!" I yelled, anger making my voice reverberate over the parking lot, the echoes seeming to take an age to die out. "Hold your fire and we'll spare your lives. I only want to talk to Panettierre."

The uniformed men and women scuttled back, using the time to regroup around the helicopter. There were maybe thirty of them left, most reloading, others barking out orders, a few drag-ging the bodies of their dead away from the stationary berserkers. I stood my ground and held my arms wide, trying to show them I wasn't a threat, trying not to give them an excuse to start firing again.

"Panettierre," I shouted, directing the words at the open door of the chopper. The rotors were spinning faster, the whine of the engine growing louder. "I know you're in there."

No response, although I saw several of the soldiers turn their heads toward the door, waiting for something. It was all the con-firmation I needed.

"Colonel Panettierre, I'm not going to ask again."

She stepped into view, dressed in surgical whites and dwarfed by the enormous helicopter. In her hands she held a radio handset, and when she spoke her voice was blasted out through the chopper's loudspeaker. I was close enough to see that same smile on her face, a half-moon of teeth as white as her overalls.

"Alex," she said, the speakers crackling. "What a surprise."

"What have you done with Zee?" I asked. The sound of the rotors was still increasing and I wondered whether she'd heard me. I started to ask again but she cut me off.

"He's here," she said. "Safe, with us."

"I won't let you take him." I took a step forward, thirty machine guns swinging my way, bristling. Impossibly, Panettierre's smile seemed to grow even wider, like there were hooks in the sides of her mouth.

"He wants to come with us, Alex. He's not like you. He wants this all to end. He's going to help us win this war." I saw her click off the handset, shout something into the helicopter cabin before putting it back to her mouth. "I'm sorry to learn you're working for the other side. I'd hoped you would have seen the light, realized where the greater good lay."

I sensed a presence, and I didn't need to look to know that there was a berserker on the roof above me. There was another approaching from the side of the building, its presence similar to the way you sometimes just know you're being watched. I couldn't see it, but I knew it was there.

"I'm not working for them," I said. "I told you the truth, that I'm going to end this. We're on the same side."

"No, Alex," Panettierre replied, her voice laced with static. "We're not. I don't know what you really believe, what you're telling yourself is going on. But look at this from my point of view. You are a convicted murderer. You started the prison break. You unleashed the monsters onto the streets. I thought you were a victim, but here you are, a monster yourself, these freaks at your beck and call. No, I don't know what you are, but you're sure not one of us."

She was still wearing that patronizing smile and it infuriated me. I focused on the berserker on the ground, imagined it grabbing hold of a soldier. My control over them must have been growing, because without a pause the beast bounded forward, snatching a victim from the crowd, holding him up by his neck. The others changed their target but they didn't fire. They couldn't get a clean shot without hitting their own man too.

"I'll make a trade," I shouted. "His life for Zee's. Hand him over and I'll let this soldier go. Then we'll just walk out of here, we can forget this whole thing."

The soldier struggled like a hanged man, batting pathetically against the berserker's grip, and a sudden pang of guilt cut through the storm of nectar. What the hell was I doing? The creature looked back at me, obviously confused, and I forced myself to focus. I wasn't going to kill him, I just wanted Zee back. I *was* doing this for the right reasons.

Panettierre looked at the soldier and for once her smile wavered. She put the handset to her mouth.

"Alex, you don't seem to have grasped what's going on here. That man, that soldier, he's willing to die for his country, for his planet, for his way of life. He will sacrifice himself because it is the right thing to do. He understands that. All these brave men and women do. Even Zee understands it. The only person who doesn't is you, and that's how I know you're not on our side."

"I'm warning you," I said, almost screaming now. "Give me Zee or this man dies."

A wave of anger surged up from my gut, so powerful my vision shaded over, like a dark cloud had passed across the sun. The berserkers behind me howled to each other in response to it, like monkeys in the jungle, and Panettierre retreated a couple of steps from the door into the interior of the chopper. Her eyes seemed to gleam in the half-light.

"If I'd known you were in charge all this time then I'd have left you to die on that tower," she said. "It's a shame. But there will be no trade today, Alex. Nor any other day. We do not negotiate with terrorists, not now, not ever."

The anger took hold, too much of it to control. Before I knew what was happening I saw the berserker's fists clench, the muscles knotting. The soldier was crushed like an empty beer can, his twitching body dropping to the floor.

"No!" I said, taking a step toward him. I wanted to run over, to fix him, to breathe life back into the man, to undo what the berserker—what *I*—had done. But it was too late. Panettierre shouted something into the cabin, then she turned back to me.

"Zee is coming with us."

The pitch of the helicopter's engines reached a crescendo and I saw the wheels rise unsteadily from the ground. I started forward, driven by fury, picturing the berserkers attacking, screaming orders at them in my head.

The twin freaks responded, but before they had a chance to move there was a deafening crack, loud enough to send a shock-wave of dirt and dust across the parking lot. The truck beneath the berserker vanished in a ball of fire and the creature exploded with it, hissing black guts spiraling out like the sparks from a Catherine wheel.

I squinted against the heat, scanning the lot, seeing the turret of a tank spin lazily around, looking for another target. The gaping barrel, still smoking, settled on me. The Chinook rose over it, banking hard, Panettierre's voice raining down on me from the speakers.

"There's a special place in hell for people like you, Alex. Enjoy it."

And her amplified laughter almost drowned out the thunder of the tank as it fired again.

EXTREME MEASURES

I THREW MYSELF TO THE SIDE instinctively, felt the heat of the football-sized shell as it roared over my head. It must have struck the hospital because it was as if the gates of hell had opened up behind me, engulfing me in fire. My thoughts were in overdrive, thousands of them stampeding through my brain before I hit the ground. The sheer volume of them seemed to have slowed down the world around me, like they'd knocked time off its rails.

I imagined the berserker on the roof leaping onto the helicopter, grabbing the rotors. Sure enough, when I glanced up through the burning air I could see it in mid-jump, its long, skinny arms flailing. There was another earth-shattering crack as a second shell thudded into the hospital, the explosion making the ground shake. It was so loud that I didn't even hear the machine-gun fire that followed, only the whisper of bullets and the erupting concrete letting me know they were aiming at me.

More thoughts, screaming at the berserkers to charge, to attack. I wasn't even thinking about what I was doing anymore, my brain on autopilot, survival mode. It was either them or me, and I wasn't going to die, not today, not before finishing what I'd promised to do.

I struggled to my feet, the heat and the noise and the trembling ground making it feel like I was on a gyroscope. But I kept my balance, ordering the berserkers to tear apart anything in their way. Then I was running, bursting from the smoke so fast that none of the soldiers could keep track of me. I cut to the side and hurdled a truck, landing on the hood of a military Hummer, using it like a trampoline to propel me toward the tank. Its turret spun, slowly, clumsily, and by the time it was pointing in my direction I was way past it, perched on its roof.

From here I had a better idea of what was going on. Another berserker—a beast that looked like a minotaur, its head too big for its body, its skin charred and smoldering, the color of coal—had appeared from nowhere. It was in the middle of the group of soldiers and it looked like it was toying with them, the way a cat does with a bird. Its skin sparked with every bullet that struck it, but just like my arm it was coated in nectar, impenetrable. Most of the military personnel were fleeing now, although some had sunk to their knees, their eyes empty of emotion, as though their brains had just been switched off.

The helicopter was in trouble, thirty meters over the ground and spinning out of control. I squinted into the setting sun to see a berserker clinging onto the sides, its fist lashing out at the forward rotor. There was smoke churning from it, the blades whining. Every time it came full circle I caught sight of the pilots behind the windshield, and I imagined Panettierre there, her terror. The thought made me laugh, an insane chuckle that rose up my throat like bile. I'd completely forgotten that Zee was in there too.

There was a grunt as the tank started to move forward, the turret turning sluggishly back and forth in a vain attempt to knock me loose. I raised my right hand, the blade glinting—half sun, half fire—then I brought it down in the gap between the hatch and the roof. It slid in like a knife through butter and I wrenched it back out with the ear-piercing squeal of sheared steel. The round hatch popped open, revealing two faces inside blinking up at me.

The sight awakened a distant memory of solitary confinement, back in the prison, and for a moment I hesitated. The soldiers inside the tank were little more than kids, a few years older than me. They were just following orders, like Panettierre had said. They were fighting to save their world from the freaks that Furnace had unleashed on it.

I took my eyes off them, saw the charcoal berserker with a young soldier in its jaws, pumping nectar into his veins, turning him into a rat; saw the helicopter clip the hospital roof, spiraling into the smoke; saw the ground littered with corpses, most no longer recognizable as human . . .

This was wrong, it was *wrong*.

There was a snap, like bubble wrap, a bullet striking my blade and ricocheting away. Another one, the round catching me in my stomach. Inside the tank one of the soldiers was pointing his pistol at me, ready to squeeze off another shot.

Another vision flared up against reality—a group of people in an orchard, condemning a boy to die, a boy like me. Just like that kid, I had been abandoned, and I would have my revenge.

Once again the nectar reacted before I had time to stop it, my hand slicing back into the tank, skewering the man. I hauled him out like he was stuffed with feathers, flicking my arm and sending him soaring gracefully into the air. I didn't look to see where he landed, reaching in with my other hand and grabbing the second soldier by the head.

My fingers weren't fully formed yet, not even close, but I managed to pull him free, then throw him to the ground. He scrambled away and I let him go. He wouldn't get far.

The troops had been completely routed, a handful of survivors retreating in all directions. I would have ordered the berserkers after them but I didn't need to. They were in their element, uttering chirruped cries of delight as they bounded between their victims until not a single one of them was left alive.

I jumped down from the tank, my head thumping, each frenzied heartbeat painting a network of black veins over the world. I could feel the emotions on the other side of the nectar, building up like water against a crumbling dam. I shook my head as if I could chase them away. There wasn't time to think about what I was doing, only why. The means didn't matter, only the end. The end of *him*.

I was halfway back toward the hospital when I heard somebody coughing, so hard it sounded like they would puke up a lung. I lifted my hand, prepared for an attack, but the lopsided shape I saw stumbling from the smoke was unmistakably Simon. I ran to him, guiding him away from the inferno.

"What happened?" he asked, rubbing a bruise on his forehead. "One minute you jumped out the window, the next I came around in a room somewhere and the whole hospital was burning down."

"Everything's okay," I said, and for some reason I was relieved that he hadn't seen what had happened. It was better that way. We picked up speed, walking around the side of the building, language coming back to me as the roar of the nectar faded. "Zee's chopper ended up over there somewhere. Looked like it might have gone down pretty hard."

"It was a big bird." Simon coughed. "Should be okay, unless those things got to him first."

He nodded toward the coal-black berserker. It seemed to have run out of things to kill because it was squatting among the dead, licking the blood from its fingers, looking more than ever like some monstrous cat. I panicked, and without meaning to I pictured the helicopter on the ground, Furnace's freaks tearing into it, killing everybody inside. The beast must have seen it as a command because it lifted itself off its haunches, running toward the hospital on all four limbs.

"No!" I shouted, making Simon jump. I stopped, screwed my eyes shut, called the berserker back, called them all back. *Don't touch him,* I said, showing them Zee's face. *Don't you dare touch him.* The monster stopped, looking at me, its head cocked. It waited until we were close, then it joined us, loping alongside like a giant pet. The remaining pink twin also jogged over, a dozen holes in its torso and one of its arms missing. It didn't seem to be in pain, though, as it sniffed the other berserker curiously before walking with us. Simon stuck to my side the same way a kid does to their mom when walking down a dark alley, so close I thought we were going to trip each other up.

We reached the end of the parking lot, following the path around the side of the hospital, heading toward the main entrance. There were thick plumes of smoke rising from every direction and I offered a silent prayer that none of them were from the chopper. What if it had crashed badly? What if everyone on board had been killed? If Zee was dead, if I had murdered him, I'd run my blade through my own skull right here and now, promise or no promise.

Halfway along the main building we met up with the blacksuit. He too was covered in blood, and it wasn't his own. He was brushing his hands together like he was celebrating a job well done.

"Saw it pass overhead," he said when I told him where we were going. He took the lead, sprinting, and we covered the rest of the distance in a second. We heard the chopper before we saw it, the muted bleeps of its alarm like a heart rate monitor, telling us it was still alive. I skidded around the corner so fast that I slipped on the gravel, tumbling. Simon helped me up and together we ran into the manicured garden where the bird had landed.

Smoke gushed from the rotors—which were still trying to turn even though the helicopter lay on its side, its blades broken—but luckily there was no fire. The door was open, now facing the sky, a couple of soldiers perched on either side helping people out. A third was obviously on sentry duty on the ground because when he saw us he lifted his weapon.

"Here they come!" he yelled, pointing the rifle this way.

By the time my reactions had kicked in the blacksuit was already on the move, covering the last twenty meters faster than the soldier could pull the trigger. He sent him flying with a punch, the gun clattering out of reach. I ran past the blacksuit and leaped onto the upturned body of the helicopter, Simon by my side. The coal-black berserker followed, so heavy that the metal walls of the chopper groaned, bending inward. I commanded it to stay still and it obeyed, watching me with its silver-dollar eyes.

The soldiers had guns, but they knew when they were beaten. They threw their pistols to the ground, holding their hands up, and I could see in their eyes that they realized they were about to die. They were scared, but they were defiant too.

"I don't want anyone else to get hurt," I said, holding my own arms out. "This has gone far enough." The men didn't reply, just glared at me. If looks could kill I'd be long dead. I pushed past them, peering down through the open door to see people there, staggering back at the sight of my face. I turned to Simon. "I'm going in."

"I'm coming with you," he stuttered back. "No way I'm staying out here alone."

I nodded, then spoke to the soldiers: "If either of you moves, that thing will eat you. Okay?"

The berserker grunted on cue and the men nodded in tandem. I checked to make sure the blacksuit was still there, keeping watch, then I jumped down through the open door.

It was hard to see through the smoke, my eyes watering as soon as I was inside. I could just about make out the blurred outlines of ten, maybe fifteen people clustered at the back, a mixture of medical and military uniforms. I waited for the gunfire to start, my bladed hand up to shield my face, but it didn't come.

"Alex?" somebody said.

"Wait! Zee!" came another voice, this one female.

Then a tiny shape in army fatigues was running toward me. Zee's arms wrapped around my waist, his smile beaming up at me. Another figure stepped out of the group, also wearing camouflage. She took a couple of steps forward, hesitated, then followed Zee. It took me a while to recognize the girl, the same one who had given me the St. Christopher medallion. Her eyes widened when she saw how I had changed, what I had become, but she didn't shy away.

"Lucy," I said. "Zee—you both okay?"

Another voice answered for them, Panettierre's. She stood in the middle of the group, that smile finally wiped from her face.

"You just don't give up, do you?" she spat. There was a clatter from overhead, then a strangled yelp as Simon tumbled into the helicopter. He saw Zee, the pair of them hugging briefly, slapping each other on the back. Panettierre waited for them to finish before continuing. "Are you happy now, Alex? Are you happy with the blood of my men and women on your hands, happy to have brought the world to its knees?"

"No," I said. "Not yet. There's something else I've got to take care of before you'll see me smiling."

I lifted my right hand, extending it toward Panettierre. She flinched, but she didn't move. There wasn't anywhere for her to go. A flurry of cries and gentle prayers rose up from the people around her, a couple of them collapsing to the ground. But when Panettierre spoke her voice was strong.

"Then you'd better do it. You'd better kill me. Because I'll keep coming after you, Alex. We need him. If he's immune to the nectar then we can find a way to make others immune too. We need him to find a cure."

"You need to butcher him, you mean," Lucy spat back, jabbing her finger toward the colonel as if she wished her hands too were weapons. "You were supposed to be helping us, not killing us."

"We went through this," Panettierre replied, the edges of her voice fraying. "You agreed to it, Zee. You understood that sometimes sacrifices have to be made, that some people have to die so that others can live."

I looked at Zee and he shrugged.

"Pretty hard not to agree to something when there's a gun pointed at you," he said. "I'm all for ending the war, for things going back to normal. But, you know, I'd rather find a way of doing it that doesn't involve me lying in pieces on an operating table."

"Amen to that," said Simon, waving the smoke from his face. "Come on, let's get out of here while we still can."

"Hang on a sec," I said, starting forward, holding my arm out like a spear, the point at Panettierre's throat. One thrust, that's all it would take. Somebody like Panettierre didn't deserve to survive this. She was a killer, worse than the rest of them; she was a monster, a Warden Cross in the making. In her head she probably thought she was saving the world, in her heart she wanted power, she wanted the nectar. I'd have bet my right eye that if she was offered the chance to swap places with Alfred Furnace, to be at the head of his army, she'd have accepted without hesitation. She deserved to die.

I felt a hand on my arm.

"Stop it, Alex, she's not worth it," said Zee. His grip was kitten-weak, and yet it anchored me like steel—as though his fingers were passing right through the twisted flesh of my new body, wrapped around the old me, the *human* me. "There's been enough blood spilled today. Come on, leave them."

I met Panettierre's eyes, just pockets of darkness in the unlit interior of the chopper.

"I meant what I said," she hissed. "I won't stop coming after you. You know all about promises, Alex, and that's mine. *I won't stop.*"

I glanced at Zee, who was shaking his head. Then I looked at Lucy, and at Simon. They stared back, and I knew what they saw: a monster, bent and twisted almost beyond recognition, drenched in blood. My hand dropped as I pictured myself through their eyes, a freak, a killer. And suddenly I was so full of shame that I couldn't breathe. It was as if that dam had finally broken, the barrier of nectar crumbling, the emotions sluicing through. I would have cried, I think, if I'd remembered how. Instead I just stood there, feeling hollowed out.

Zee must have sensed it, because his grip on my arm tightened and he pulled me back, pulled me away.

"Let her come after us," he said softly. "Worse people than her have tried."

"And it's not worth another death on your conscience," added Lucy.

She was right. I felt like one more murder would mean I'd be lost completely, the last, broken pieces of me sinking into the nectar, forever gone.

"But if she tries to stop us getting out of this hospital then you have my permission to kill her ass good and dead," said Simon, looking back at Panettierre. "Does that work for you?"

She held her hands out in mock surrender, her smile like a badly painted doll's. Simon climbed out of the chopper first, his hand dropping down to help Zee, then Lucy. I paused, staring back at where Panettierre stood. It was insane, wasn't it? Letting her live? Every instinct was telling me to finish her off, not just as payback for what she'd done but as protection against what she had promised to do.

But I didn't, even though some part of me knew that decision would come back to haunt me. I left her standing there, draped in shadows, her hatred and her anger an invisible tide that seemed to lower the temperature in the helicopter by a good ten degrees. I launched myself up, grabbing the lip of the door with my good hand, hanging there for a moment.

From the darkness, Panettierre spoke. And I don't know whether it was coincidence or fate that I'd heard those words before, so long ago in another life, in a stranger's house after Toby had been shot, as I was being framed for his murder, pushed out onto the streets by the blacksuits. Either way it turned my blood to ice, the chills chasing me along with the echo as I pulled myself back into the sunlight:

"Good luck, Alex. Run as hard as you can. We'll see you real soon."

DECISIONS

I CLAMBERED OUT of the chopper thinking we were under attack again. Lucy was screaming, Zee too, and they both looked like they were about to throw themselves back through the hatch.

It took me only a moment to identify the source of their panic—the berserker that was perched on the upended chopper. Its hackles were raised, a loose growl emanating from its throat, although it seemed to be in control of itself. It took a lot longer than a moment—almost a full minute—for me to calm the pair of them down enough to explain what was going on.

"You're telling me you can *control* it?" Zee asked, his face warped by disbelief. I focused, silently ordering the beast to keep its distance, give us space. It did so, hopping back down to the ground and retreating to a flower bed, staring aimlessly at the setting sun. Zee opened his mouth but I knew what he was going to ask.

"I don't know how," I said. "I just can. The berserkers have saved my ass. They saved yours too."

"You mean the one on the helicopter?" Lucy asked. "The one that brought us down?"

"Yeah."

"You told it to jump onto a helicopter and it did?" Zee asked. "I didn't even think they understood English or anything."

"They don't." I struggled, unsure how to describe it. "It's like they can listen to my thoughts, like I can send messages to them. Not words, just images, like I can transmit things into their heads."

"The same way Furnace can?" said Zee, the words making my skin crawl.

"No," I stuttered, breaking eye contact, trying not to think about the implications of what Zee was suggesting. "It's not the same. I'm not like him."

"So the berserkers are your pets now?" Lucy asked.

"There's a blacksuit with us too," I said, trying to ignore the venom in her voice. "But go with it, okay? He can help us get out of here." I lowered my voice so the suit below wouldn't hear. "He might be able to get us to Alfred Furnace."

There was movement inside the Chinook, and voices. I jumped to the ground, offering my hands to help Zee and Lucy. They saw my arm, like a sharpened stake pointing at the heavens, and not surprisingly they shook their heads, making their own way down over the wheels. Simon followed them, landing beside me. He looked at Zee, then at Lucy, frowning.

"How come you guys got cool uniforms?" he muttered, looking down at his bedraggled clothes. "No fair."

The blacksuit appeared from the other side of the helicopter and for a moment we all stood there awkwardly, nobody quite sure what to say. It was the blacksuit who broke the silence.

"This is touching," he muttered. "Friends reunited. Do you want me to find you all a room, or are we okay to go?"

"I thought you guys weren't clever enough for sarcasm," Zee said, although he was standing behind me, peering at him past the crook of my elbow. The blacksuit sneered, then turned and started jogging away from the burning building. We trod in his shadow, the two berserkers loping along behind.

We crossed the garden and reached a small rotary, a sign telling us that this was the way out. I must have glanced back a hundred times as we went, checking the chopper doors, waiting for Panettierre to appear with a rocket launcher in her hands ready to blow us all to kingdom come. But there was no sign of her, and five minutes later the hospital was out of sight behind a bank of trees.

"Should have let me kill her," I mumbled beneath my breath as I ran to catch up with the others.

We found ourselves on a main road, all four lanes deserted. The only vehicle in sight was an army truck parked by the hospital gates, and the blacksuit ran over to it, his gown fluttering as he disappeared into the cab.

I looked to my left, to where a vast, black cloud hung over the city, like something from one of those horror films where weird forces are unleashed from the skies. Except the cloud was nothing more exciting than smoke, so much of it that it looked as if night had fallen over those few square kilometers, putting up walls of darkness and threatening never to let the sun in again. The pain in my head pointed right toward it, no matter which way I turned. It was like there was a leash inside my skull, a wire that wanted to pull me in that direction. I had an idea that a leash was *exactly* what it was.

"What's the plan?" Zee said, his eyes wide as he took in the cancerous horizon.

"You know what the plan is," I replied. "It's the same as it's always been."

"You're going after him," said Lucy, standing on my other side. "You're going after Furnace."

"What choice is there?" I asked. "Look at the city, guys. It's a graveyard. And how far has it spread?"

"Far," said Zee. "We saw the news reports while you were zonked, back when the news was still being broadcast. It's pretty much nationwide now, over the borders too. The whole country has been quarantined."

"They say the death toll is in the millions," said Lucy, almost choking on her own words. "And that's not including the . . . the kids that have turned."

She looked at me and I could see the hate there, gone in less than a second as she got it under control, but still simmering underneath. She let her head drop, swallowing hard, and I got the impression she was biting her tongue. Zee walked to her side, slotted his hand into hers and squeezed. She didn't let go. Another pang of jealousy twinged inside my chest and I thought about how different things might have been if Zee had been the one to change and I was still normal. The dream was too painful and I tried to pretend it didn't exist, turning back toward the city.

"There's only one thing we can do," I said. "Going to the police, to the army, it won't work. We know that now, they'll just try to kill us, and for what? To make monsters of their own." Nobody argued. How could they? We'd all seen it for ourselves. "And we can't hide. Not forever. The country's gone, finished. No matter where we go, we'll never be safe."

"We could find a boat," said Lucy. "Try to get abroad."

I realized something was glinting, throwing light against her skin, and I remembered the St. Christopher medallion around my neck. I was amazed it was still there after what I'd been through, and I hoped it was a good omen.

"You made me promise something when you gave me this," I said, touching it tenderly with my new fingers. "You made me promise that I'd make things normal again. I will, I'll do that by killing Furnace. I've promised it to you, to everyone. I'm not going to give up on that."

She looked at the medallion, hypnotized by it, then she nodded.

"But you can go," I said. "I'd understand."

Zee, Lucy, and Simon exchanged glances, and they must have been reading each other's minds because they all shook their heads as one.

"Let you get all the credit?" said Simon. "No way, man. I want my medals too."

"Even if you have to risk your life for them?" I asked. He spluttered, waving the thought away with his bigger arm.

"You kidding? We've broken out of the world's worst prison, killed the warden, fought his berserkers and lived, taken on the army and won. How much more dangerous can it get? Compared to all that I bet Furnace is a total pussy. Let's find him and get this over with."

It was impossible to resist his enthusiasm, and before he'd even finished speaking the four of us were laughing.

"A total pussy, eh?" I said, my chest heaving. I wondered if Furnace was listening in on the conversation the way he often seemed to, wondered what he thought of the insult. I was tempted to ask him, but I didn't dare. Our laughter was just a rowing boat floating on a lake of fear, ready to be sucked under at any time. The thought of meeting him still terrified me, made worse by what I'd seen in my visions—the boy with the stranger's blood. I settled for saying, "I hope you're right."

"I'm right," said Simon. "I can feel it. He'll cack his pants when he sees us, when he sees what you can do with his berserkers."

"Yeah," said Lucy, giggling. "He'd better have plenty of bog roll, wherever he is."

And then we were howling, so much that I almost couldn't stand upright, so much that we didn't even notice that the blacksuit had started the truck's engine until he pulled it up next to us. He peered out the window, one eyebrow raised, and the sight of him staring at us like a stern parent made the laughter come even harder, until I was doubled over and thinking I'd never be able to take a breath again. I leaned against the side of the truck, wheezing, the tears rolling down my cheeks, the berserkers watching us with intense curiosity, uttering bizarre, chuckle-like grunts of their own.

I don't know how much later it was that we managed to collect ourselves, climbing inside next to the blacksuit. I pulled myself into the passenger seat, only just able to fold my mutated body into the space, my head scraping the ceiling. I reached down, flicked a lever, and rolled the seat backward, earning a yelp from Zee as he, Lucy, and Simon climbed onto the rear seat.

"Leave me some room," Zee squawked. "I'm being crushed."

"Stop moaning," I said. "You've only got little legs."

But his muttering didn't stop, and with a sigh I reached down again, fiddling with the seat until it finally jolted forward a few centimeters. It almost had us all in stitches again.

"You comfy?" asked the blacksuit with more than a little sarcasm.

"I think so," I said. The laughter had left me utterly exhausted, more so than the fighting, more than the fear and the anger. It wasn't surprising, really. I mean, you give more of yourself to laughter than you do to anything, I think. I looked out of the windshield, the overcast city hanging in front of us, so dark it seemed as if somebody had drawn a blind down over the truck. "So where are we heading?"

The blacksuit just looked at me.

"What?" I asked.

"How the hell should I know?" he said eventually. "You're in charge. You're the one he's been talking to. He hasn't told you where he wants you?"

He had, I realized. He was telling me right now in the throbbing pain that sat smack bang in the middle of my forehead, that leash tugging on the flesh of my brain, pulling me forward.

"Head south, through the city," I said.

"You sure?" the suit asked, putting the truck in gear and gunning the engine.

An image flashed up, coating reality like a layer of grime—an island, waves crashing against its cliffs—there for less than a second, then gone. And if I hadn't been certain before I'd seen that, I definitely was afterward.

"I'm sure," I said, blinking the echoes of the image away. "South. The coast. That's where Furnace is."

And I knew something else too, something just as impossible, and yet just as undeniable.

"He's waiting for us."

CITY OF THE DEAD

THE CITY WAS A PLACE of ghosts and dead things, and we drove through it in silence.

I couldn't believe what I was seeing through the filthy glass of the truck's windows. It was as if every living thing had been sucked from the streets and the buildings, leaving an empty shell, a dried husk that withered and crumbled in every direction. We headed south on the highway, toward the heart of the city, the suburbs on either side of us deserted. Then the tower blocks began to drift out of the smog, some of them still on fire. They stood like flaming torches, their pillars of smoke like the bars of a cage that imprisoned the city.

The two berserkers kept pace with the truck, even though we were traveling at over fifty miles an hour along the short stretches of road that were clear. They thundered along on all fours—or all threes, in the case of the one with the missing arm—occasionally vanishing from sight every time they caught a whiff of something that might be alive, but always catching up with us.

We had to slow down the farther in we got, the streets littered with cars and corpses. Most of the buildings here had burned out completely, looking like blackened stumps of teeth coming loose from the concrete. I recognized some of them, or at least I thought I did. Most were just shadows of what they'd once been.

The ground was scorched, still radiating heat, so much of it that I thought we were in danger of spontaneously combusting. The smell was the worst thing, though, a mixture of burning rubber, superheated concrete, and the unmistakable rancid tang of decaying meat. It clawed its way down my throat, a fist inside my guts. If I'd had anything inside me I would have puked.

The truck was big enough to shunt most of the stationary cars out of our way. When we came across something bigger I called in the berserkers, commanding them to clear a path. It was difficult, and they didn't always seem to want to—as if the only orders they found easy to follow were the ones that involved bloodshed. But with a little patience they managed to obey, even working together to shift a massive oil tanker out of the road.

"Might even be able to house-train them," said Zee as we watched the gleaming metal cylinder bounce down a hill, shedding gasoline as it thumped into the side of an office block. It detonated a few minutes after we started moving again, the shock wave shunting us along the street. I looked at the fireball in the rearview mirror, wondering whether there was anyone else left alive to see it.

"This can't be real," said Lucy as the truck roared into what I vaguely remembered as being the theater district. The vast stone obelisk outside the doors of the underground station here had been sheared clean in half and now lay over the main road. We slowed to a crawl, and we were almost level with it before I realized that there were corpses propped along its length like dolls on a shelf. "I was here, like, three weeks ago. With my mom. We came to see *Grease Revival*. Feels like, I don't know, a million years ago. Now I don't even know if she's . . ."

She put a hand to her mouth, screwing her eyes shut. She wasn't crying, though. It looked like she'd done enough of that. There probably weren't any tears left in any of us. Or so I thought.

"Your mom will be okay," Zee said. "We'll find her."

Lucy ignored him, leaning forward and grabbing the back of the driver's seat, spitting her words at the blacksuit as we drew level with the enormous pillar.

"You like what you see?" she demanded. "Is this what you signed up for? Look at those people. Look at them!"

He did, turning his head and studying the bodies, their unblinking eyes reminding me of crows along a telephone wire. And when he laughed, a deep grumbling chuckle the same volume and pitch as the truck's engine, Lucy lashed out, slapping him around the head again and again, screaming at him. The truck lurched as he tried to bat her away, both Zee and Simon having to force her back into her seat.

"Better keep her under control," the suit said, pushing down on the pedal and turning right at a junction. "Unless she wants to end up dead out there too."

There was something in his voice, though, not quite a tremor but close—and when he turned the next corner I noticed that he was gripping the wheel so tightly that his knuckles had turned the color of old parchment.

"Bastard," hissed Lucy from the back, her fists landing in her lap. "You'll get yours. We won't always need you, you know."

It was only a few minutes later that we saw our first rat. It came out of nowhere, launching itself over a pile of rubble and hitting the side of the truck so hard that it bounced off, sprawling on its ass like an upturned bug. It didn't seem like it could remember how to get up, and we all watched it squirm and wriggle as the blacksuit drove us on. The image of the rat's face, though, stayed with me long after it had disappeared from sight—a girl, no older than ten, one of her pigtails still in place and her red-rimmed glasses hanging around her neck on a cord.

There were others here too, their dark eyes watching us from the gutted buildings. A couple more attacked, but they were weak and slow and the berserkers quickly put them out of their misery. I realized that they must have already been close to death, or they would have left this place long ago, following Furnace's clarion call as he ordered them to spread out, to attack new towns and new cities.

Or maybe they hadn't moved on because some part of them remembered being happy in the city, because deep inside them, past the overpowering strength of the nectar, they remembered who they were. Not for the first time I thought how unbearably cruel it was that the nectar only worked on kids, that adults were spared its power. I watched the faces of Furnace's children stiffen once the berserkers had finished with them, prayed to a god I didn't believe in that they were going somewhere good.

By the time we reached Monument Bridge the smoke-paled sun was disappearing behind the handful of skyscrapers that still remained. The blacksuit flicked on the truck's lights, painting the ruined city in an eerie, flickering glow, like the ghosts of the dead were rising from the steaming tarmac. He kept the same slow but steady speed as we drove over it, the thrum of the tires changing pitch. Beneath us the river was as black as tar, but there were

things moving in the water, bloated shapes bobbing up and down
with the tide.

"Stop here a minute," I said to the suit. He mumbled something but he obeyed, pulling the truck to a halt in the middle of
the bridge. I struggled to unlock the door, my new fingers not
quite up to such a delicate task, eventually managing to swing it
open. I walked to the barrier and peered over the edge.

"What is it?" said Zee, running to my side. "We probably
shouldn't stop here. It's not . . ." And then he looked down and the
words dried up in his throat.

The river was swollen with corpses, hundreds or maybe thousands of them, all floating slowly under the bridge like logs. The
ranks of the dead were so thick that I could barely make out any
of the river's surface, their flesh and tattered clothes rippling in
cruel imitation of water. Countless gulls and other birds sat on
the bodies, riding their portable feasts downstream—their screams
so loud, so much like human cries, that for a terrifying moment I
thought the dead were calling out to us.

"There's so many of them," Zee whispered. "How can this have
happened?"

I shook my head. There was no answer I could give. I turned
away, my shoulders slumped, but Zee grabbed my arm and pointed
at something in the water.

"What's that?" he asked. "Down there, look."

I followed his finger, struggling to make out what he meant.
Then I saw it, a shape pushing itself up between two corpses, a
body the color of wet bone, two spiderlike arms jutting up, wrapping themselves around what had once been a woman in a red
dress, lazily pulling the body beneath the water. The creature's

head was the last thing to submerge, and it seemed to gaze up at us through wide eyes blackened by nectar. Then it was gone, the bloated dead filling the space where it had been.

"Was that a berserker?" Zee asked, pulling his army jacket tight around his throat. "They're in the water too?"

I walked back to the truck, my brain trying to simultaneously make sense of and forget what I'd just seen. Lucy and Simon were peering out the window, looking at me expectantly.

"It's nothing," I said before they could ask. "Forget it. Let's move."

I jumped back into the truck, slamming the door. The blacksuit had kept the engine idling, and when Zee had clambered in he set off again. The headlights were bright, but the smoke muted their glare, like we were driving through fog. Then the near-invisible sun finally dipped below the horizon and night fell instantly, as if somebody had flicked a switch. I realized that none of the streetlights were working. Outside the truck the berserkers howled to each other, and there were other noises too, distant shrieks and calls, creatures celebrating the darkness. The city was obviously less deserted than I'd first thought.

"Which way now?" the blacksuit said when we reached the end of the bridge, stopping at a set of traffic lights even though they showed no color.

"Keep heading south," I replied, thinking about the island.

"Is it safe to be out here in the dark?" Lucy asked, sitting forward. "Maybe we should find a place to take cover."

It was so gloomy that it looked as if the world outside the truck's windshield had been erased. The blacksuit squinted into it, gently revving the truck's engine. Something shrieked, the noise dropping down from above. I pictured the buildings here, the rats that crawled inside, waiting to pounce. The suit must have been thinking the same thing because he nodded.

"Let's just get out of the city," he said. "It will be safer on the other side."

He pushed us forward, around the hulking shell of a tank that loomed up in the middle of the street, taking a road that angled diagonally to our left. One of the berserkers that was escorting us—the minotaur lookalike—shot off to the side, its giant fists flailing at a shape there, but I couldn't see what it was.

"How come the rats still attack us?" I asked the blacksuit.

"Because their brains have turned to mush," he replied without hesitation. "They're Furnace's version of a biological weapon, a short-term measure to overwhelm and subdue the enemy. Their sole thought is violence, to attack, to bite, to spread the nectar into their victims."

"Like a virus," I said.

"Yeah, like a virus. They don't care who they infect. Adults will die, because the nectar can't take with them. It eats them from the inside out. Most kids will turn into other rats, but some will go beyond that."

"Berserkers."

The suit nodded, picking up speed as the roads began to clear. The noise of the engine rattled the whole truck and I had to lean in to hear what he said next.

"The ones we can catch in time, that we can program, operate on, will become blacksuits. But there aren't too many of those yet, there's been no time. This is phase one, shock and awe. These rats aren't designed to live very long, a few days, a week at most, then the nectar dries out. Some of them can keep going for longer, if they remember to feed, and if they can work out that drinking more nectar keeps them alive. That's unlikely, though. That much nectar pumped into them so quickly, it ravages them, snaps their mind clean in half. They won't even know they're still alive."

"But they're just kids," I said, unable to believe what I was hearing, even though I'd already known that was the truth. "Like me, like *you*."

"They're nothing like me," he growled. "They're not even animals, they're weapons. You don't feel sympathy for a bullet once it's been fired from a gun, so why feel any for a rat once it's served its purpose? Only the chosen few get to become blacksuits."

"Don't you remember anything from your life, though?" I asked. "From before you were turned."

The blacksuit flashed me a warning look, his eyes like sharpened steel.

"I had no life before the tower," he said. He must have been one of Furnace's soldiers, not the warden's, turned in the tower in the city, the one that had been destroyed with me almost still in it. "Furnace is my father. That's where the elite forces were created, not like Cross's pathetic half-breed spawn inside the prison." He returned his attention to the wheel. "Which is why I'm so surprised that Furnace has chosen you, a prisoner—not quite blacksuit, not quite berserker, not quite anything."

We swung onto the southbound highway, using the hard shoulder to avoid the cars and vans that had been abandoned on the main roadway. Something about this road was familiar but I couldn't put my finger on it. Not that I really had fingers.

"So why *does* he want me?" I said, watching the speedometer smoothly circle the dial, taking us up to sixty. The blacksuit shrugged, opening his mouth as if he was about to spit, hacking up words instead.

"Beats me. Maybe it's because you're such a freak. Usually when people get to berserker size they lose their minds, and you haven't. You're a failure, and maybe he wants to see you for himself, learn from his mistakes, before he puts you down."

"He's not going to get to do that," I said.

The blacksuit smiled, the gleam of his teeth and his eyes brighter than anything outside the windshield.

"Yeah, you tell yourself that."

I felt something squirming in my gut, but I wasn't sure whether it was anger or fear or a combination of both. I swallowed hard, trying to bury the sensation before it could fire up the nectar again. I could feel the poison in my veins but it didn't show any sign of waking. Either that or I was getting better at controlling it. Something flashed by outside, a green sign, and without knowing quite why I said, "Take the exit ramp."

The blacksuit pulled off the highway, accelerating up a hill and blasting onto a rotary, taking the exit that I pointed to. The pain in my forehead shifted to my temple, telling me I was going the wrong way. Somebody shouted something from the backseat and I had to turn around, asking them to repeat it.

"I said, where are we?" yelled Simon.

I wasn't quite sure, but something was telling me to go this way. Not Furnace but something different, some other indefinable instinct that made me direct the blacksuit down a long, sweeping residential road, past a row of shops and over a second, smaller rotary.

"Somewhere safe," I said eventually. "Somewhere we can spend the night."

"But where?" Simon asked again.

We turned right, houses on both sides but no sign of life

anywhere other than the occasional hungry-looking cat watching us from the shadows. I guided the blacksuit down three more roads, each shorter and narrower than the last, and it was only when we pulled into a street packed tight with semidetached houses that the memories came flooding back. They cut through the constant white noise of the nectar, the way they always seemed to eventually, and I finally understood where I had brought us.

The truck pulled to a halt right outside it, almost bumper to bumper with the little blue car I knew so well, the one I had named Humphrey when I was eight. Next to it was a tiny garden, untidy but packed with spring blooms, a cobblestone path leading up to the front door. It stood open, welcoming me back.

"It's my house," I said, turning to face them, tears in my eyes. "I'm home."

HOME

THE BLACKSUIT FOUND a flashlight in the truck for Zee and Lucy to use, though the full moon made it almost redundant. I looked at the house, bathed in a soft silver glow. It was just as I remembered it, only not. As though somebody had studied my memories and used them to create a replica of my house, getting it almost perfect but messing up the small things, the details.

The garden was too overgrown, the grass ankle length. It had been one thing my dad had always insisted on, keeping the small patch of green in good shape so the neighbors wouldn't complain. A memory floated to the surface, so painful that it might have been barbed—me as a kid, half my age now, helping him and my mom plant the rosebush that still sat by the low wall against the street, the one time they hadn't told me off for getting mud on my trousers.

The thought made me feel like I'd been punched in the solar plexus and I had to fight to stop from doubling over. I suddenly wondered what good could come from being here. Maybe we should just get back into the truck and keep driving, find somewhere else to take shelter. But Zee and Lucy were already at the front door, peering inside.

I followed cautiously, taking in more of those flawed details. A couple of the windows had been smashed, a pool of glass lying in the flower bed. Through the holes I could see that the curtain pole in the front room had been pulled out of the wall, lying diagonally and concealing the interior with rumpled velvet drapes. Another memory cut through the surface of my brain, the way my mom would draw those curtains every night at dusk, the smell of the dust wafting through the living room as we sat down to eat dinner in front of the TV.

"I don't think anyone's home," said Zee. I waited for the relief, but instead it was sadness that gripped me. I guess some part of me had hoped they'd still be here, my mom and dad, even though they wouldn't recognize me now, even though they'd see me as a monster. I just wanted to bury my head in my mother's chest the way I always did when I hurt myself, feel my dad's arms around my shoulders. Between them, they had once been able to make everything bad go away.

But that had been a long, long time ago.

"You sure you want to go in?" Lucy asked me as I approached the door. She reached out and touched my arm with her fingertips, leaving them there for a moment. "You don't know what you might find."

"It's okay," I lied. "Let's just get out of the street before something sees us."

Zee and Lucy entered first, the flashlight cutting through the gloom. I walked after them, having to stoop under the doorframe that I had once struggled to touch on my tiptoes. The door itself had been forced open, the wood split by a crowbar, flecks of red paint like dried blood on the welcome mat. Burglars, probably, I thought, trying to ignore the irony. Whoever it had been was long gone, though. I could sense that the house was empty the moment I stepped inside, the air cool and still, undisturbed.

But then I took a breath, and the house was suddenly full. It was the smells, ones I never thought I'd experience again, reawakening the child inside me, like they'd been left here to help me remember, like they'd been left here so I could imagine my mom and dad back into existence: the wax from my dad's Barbour jacket, hanging on a hook in the hall, reminding me of holidays in the country, clambering over stone walls and traipsing through muddy fields; incense from the bathroom, because my mom had always insisted we light it after we'd done our business; the herbs in the kitchen, the scent of basil filling the house with memories of the times I'd helped her cook, pulling off the leaves and smelling them on my fingers for the rest of the day.

And dewberry, stronger than anything else, so strong and so fresh it could have been ebbing from the very structure of the house. My mom had worn it every day, some kind of moisturizer or something, and I'd never really noticed the fragrance before now. With that smell she was there, they were both there, standing in the hallway, smiling at me in a way they hadn't done since I became a criminal, since I broke their hearts.

I clamped my eyes shut, holding the image there, praying, praying, praying that if I willed it enough, if I really believed it, that all of this would go away. Maybe I could open my eyes and they'd really be there, I'd never have stolen that twenty quid all those years ago, never have broken into that house with Toby, never have been buried alive in Furnace Penitentiary. I could just wake up and be that kid again, the one who helped his mom cook and his dad plant rosebushes and who just wanted to learn magic tricks.

Please, I said to them, and I'm not sure if the words were spoken out loud or just in my head. *Please let me come back. I'm sorry, you know I am. I don't look like me anymore but I still am, it's still me. Please, Mom, I just want to come home.*

It was too much, my stomach churning and my head spinning. My grief was like an engine inside me roaring to life, tears rolling down my cheeks, my body racked by great, heaving, bittersweet sobs.

My mom and dad held out their hands to me, and I fell toward them, feeling like I could shed this body, step out of it like a crab from its shell, walk right back into my old life.

There was a crash, a tearing sound, and I opened my eyes to see that my bladed hand had slashed through the coats in the hall, knocking over the telephone table and sending the glass key bowl flying. The shot of adrenaline rocked me, and I looked back at my dad, ready to apologize, to say it was an accident, to say I'd pay for a new one.

But they were gone, of course. The engine of my grief stalled and I stood there, in the hall, blinking away the tears, my mouth hanging open, feeling like I had been wrung dry, every last iota of strength squeezed from my pores.

I felt a hand on my arm, looked down to see Zee there, moisture pearled in his eyes. He was biting his bottom lip, trying to hold back his own emotions, but he still managed a half-smile. I realized everybody else was watching me sadly. Even the blacksuit seemed to have run out of cruel remarks.

"Come on," Zee said, his voice cracking. "Let's find you a place to sit down before you fall down."

I didn't answer, just let him guide me through the door to the left into our small sitting room. I knew what to expect this time, trying to build a wall against my senses, but I could still feel the memories there, hammering on it, demanding to come in. I collapsed onto the sofa, my arm splayed halfway across the floor, and I just sat there trying not to think, trying not to exist, trying not to breathe in the smells, those ghostly echoes, the last thing that remained of my mom and dad.

I DON'T KNOW how much later it was that I started to come around, drifting out of my exhaustion to see that I was alone in the night-filled sitting room. I could hear voices coming from somewhere, though, and with no little effort I managed to push myself from the sofa to try to find them.

Gentle firelight flickered from the kitchen, and I stumbled toward it to see Zee, Simon, and Lucy inside. They were sitting around the breakfast table, the candles between them drenching the room in warmth. They looked up when they heard me enter, welcoming me with a parade of sympathetic smiles. They all looked exhausted, and I wondered if they'd been talking about their own homes, their own families.

"Hey," said Simon. "How you doing?"

"We thought we should leave you alone," Zee said before I could reply. "You looked like you could do with some space."

I used my left hand to pull a chair out from beneath the table, sitting in it.

"Thanks, guys," I said, shivering. "It's just, you know, weird, I guess. Being back here."

They nodded.

"Just making a cuppa," said Lucy. I could hear bubbling, realized that there was a saucepan of water heating up on the stove. The electricity was out, but the gas was obviously still working.

"Nice to see gas being used for something other than blowing stuff up," I said. Zee smiled and I could see in the brightening of his eyes that he was remembering when we'd used the gas to blow up the chipping-room floor inside Furnace Penitentiary, a lifetime ago. Lucy frowned, looking like she was going to demand an explanation, then obviously deciding not to. She got up, adding another cup to the ones that were already on the counter.

"Can you drink tea, or will it make you puke?" she asked. I didn't honestly know the answer to that. My system couldn't handle ordinary food anymore because of the nectar—as Lucy knew all too well after watching me throw up a burger on the day we'd met her—but I could still drink water.

"Only one way of finding out," I said.

"Gotta still be able to drink tea," Zee said, shaking his head. "Might as well top yourself right now if you can't."

"Where's the suit?" I asked.

"Outside," said Simon. "Said he's keeping watch, but I think he's gone to find some new clothes. Just as well, really. I mean did you see that surgical gown thing he was wearing? Every time he moved I thought his junk was gonna fall out."

"Simon!" Lucy said, full of mock outrage, clipping him around the back of the head and doubling the level of laughter. It was weird—good weird—sitting around the kitchen table making jokes, just like having mates around after school or something.

"What?" Simon said, lifting his hands. "It's true. If there were any cops left in the city he'd have been done for indecent exposure. Speaking of which . . ."

He nodded at me and I realized I was still wearing my surgical gown too.

"There isn't a single thing in this house that will still fit me," I said, resigning myself to it.

The pan began to rattle and Lucy wrapped a tea towel around the handle, lifting it up and carefully sharing the water between the cups. The tea-infused steam was another smell that brought back a fistful of memories, and I let them come. Better to open the door for them, even if they're sad, than to let them burn your house down from the outside. I pictured myself standing right where Lucy was, years and years ago, making my first ever cup of tea, a surprise for my dad. It had been half milk and half warmish water, with the merest dip of a tea bag in it, but he'd told me it was the best cuppa he'd ever had.

"You guys find something to eat?" I asked. "I'm sure there's stuff in the cupboards."

"Zee's already gone through a whole pack of cereal bars," Lucy said, opening the lightless fridge and pulling out a bottle of milk. She sniffed it, pulling a face. "Probably not the freshest it's ever been but it'll have to do."

"He's also eaten a can of cold beans and a packet of cheese slices," Simon said.

"I was hungry," Zee protested.

"You're always hungry," muttered Simon, smiling. "Oh, and we found something on the fridge, we're not quite sure what it is but it looks like it could be evidence of a new monster, something truly awful that Furnace has been saving. I'm not sure if I should even show you, it's so horrendous."

"What?" I asked, genuinely confused. Simon handed me a photograph, and I flipped it over to see a kid, maybe six years old, beaming at the camera, half his teeth missing, his hair a mess, a pair of black glasses perched unevenly on his small nose. At first I didn't recognize him, then I looked at those eyes, the ones that had stared back at me from the mirror for fourteen years of my life, before the warden's scalpels had taken them.

For an instant I was back inside that kid's head, at school for the yearly photo, my whole class there with me. I remembered that day, the flash of the camera leaving traces on my vision for the whole of lunchtime. It seemed impossible that the same kid had somehow grown into me, this twisted beast of torn flesh. Simon was right, that kid had become one of Furnace's monsters, something truly awful. I put the photo on the table, pushing it away, swallowing the bile back down.

"Whoa, sorry, man," said Simon. "It was just a joke, I didn't mean anything by it."

"It's fine," I said. "Just feeling a little fragile right now. Don't worry about it."

"Here you go," said Lucy, placing a cup of tea in front of me. "This should help."

I looked at the tea, worried that if I tasted it I'd break down into another fit of tears. I pushed myself up, using my bladed hand as a crutch.

"I'll be back for it in a bit," I said. "I just want to take a look around, make sure nobody's here."

"Already done," said Zee. "We searched the place top to bottom."

I nodded at them, walking back into the hall. It was a small house, and the only other room downstairs was the dining room. My dad had used it as an office, and when I ducked my head inside I saw it was still packed full of paperwork and books, receipts and bills and other stuff piled high on every available surface. I left it all alone, making my way slowly up the stairs. I was so tall now that I had to crouch beneath the landing, the sheer size of my arm making it awkward. I got there eventually, checking out the bathroom and my parents' bedroom, plus the small storeroom that was also heaving with junk.

My bedroom was at the end of the hallway. I'd taken the chunky "ALEX" stickers off the door a while back, but their outline was still there in the flaking paint. I put my good hand against them, assaulted by my past, the tide showing no sign of stopping. It hurt, but I welcomed the pain because it meant I was recovering. It was the same pain as surgery, only this time I wasn't being hacked apart by blades, I was being repaired by memories. Each one chipped away a little more of the warden's work, turning me back into the kid I'd been before.

I looked in, my silver eyes peeling apart the darkness. It was a lifetime ago that I had last been here, but I remembered it like it was yesterday. Of course I did. It was my last day of freedom. I had gotten up that morning knowing I was going to burgle a house, relishing the thought of something for nothing. My bed had been made since then, and the old clothes I'd left strewn across the floor had been washed and folded, but nothing else had been touched. The same posters hung on the wall, the same DVDs and video games littered my desk, the same drawers stood open.

I walked inside, barely able to stand upright without hitting the ceiling. I was so tall that I could see on top of the wardrobe. There was a pile of magic kits there, the cardboard boxes torn and dust-covered, a home for spiders. I could never quite bring myself to throw them away.

I thought about getting them out now, taking a card trick downstairs to show the others. I could probably still recall how to do the simple ones. But even as I was reaching up for them I saw my hands, realized I'd never do a magic trick again. Although the fat digits on my left hand seemed longer now, more fully formed—the changes were too slow to see, like a plant growing. I sighed, my bladed arm thudding to the carpet.

I went to leave and that's when I saw it, on my desk. It was a photograph, and I almost didn't register it until I remembered that I'd never kept photos in my room, too embarrassed about my family to display them to my mates. I walked over and picked it up with my new fingers.

It was my mom and dad, on a pier in the middle of a summer's day, both of them holding ice creams and smiling with cream-covered lips. My dad's cone didn't have any ice cream in it because it had just fallen out, tumbling over the edge into the waves. In between them was me, older than in the picture downstairs, age ten or eleven. No, I was twelve. I knew that because it was the last week of the holidays, before I'd gone back to school, before I'd stolen that twenty quid from Daniel Richards. Before I'd changed.

We looked so happy that it was almost artificial, like somebody had Photoshopped it. But we *had* been happy back then. That summer, that day on the beach, it had been one of the happiest days of my life. I felt the tears clustering again, that awful pressure in my throat like something huge was crawling up it, trying to get out. My parents had left this photo here for me; they must have believed I'd come back.

Beneath the photo was a pile of paper—legal documents, by the look of them. I read the header on the first page: *Alex Sawyer—Appeal Hearing Denied.* It was the same on the second, and the third. There were seven in all. Seven times that my parents had tried to appeal my sentence, get me out of Furnace, all rejected. I couldn't believe it.

I put the photo down, my hand trembling, then thought better of it and turned it over. On the back were three neat lines in blue ink, and I recognized the small, sloping capital letters as those of my dad. I read it once, my legs buckling, dropping me to my knees. I read it again, so many tears now that I couldn't make out the words, couldn't be sure they were real. But they were, I didn't need to see them to know what they said. Those three lines of text were engraved on my mind, on my heart. I would never, ever forget them.

ALEX, WE'RE SORRY.
WE FORGIVE YOU, WE HOPE YOU'LL FORGIVE US TOO.
WE LOVE YOU SO MUCH. —MOM AND DAD

TEA

I HEARD A GENTLE COUGH from the landing and realized I was no longer on my own.

I let the last few sobs fall out, my eyes burning under the pressure of so many tears. I used my sleeve to wipe them, looking up to see a blurred shape in the doorway. I felt suddenly ashamed, clambering to my feet with an embarrassed cough.

"Sorry," I said, blinking until the figure focused. It was the blacksuit, his silver gaze like two coins embedded in the darkness. I expected him to make some sarcastic comment, to tell me I was weak and pathetic, but instead he just stood there, even more awkward than me. I realized he was wearing a baggy tracksuit that he must have found in another house along the street. His feet were still bare. It wasn't easy finding shoes to fit when you were a blacksuit. "You okay?" I asked.

"Yeah," he said, his voice weak.

But still he didn't move. I took a step closer, trying to make out his expression.

"You don't look it," I said. "What's wrong?"

He ran a hand through his hair.

"I just . . ." he started, and I could see how hard this was for him. "I think I remember something."

"About your life?" I said. He shook his head, but it wasn't a denial, more like he was trying to shake the thought away. His gaze was locked on something on my desk.

"That computer," he said. "It's for games, right? I seem to remember playing . . . Only . . . It wasn't me. It couldn't have been me."

"Don't fight it," I said. "Let the memories come. They're the only thing that can save you."

It was obviously the wrong thing to say, as the blacksuit's face suddenly tightened, his sneer returning. He wiped his sleeve over his mouth, his teeth flashing.

"Save me?" he said, his voice filling the room like distant thunder. "You really believe that? Furnace already saved me, saved me from a weak and pointless life like this. He turned me from a child into a soldier, into a superhuman. You think I'd want to leave this war and return to living like an insect?"

He spat onto the carpet, but there was still uncertainty in his expression, in the way he blinked too fast, the way his Adam's apple bobbed. Something was growing in him, a seed of a memory pushing free from the nectar of his mind. Sooner or later it would bloom.

"We leave at dawn," he said. "So if you want some rest, you'd better get it now."

I pushed past him, heading down the stairs and back into the kitchen. Lucy and Zee were sharing a packet of raisins that they had found, washing them down with tea. They both looked half-dead, their eyes ringed with shadows. Simon had already given in to sleep, folded over the table with his head in his hands, snoring gently.

"Find what you were looking for?" asked Zee. I sat down, remembering the photo in my hand and sliding it over the table. Lucy picked it up.

"Is this really you?" she asked, smiling at the image of me and my parents.

"Look at the back," I said.

She turned it over, her hand going to her mouth as she read the words aloud.

Zee smiled at me. "I knew they weren't as bad as you kept making out," he said. "You can thank them for this when you see them."

I thought of the river of corpses and I knew I'd never see them again. Not in this lifetime, anyway. There was a slap of feet and the blacksuit entered, leaning against the counter.

"Nice tags," said Zee, nodding approvingly. "Does this mean you're a 'tracksuit' now?"

The blacksuit scowled.

"Seriously, though," Zee went on. "If you're gonna be hanging around with us then we should at least know your name. You remember what it is?"

"We don't need names," said the suit.

"Fair enough," said Zee. "I guess we'll just have to make one up for you. How about Bob? No? Norman? Maybe Algernon." We could all feel the anger from the blacksuit boiling up like water, the heat in the room seeming to rise. Zee decided not to push his luck, ending with a muttered, "Bob it is, then."

"Why *are* you hanging around with us?" Lucy asked. "I mean, days ago you lot were trying to kill us, and now you're here as, what, a bodyguard?"

"I'm just following orders," he said, and his contempt was un-mistakable. "Alfred Furnace made it clear that your compadre here is his new general. That means we have to do what he tells us."

Lucy looked at me, one eyebrow raised.

"You're his new *what*?" she asked.

"I'm not," I replied. "It's because I killed the warden. I don't know what's going on, but I can tell you this right now: I'm not Furnace's general. I never will be. I'm still going to find him, and then I'm going to kill him," I blurted out. "That's the only way this is going to end."

I looked at the blacksuit, worried that I'd said too much.

"Oh, don't worry." He grinned. "Furnace has told me all about your little plan."

"So he talks to you too?" I asked him, genuinely curious. I picked up my tea, taking a big sip. It was only lukewarm, but it still tasted like heaven in a cup. I waited for the kick in my guts, for the puking to start, but my system must have just thought it was water because it settled pleasantly in my stomach. "The same way he talks to me, inside your head?"

"He gives me my orders," he replied. "That's all there is to it. I keep you alive—we all keep you alive—and get you to him."

"And then what happens?" I asked.

"That's up to Furnace," said the suit.

"So let me get this straight," said Lucy, talking to me. "Furnace knows you want to kill him, and yet for some reason he appoints you his general and does his utmost to help you find him. Some-thing here doesn't add up."

She was right, but when I tried to think about it my head felt weird, like I couldn't get it in gear. It did seem strange that

Furnace was so desperate to meet me face-to-face, despite my vow. It was better not to think about it. Thinking could get you killed. I drank the rest of my tea in one go, the taste seeming to wash a little of the confusion away.

"You know, Lucy's right," said Zee, his forehead creasing. "Furnace wanted you to go to the tower, back in the city. You thought you were going after him then, but instead you had to face the warden. He wanted you to beat Cross. That's exactly how he planned it."

"So?" I said.

"Furnace is clever. He knows what he's doing. If he's making it easy for you to reach him then there's a reason for that, it's part of his plan. He wasn't in the tower, he might not be waiting for you now, either. Maybe he's leading you there to fight something else, something *worse* than Cross."

"He's there," I said, and I wish I could have been as confident as I sounded.

"I'm just saying, that's all." Zee slumped back in his chair.

"But I already told you, we don't have a choice."

"I know," said Zee. "I know. But be careful, Alex. Things might not be what they seem."

Quiet held the room for a moment, all of us trying to work out what was going on. I glanced out of the window, saw the tiny backyard there drenched in night, and beyond it the street where I was finally caught by the police. On that night, so long ago, I'd thought that if I could just make it past those cops, back into the kitchen, then everything would be okay, I could forget about what had happened and go back to my life. Well here I was. Surely now the nightmares would go away. All I needed was a plan. But every time I grasped for an idea it sank back into the fog of my thoughts.

"Let's get some sleep," I said, giving up. "Maybe it will be clearer in the morning."

"We leave at dawn," the blacksuit said again. "There's no time to waste. I'll take watch."

"Thanks," said Lucy, and I could tell she meant it. "There's a cup of tea there for you, if you want it."

The suit looked at the steaming mug on the counter, then back at Lucy, and I could see the surprise registering in his expression. It was only there for an instant, hidden behind Lucy and Zee as they traipsed out of the kitchen and into the lounge, but it was unmistakable. Simon stayed where he was, still fast asleep.

"Night, Bob," chanced Zee. "Enjoy your tea."

"I don't need tea," the blacksuit shouted. I nodded a good night at him and walked after the others, trying not to smile when I heard the scrape of ceramic and the fast, deep gulps that followed echoing after me down the hallway.

CRUELTY

I DIDN'T REMEMBER FALLING ASLEEP—didn't even remember where I'd sat down to rest—but I must have, because I was dreaming again.

I was dreaming of the boy.

He gazed down at me from a throne of corpses, their bodies stacked so high that I almost didn't see him perched on the top. The dead were dressed in clothes that should have belonged in a museum, and I noticed that some of them wore armor, sightless eyes peering out from beneath cone-shaped helmets. All carried horrific wounds, their blood pooled around the mound like a moat. When I looked to my left and right I made out a battlefield filled with piles like this one, cairns of the countless dead.

The boy himself, Alfred Furnace, looked like he had been bathing in blood. It coated every inch of skin, making his hair stand upright, slick with gore, and when he smiled at me I could see it on his teeth. His eyes were empty wells, puncture wounds in his head, their depths endless. And yet I knew he was looking at me.

"You did this?" I asked him, my voice whipped away by the wind. I tried to move just to see if I could, but like in my other dreams I was paralyzed, stuck fast in the bloodied mud of the field. "You killed these people?"

They killed me first, he answered, and it was as if all the dead were speaking, their voices loud enough to crack the earth. He cocked his head, and it felt like a demon was watching me.

"Is this a memory too?" I asked, thinking back to the visions I'd had of the orchard. Furnace nodded. He wiped a hand across his face, mopping up the blood, and for a second he looked like a kid again, his features crumpled. Then those eyes came back into view, blazing darkness.

This was my life, he said, making my ears ring.

"But how could you do this?" I asked. Not that I needed to. I already knew. I could see the stranger's blood at work inside him, his veins so dark they looked like tattoos. He followed my line of sight.

He sacrificed his blood so that I could live, he said, and I knew he was speaking about the stranger in the orchard. *But he lives within me now. I can feel him there.*

"But what was it, that thing?" I asked.

Furnace laughed, the sound of a soul tearing in two.

You don't need me to answer that.

I shook my head, more bewildered than ever, trying to understand what he was saying. But all I could see were the faces of the dead, the people Furnace had killed.

"There's . . . there are so many of them," I whispered.

Not yet there aren't, but there will be.

I felt the ground begin to shake, like an earthquake. I turned as best I could, looking over my shoulder to see what I thought was a tidal wave surging across the field. Then I saw the figures in it, realized that it wasn't a wave but an army, hundreds of men charging this way. There was a grunt as Furnace leaped off the mound of bodies, landing by my side and grabbing my face in his hands. His fingers burned, blood steaming from his superheated flesh, and there was no escaping his bear-trap grip. He forced me to watch as the army approached, a hundred meters away now and closing fast. Most were holding spears, some had swords. Others must have had bows because an arrow thumped into the soil close to where we were standing, more following, turning day to twilight.

I struggled. I knew this was a dream, but it felt so real. If I didn't move now, then I would be trampled to death, or impaled on a hundred blades.

"What are you doing?" I screamed, the men now fifty meters away, so close I could see the spittle flying from their howling jaws. "Let me go!"

They cannot harm us, Furnace said. *I will not let them.*

And then he was off, running at the army, leaping into it with a cry that threatened to knock the heavens loose. A fountain of blood spewed up from the middle of the crowd, turning the sky red. It seemed to bleed into my vision, drowning the world in color. But it didn't matter that I couldn't see. I was safe now that Furnace was here.

THE WORLD FELL SILENT and I opened my eyes again. I was still inside the dream, but my location had changed. I was in a barn of some kind, straw on the floor, ancient farm equipment on the walls, moonlight streaming in through the single skylight. And I wasn't alone. There was a group of people here, three men and a woman. They were passing a jug between them, and they all looked drunk. Their flushed faces and toothless grins were directed at a shape on the floor, a small figure that curled into itself as they kicked and spat at it.

It was a kid, my age I think, his pale flesh covered in bruises. He was painfully thin, his brittle bones pushing against his parchment skin, his bird-wing shoulders shaking up and down as he cried. I tried to help him, feeling the nectar power up inside me. But I still couldn't move.

We are so cruel, Furnace said, and I turned my head to see him standing beside me, his body now clean of blood, watching the attack with his empty eyes. *We hurt and we kill, all for what?*

"Save him," I said, expecting the men and woman to turn at the sound of my voice, to see me there. But they just howled their banshee screams at each other, delighted by their brutality.

Would you save him? Furnace asked.

"Of course," I shouted back. And I would have. I'd be saving him now if the dream hadn't been holding me back.

What if it's too late?

"But it isn't too late!"

The four adults continued their drunken assault, even though the kid now lay still. The anger inside me surged, so much so that I almost managed to move a foot, the sheer force of the nectar shredding the dream. But Furnace was already stepping forward, a throbbing, doglike snarl emanating from his throat. The men and woman heard it, staggering away from the body on the floor. The jug dropped, shattering, as they retreated. But there was nowhere to go.

Furnace knelt down beside the boy, lifting his head in his hands. He was still alive, but only just and not for much longer. There could be no helping him.

And suddenly I understood what Furnace had meant when he'd

asked me if I would save him. He hadn't been talking about pro-
tecting him from his attackers, he had been talking about *bringing
him back*. I watched as Furnace pulled a knife from his belt, jabbing it into one of the charcoal veins in his wrist. A bead of tainted
blood appeared, then another, and by the time the flow had started
he had pressed his arm against the kid's mouth. The boy drank
hungrily, sensing perhaps that this was the only way he could survive his injuries. I wanted to tell him to stop. But what choice did
he have? Was death really better than this?

Furnace turned to me as the kid suckled from his wrist, the
vortexes of his eyes burning with cold heat.

Would you save him? he asked again, and even though I understood his true meaning I still nodded.

"Of course," I said, softer now. Furnace smiled, and there was
no malice there. He peered down at the kid, whose own veins
were now beginning to pulse black.

He reminded me of József, he said. He pulled his wrist free, a plug
of nectar already forming over the wound. The kid had drunk
deep, however, thrashing on the hay-covered floor as the poison
took control of his system. Furnace held him tight, smoothing
back his hair, brushing straw from his face. *So I made him my new
brother.*

The drunken woman made a break for it, her eyes like saucers
as she bolted toward the door behind me. She didn't stand a chance.
The kid sensed her movement, scrabbling up and throwing himself at her. He took her legs out with one swipe, sinking his teeth
into her throat. He was on the move again before the first spurt of
her blood could hit the floor, destroying the three men with ferocious, terrifying speed.

When he had finished, he scuttled back to Furnace on all fours, gazing up at him the way a dog looks at its master, a look that was still heartbreakingly human. Furnace took him in his arms again, holding him, the blood cooling around them. Then he looked at me once more, extending his other hand, welcoming me into the embrace. And it was a good thing that I couldn't move, because I would have gone to him.

Furnace smiled, and even as this dream began to fade I heard him speak.

He was the first.

ANOTHER ABYSS of silent darkness, deep sleep. And then I was dreaming once more.

This time I dreamed of the island.

I hung over an ocean, the waters kicked up by the wind into a frenzy of churning silver blades. Above, the sky was so overcast that it could have been carved from rock, seeming to sink down, as if to crush me. The island sat between the sea and the sky, a fist of rock whose sheer cliffs protected it from the onslaught of the elements. Perched on those walls of stone was a mansion whose crooked turrets rose like fingers toward the encroaching clouds. More than anything else it reminded me of the Black Fort, the building that had plugged the only entrance to Furnace Penitentiary. All around it were knuckled shapes, impossibly big, that prowled the cliffs and watched me with eyes of silver and black. Their forlorn cries were as loud as the pounding surf.

I looked to my side, knowing I'd see Furnace there. He was older now, much older, his face creased and wrinkled, his long beard flecked with gray. And yet I could still see the boy beneath the aged flesh. There was no mistaking the child that this had once been.

I thought back to the last dream, already untangling like cotton threads in water.

"How many have there been?" I asked, thinking of the boy in the barn. Furnace's dark eyes never left the island, as though he was waiting for something to appear there.

Too many to count, he said, his voice louder than the waves and yet still that same whisper. *Too many to remember.*

"Were they all like him?" I asked. "Like that first boy?"

No, Furnace said. *Most were like him; they had a choice between death and something wonderful. You were like him.* I thought back, trying to peer into my own memories, but already I was forgetting the truth of what had happened to me. Would I have died in the prison if the warden hadn't chosen me, changed me? Probably. Furnace's words knocked my train of thought off the rails. *Others were not. Others were happy in their old lives, they did not want to change.*

"And you forced them?"

No more than any child is forced to grow up, to accept his responsibilities.

The ocean seemed to swell at the sound of his voice, giant waves breaking against the island's cliffs, drenching the mansion in mist and rainbows.

"Where is this place?" I said.

My home, he answered. I looked back at him, at this boy locked inside an old man's skin.

"Why are you showing me this? You know what I'm going to do when I get here. I'm going to kill you."

Furnace inhaled, then turned to face me. Those eyes, or at least the place where his eyes should have been, burned black, like two gaping holes in the very fabric of reality. When he smiled, it was with sadness.

I know, Alex.

"What do you mean?" I demanded, trying to turn to face him but unable to move the lower half of my body. My mind was just as rooted, unable to flow, to grasp what I was hearing. "Tell me what's going on."

There's no time, he said. *You have to go.*

"Go where?" I said, frustration shunting me to the edge of tears again. "I don't understand."

Go now, it's not safe. They have come for you.

"Who?" I asked, looking around me. "I don't see anyone."

Furnace reached up, his hands around my face once again. This time the pain of his searing flesh tore through my sleeping head, stripping the dream away. The waters of the bay rose, defying gravity, until all that remained in the churning void were two eyes like whirlpools and that timeless voice.

They're here.

REUNION

"THEY'RE HERE."

I spat out the words as I woke, still feeling the spray of mist on my skin, hearing the rumble of the ocean. I was sitting in the chair in the lounge. Zee and Lucy were asleep next to each other on the sofa in their matching military uniforms, his head on her shoulder. The dreams were already fading, bleeding into the corners of my mind, but they had wound my heart up like a clockwork toy, letting it loose at what felt like a million beats a minute. I rubbed my hand against my chest, trying to calm it before it jumped right out of my throat.

Zee snorted gently, one eye opening.

"You say something?" he slurred.

I let myself fall back into the chair, shaking my head, my pulse slowly returning to normal. It had just been the nightmares, those fears crossing the threshold between sleep and reality. A weak, smoky light was filtering in through the window, past the tangle of curtains. It was dawn. There was nobody here apart from us.

So why could I still hear the ocean?

I stood, walking out into the hall, toward the front door. That roar was getting louder, sounding less like the sea and more like a distant storm pulling itself over the horizon. Outside it was even clearer, making the remaining glass rattle in the window frames. I could hear car alarms too, triggered by the trembling ground.

It seemed as though it was barely morning, half the world hidden in an eerie gray half-light, but I could see the disc of the sun above a rooftop on the other side of the street, so drenched in smoke and cloud that I could look right at it without even squinting.

"Everything okay?" Zee had followed me out and was standing in the doorway, still looking half-asleep. He wiped his eyes, yawning. "Hey, your hand's looking better."

I lifted my left arm, seeing that my fingers—or at least those three nubbins of charred flesh that were becoming fingers—had grown another inch when I was asleep. I lowered it again. Right now there were more important things.

"Can you hear that?" I asked. Zee cocked his head one way then the other.

"Yeah, what is that? Sounds like Simon's snoring."

"Go wake him up," I said. "Lucy too. We should get out of here."

"Why?" asked Zee, and I had to stop myself from saying *because Furnace told us to*.

"Just do it," I said. He saw the look on my face and ran back inside without asking any more questions. The fleshy pink berserker roosted on a car on the other side of the street, examining the stump where its arm had once been. There was no sign of the minotaur-like one. I stepped out of the garden, looking for the blacksuit, eventually finding him inside the truck. He too was asleep. I pulled open the door, the squeal of metal making him jump so hard his head hit the ceiling.

"What's going on?" he asked, rubbing his scalp. Then he heard it for himself that distant rumble, and straightened up in the driver's seat. "What is that?"

"Trouble," I said. He nodded, turning the keys and making the truck start with a lurch. The engine was loud, but even that didn't quite drown out the noise from outside. The berserker clambered down from the car roof, sensing that we were about to move. I commanded it to stay alert, to keep watch for any sign of danger.

"We ready to go?" the blacksuit asked, scanning the sky and the muted sun. "We're running way behind."

"The others are coming," I said, willing them to hurry up. I looked at him, realized that he was wearing a thousand-yard stare.

"You okay?" I said. He seemed to snap out of his trance.

"I was dreaming," he replied. "I haven't had a dream since . . . Not since the tower."

"Was it Furnace?" I asked, thinking of my own nectar-inspired nightmares. But the blacksuit shook his head.

"No, I was dreaming of a house," he said. "Of a family. I think I was dreaming about *my* family."

I could see the confusion in his eyes, the pain, the fear, and it made my heart bleed—because I had felt it too, that tug of war between the nectar and the memories, between Furnace's promise of power and those fleeting glimpses of a life you had all but forgotten. I wondered how many of the blacksuits had felt their new masks slipping, had dreamed of the children they once were. He gripped the wheel as if he was holding on for his life, as if letting go would mean spiraling into an abyss.

"I was dreaming of my name," he said, almost choking on the words. There was a crunch from the house, Zee, Lucy, and Simon slamming the door behind them as they jogged across the garden to the truck. They clambered in, all of them asking questions. I kept my eyes on the blacksuit.

"Your name?" I asked. "You remember it?"

He nodded, his silver eyes blinking in the gloom.

"It's Sam," he said, his voice hoarse, breaking up. "I don't know how I could have forgotten it for so long."

"Welcome back, Sam," I said, clapping him on the shoulder. I turned to the others.

"All set?"

"Let's scram," said Zee, buckling up. Sam put the truck in gear, pulling off down the road. The berserker bounded along beside us on the sidewalk, its nose twitching as it sniffed the air. By the time we'd gotten to the end of it the rumble was closer. It sounded like a stampede, the noise of a thousand animals running at once. Or the roar of an approaching army. I thought of my dream, the memory of the troops who were charging at Furnace, the murder in their eyes.

"You know where we're heading?" Sam asked. All trace of emotion had gone, his steely eyes focusing on the road as he edged the massive truck around a corner.

"Get us back on the highway," I answered, the pain in my head burning, as if it was physically pulling us all along. "We should keep heading south."

"No prob—" he started, the words dying in his mouth as he turned left at another junction and almost drove the truck straight into a tank. It was bombing down the road toward us, its squeaking tracks gouging massive craters in the tarmac, crushing the cars that sat there. The immense black hole of its gun was pointing right at us. Sam swore, wrenching the steering wheel and bumping us onto the curb. I saw the berserker fly past, heading straight for the tank, and I called it back. Berserker or not, it wouldn't last long if that cannon went off.

"Hang on!" Sam yelled, bringing the truck around so sharply that its right-hand wheels came off the ground, threatening to spill it over onto its side. It demolished a wall, plowing through a garden, and then we were speeding back the way we'd come, accelerating so fast I thought I'd left my guts behind me.

"How did they find us?" Simon asked, all of us apart from Sam staring back at the tank. It had a clean shot but it didn't take it, pursuing us as we screeched around a bend, trying to find another route. We hadn't gone far before Sam slammed the brakes again, so hard that I almost decapitated myself on the open window. I turned in time to see an army truck, the same size as ours, appear at the junction we'd turned off moments ago, its tires smoking as it skidded to a halt.

"Keep going!" I yelled, pointing down the road. It wasn't like we had much of a choice. Sam floored it, each speed bump threatening to rip off the vehicle's undercarriage and send us soaring into space. I looked back, saw the berserker tearing through the cabin of the other truck, doing what its kind did best. It was chasing after us again in seconds, leaving crimson footprints on the road.

We had a bit more warning about the second tank. It was sitting at the end of the road in full view, its turret pointing our way. This one did fire, although the shot went well wide, thumping into a house to our side hard enough to rip out the inside walls, causing the entire building to fold in on itself like it was made of cards. Sam spun the wheel to the left, sending us up a narrow side street, the truck sparking like an angle grinder as we scraped the parked cars on either side.

There was a junction up ahead, another military truck sitting to the right. We turned left, the road here much wider, and it was only when a third tank wheeled into view, forcing us to take the next right, that I realized what was happening.

"We're being herded," I said.

"Herded?" asked Zee, leaning forward as far as his seat belt would let him.

"Like sheep," I said. "Turn right up here."

I pointed toward the next junction, a military truck parked across the right-hand road, the left one clear. Sam shook his head.

"No way," he grunted, using his body weight to pull the truck to the left. He realized his mistake as soon as he'd made it. Ahead was a dead end, a massive army truck spanning the gap between the shops on either side. Three armored Hummers were parked in front of it, all equipped with cannons.

And standing on top of the middle one was Colonel Alice Panettierre.

MERCY

SAM FLIPPED THE HANDBRAKE, bringing us to a messy halt twenty meters away from her. He slung the truck into reverse but I knew it would be no good. I could hear that rumble again, closing in tight behind us. Sure enough, when I looked out of the window I saw one of the tanks there, pinning us in. There was nowhere for us to go.

Sam swore, thumping the wheel. I heard the berserker clamber up the truck, its weight causing the ceiling to dip in and the suspension to groan. We all glared out of the windshield at Panettierre. She was wearing a military outfit now, beige combats, and she gripped the mounted cannon so hard that even from here I could see her knuckles were white. There were men and women standing on the trucks next to her, all armed.

"I told you we should have killed her," I said, the nectar turning my voice to a growl.

"Still might get your chance," replied Simon.

I wasn't so sure. We'd beaten her before, yes, but I'd had three berserkers then. I sent out a message to them, a call to arms for any of Furnace's creatures that might be nearby, but right now I couldn't see or sense any other than the one above us. No, Panettierre had the upper hand, and she must have known it because she wore that same smile, the one that seemed friendly until you noticed that there were too many teeth.

"I'm sorry, Alex," Panettierre shouted, gripping her rifle. "I told you I couldn't let you go."

At the sound of her voice the berserker threw itself off the roof, flying right at Panettierre. She was too quick, pulling the trigger while it was in midair. I had been wrong. It wasn't a cannon at all, it was another grappling gun. There was a crack of pneumatics then the harpoon punched through the berserker's stomach, trailing a rope behind it, making the creature spin almost gracefully.

It landed in a heap, black blood gushing from the wound as it tried to get up. But its one arm struggled to hold its weight and after a second or two it collapsed back down. It turned its eyes to me, blinking, a dozen angry wounds opening up in its skin as the soldiers opened fire.

Anger boiled up my throat, made even worse by my own helplessness. The creature still fixed me with that forlorn gaze, one eye now sealed shut by nectar. If I went to it, though, then I'd be cut to pieces too. Panettierre must have been able to read my emotions because she began to laugh.

"It's not so much fun, is it?" she said. "When you watch your own troops getting slaughtered."

She pulled herself out of the Hummer's gun turret, hopping down onto the hood and taking her pistol from her belt.

"Don't you dare," I said, too quietly for her to hear. She aimed the pistol at the berserker and fired off a couple of shots, both of them crunching through the back of its head. It opened its mouth, a soft moan falling out along with a torrent of nectar. Panettierre pulled the trigger again, catching the beast in its neck. This time

I reached for the door handle, my fury almost too much to contain. Zee grabbed my shoulders, rooting me in place.

"To think you value this monstrosity more than a human life," Panettierre said. "This mindless freak, worse than an animal. To think you'd sacrifice all those men and women, all my soldiers, for *this*."

She unleashed another round, this one taking off the berserker's ear. It was still looking at me, pleading, its fingers stretched out toward the truck.

"We have to help it," I said.

"How?" asked Simon. "We step out there, we're as good as dead. Leave it, Alex. It's only a berserker."

But it was more than that. It was a child. Torn open and patched back together too many times to be recognizable, yes, but it had once been like me, like all of us. Right now its face was so mutated it was almost alien, but its expression of pain and fear was as human as anything I'd ever seen. It was the expression of a kid who just wanted to go home.

It was that thought that let me know what I had to do next. I locked eyes with the berserker, entering its thoughts, trying to calm it. I could sense the emotion there, like a raging storm inside its head, but past those dark clouds was a crack of sunshine, as if the heavens had opened. Through that crack, I realized, were its memories. In that sliver of golden light lay the kid that this berserker had once been.

"It's okay," I said. My voice was barely audible, and yet I knew it heard me. "Don't be afraid of it."

I guided the berserker toward the light, ushering it there, and I could feel its heart lift as it pushed through the darkness, as it remembered. It seemed to slough off its new body, step right out of the mind that Furnace had created for it.

Are you sure? I heard Furnace ask. *It will die.*

"I'm sure," I said, holding on to the creature inside my head, holding on until with one final, shuddering sigh the berserker—the kid—disappeared. Outside the truck, on the street, the creature's eyes had dulled to lead, its chest still.

"What did you do?" asked Sam.

"What I had to," I replied, pushing the sadness and the confusion down inside me where it couldn't do any harm.

"Oops," sneered Panettierre, lowering her pistol to her side. She turned to the truck next to her, to a man holding just about the biggest sniper rifle I had ever seen. He pointed it our way.

"What now?" Lucy asked.

"If we hit those shops hard enough we might make it through," suggested Sam.

"Might end up in a ball of flames too," Simon replied. "Besides, company's on its way."

I could hear helicopters in the air above us, the beat of their blades like a sonic pulse in my head. I doubted we'd be able to evade them, being the only moving vehicle in the whole city that Panettierre didn't control.

"We might be able to bargain with her," said Zee. "I mean, you know where Furnace is now, right? Maybe we can give her his location, or lead her there, something like that. Let's just see what she wants."

"Just give us Zee and you can go," Panettierre yelled down from the truck, her timing impeccable.

"Okay, maybe not," Zee said, laughing without humor.

"We need you, Zee," Panettierre went on. "We need your resistance to the nectar. Turn yourself in and we'll let your friends live, that's a promise."

"We had enough of your promises in the hospital," I shouted back.

"I admit, we got off on the wrong foot," Panettierre said, not missing a beat. "But we don't have to resort to surgery. There are other ways. Please, Zee, at least talk to me."

"Can any of you drive?" asked Sam.

"I can," said Zee.

"Yeah, me too," said Lucy. "Why?"

"She's not going to let us go," he went on. "Any of us, even if we do what she says."

"You think?" asked Simon, his voice laced with sarcasm.

"The only important thing is that we get you to Furnace," said the blacksuit. "I don't know why, but it's the right thing to do."

"You sure about that, Sam?" I asked, meeting his eye.

"I don't know whether he's going to kill you, or you're going to kill him. All I know is that for some reason the two of you meeting is the only way this war is going to end. If that doesn't happen, if she takes you, then nobody wins, everybody dies."

"Zee?" yelled Panettierre. "I'm going to give you to the count of five, then we're coming to get you. And trust me, you don't want us to come and get you. Because we can do this the easy way or the hard way, Zee. And if we do it the hard way, we don't actually need you alive."

"Maybe I should just go with her?" Zee said. "Then maybe she'll let you leave. You can find Furnace and end this, get back in time to save me. Yeah?"

I'll come for you. I'd spoken those words a lifetime ago, to Donovan, the night the blood watch had dragged him off. I'd allowed him to be taken and he'd died. I wasn't going to let the same thing happen to Zee. And I wasn't the only one.

"No way," said Lucy. "I won't let them put their knives anywhere near you."

Everybody ignored Simon's gentle wolf whistle.

"One," yelled Panettierre from outside. The man with the rifle peered at us through the enormous scope. Other soldiers were doing the same, a flurry of laser sights dancing around the truck, reminding me of the red flecks inside Furnace's nectar. The thought was making my blood churn, my body powering up, ready for combat.

"So what do we do?" I said. "Charge at them?"

"No," whispered Sam. "You can't risk it. I'm gonna go out there, create a diversion. One of you two needs to take the wheel."

"Two," said Panettierre.

"Head for that shop there," Sam continued. "The car showroom. The glass front shouldn't give you any problems, if you're going fast enough you might be able to punch clean out the back. Then just floor it, get out of the city, get away from her."

I nodded. It wasn't much of a plan, but I sure couldn't think of anything better. The chances were we were all about to get shot to pieces, but the alternative was being back inside the hospital getting sliced and diced. I pictured Zee on the operating table, scalpels in his skin, Panettierre's scientists taking samples. It was almost too much to bear and I reached out, grabbed him with my left hand.

"We can do this," I said.

"Three."

"Why don't you come with us?" I asked Sam. "You'll die out there."

"If I don't distract them, we'll all die," he said. "This way at least you might just have a chance."

Zee reached for Lucy's hand and she took Simon's. Then Simon reached out and grabbed Sam's shoulder. The blacksuit clamped his fingers over it, squeezing gently.

"Good luck," Simon said. "Man, I never thought I'd be saying that to a suit."

"Four," shouted Panettierre. "Come on, Zee, time's almost up."

"You too," said Sam. Then he stuck the rumbling truck in gear, holding his hand out of the window. Zee was already scrambling into the front, ready to take the wheel. Sam raised his voice, talking to Panettierre. "Okay, you win. Hold on, we're sending him out."

I don't know how they spotted the lie. I guess we were stupid to underestimate Panettierre. But the moment Sam opened the door, swinging his body around to exit the truck, the windshield imploded.

Sam thumped back into his seat, the bullet passing right through his head, missing Lucy by a hair's breadth, leaving a gaping hole in the back of the truck. A mist of nectar bloomed, painting the world black. I realized there were screams coming from the back of the truck, Lucy and Simon all shouting at me to get down. I ducked as the man fired again, another bullet ripping off the top of the seat where my head had been.

Zee threw himself over Sam's lifeless body, slamming his fists down onto the pedals. The engine groaned, feeling like it was about to cut out, then it jolted forward, heading straight for the trucks.

"The wheel!" yelled Zee. I reached out and turned it, trying to remember where the shop was. I heard the crack of rifle fire, felt the vehicle buck as another bullet hit us. I risked pushing my head up, a gale howling through the broken windshield, making my eyes water. The shop was dead ahead, and I didn't even have time to shout out a warning as we barreled right through the window. Broken glass sheared into the cab, the truck still accelerating as Zee floored it with his fist. We bounced off a car, then I was hurled against the dashboard as we detonated through the other side of the shop.

The truck slowed but it didn't stop, hauling itself over the pile of rubble and debris that had once been the shop's back wall. I let go of the wheel, hoisting Zee out of the footwell and helping him get upright next to what was left of Sam. The truck stalled as he let go of the pedals but he started the engine on the move, revving hard, plowing us across a small park.

The rest of us looked back, peering through the ragged gaps in the truck to see a tank pushing its way through the remains of the shop. But it was too slow, holding back the rest of Panettierre's fleet, letting us bounce up a grassy verge onto a road. Zee took the first turn he came to, then the next, and the next, and by the time we were skidding around the fourth corner, all of us sick to our stomachs, the rumble of the army was out of earshot.

I reached past Zee, opening the driver's door.

"Sorry, Sam," I said, pushing him out. It didn't feel right, leaving him like this. But what else was I supposed to do? Find a nice spot and bury him? He hit the road with a thump, quickly rolling out of sight. The truck felt a lot emptier without him, and for a minute or so we were all quiet.

"The highway, right?" said Zee as we passed a sign. He swung onto a rotary—the same one we'd taken yesterday—and a few seconds later we were speeding down the hard shoulder again, the pain back in the middle of my forehead.

"We lose them?" he said. I looked out of the window, the road behind us clear. But I could see black specks against the overcast sky, the helicopters, probably tracking us.

"She's never going to let us go," said Simon, obviously noticing the same thing.

"Good," I said, sitting back in my seat, the cool wind on my face doing little to calm the fire in my blood.

"Good?" Simon asked. "How is it good? She'll follow us to the ends of the earth if she has to."

"She doesn't have to follow us to the ends of the earth," I said. "She only needs to follow us to the island."

I thought of it, of the creatures I'd seen on it, the berserkers that patrolled the cliffs. And I thought of Furnace, waiting there for me. He wouldn't let Panettierre harm us. He'd unleash his forces, turning her soldiers to meat, pounding their bones into the dirt. Let her come after us. This time she would receive no mercy.

"And what happens when we get to the island?" Lucy asked.

I smiled, so hard that my cheeks hurt.

"That's where *my* army is."

DEAD AIR

THE HIGHWAY SEEMED to go on forever, an endless scar that stretched from the city out across the land beyond. After ten minutes the office blocks began to grow smaller, from thirty stories to twenty, to ten, until the buildings we passed were barely taller than houses. We drove through the southern boroughs without seeing a single sign of life, as if something had reached down and scooped up every man, woman, and child in the entire area. We didn't see many corpses either, although we could smell them, the air heavy with the stench of the dead.

The truck reeked too, the inside slick with nectar, and after twenty minutes Zee pulled us off the highway into a service station.

"Can't take this anymore," he said, gagging. "I think I'm sitting on that blacksuit's brains."

He popped open the door, stepping out and taking a deep, shuddering breath.

"Hold up," I called after him. "We don't know it's safe."

I clambered out of the truck, scanning the neighborhood for rats. There were hundreds of blood-colored footprints across the forecourt, like some kind of morbid dance step routine, tattered scraps of clothing seeming to waltz this way and that, pulled by the playful breeze. It gave me the creeps, but I couldn't see any sign of danger.

"Just be quick, okay?"

Zee waved my comment away, running toward a small group of cars parked next to the shop. I saw him peering inside each one, looking for keys.

"I'm going to see if they've got clothes in there," Lucy said as she hopped down from the backseat, running in the same direction as Zee. Simon stepped out after her, stretching his legs and his back and looking up into the sky.

"They're still following us, you know," he said, his silver eyes squinting. "I can hear them."

I could too, that same endless pulse of the helicopters. I lifted my left arm, trying to extend my new middle finger, but the stubby digit didn't seem to want to rise. Simon saw what I was trying to do, lifting both middle fingers to the heavens and waving them up and down. I wondered if the chopper pilots were observing us, if they could see us from so far away. I saw the look of delight on Simon's face as he did a little dance, his fingers held high, and I hoped Panettierre was watching.

"How far behind do you think they are?" I asked when he had calmed down.

"Not far," he said. "I reckon they could easily have caught up with us by now, helicopters aren't exactly slow. I think they might be holding back, seeing where we're going. They could pick Zee up any time, but I guess they're hoping you'll lead them to Furnace."

I was thinking the same thing. In fact, I was counting on it.

"You want food or anything?" I asked him. "Because now's your chance."

"Yes, sir," he said, saluting, and then he was legging it toward the shop.

I walked over to Zee. He had managed to prise open the door of a friendly-looking van and was fiddling with some wires he'd pulled out of the steering column.

"How long?" I asked. He grunted.

"Five minutes, max," he said. "Then another couple to nab some fuel."

I nodded, leaving him to it and walking into the shop. The door was open, but the place was deserted. It was much bigger than it looked from the outside. Simon was filling a carrier bag with sweets and bottles of Coke, and I could see Lucy farther in, browsing the small clothing section. I joined her, wondering if they'd have anything that was anywhere near big enough for me. I was still wearing the surgical gown from the hospital and it was drenched in blood, nectar, and sweat.

"This might fit," she said, reading my mind and holding up a green rain poncho. I took it from her. It wasn't exactly the height of fashion, but it had to be better than what I had on now. She squatted down, rummaging in a pile of colorful trousers, eventually pulling out a pair that looked as if they would be tight on an elephant. "Thank God for the obesity epidemic," she went on, grinning. "These should do you just fine."

"Gee, thanks," I said. "I'm about to go and face the leader of an army of monsters that have torn the country, maybe the world, apart, and you want me to wear bright orange leggings and a lime green poncho?"

Lucy shrugged, grabbing her own clothes and heading toward the toilets.

"It could be worse; you might have had to face him wearing a dress."

Her laughter echoed after her, contagious, and I was chuckling as I carried my own bundle back toward Simon. He was stuffing his face full of jelly babies, watching Zee through the window. I didn't really want to ask him for help, but what choice did I have? My new hands just weren't designed for putting on clothes. I threw the pile onto a shelf by my side, then used the blade of my arm to slice open my gown, shaking the pieces to the floor and coughing gently.

"Um . . ." Simon said through a mouthful of sugar when he saw me standing there. "Is there something you're not telling me?"

The words brought back another memory—me and Donovan standing in the chipping room back in Furnace Penitentiary, dressed only in our pants, using our overalls to smuggle the gas-filled gloves across the cave. The thought made me smile, which was probably the wrong thing to do as my expression seemed to make Simon even more nervous.

"Quick," I said, glancing back toward the toilets. "I don't want Lucy to come back out and see me butt naked."

"Yeah," said Simon, putting his bag of sweets to one side. "I didn't really want to see you butt naked either."

He helped me put on the leggings first, trying not to look at the scars and wounds that crisscrossed my body like patchwork. I didn't want to see them either, but it was impossible to turn away. In places, especially my stomach and chest where I'd received the worst injuries, my skin had hardened like Kevlar. In others, black veins pulsed visibly as the nectar pumped through them, the stretched flesh so taut that it looked as though it might split at any moment, spilling my innards out onto the shop floor. My limbs too were unrecognizable, my legs like tree trunks. But I was relieved to see that everything else downstairs remained just the way it should be. Simon was obviously noticing the same thing, commenting on it as he pulled the leggings up over my waist.

"You'd think the nectar would have given you a bigger—" was as far as he got before the toilet door opened and Lucy stepped out. She was wearing a black tracksuit and brand-new sneakers, and when she saw us standing there she covered her eyes.

"A little warning would have been nice," she said, quick-stepping across the shop and out the door. We laughed, Simon pulling the poncho off the shelf and getting me to bend down as he slotted it over my head. He had to make a couple of holes in the fabric so I could put my arms through, but other than that it fit perfectly.

"How do I look?" I asked, wiggling my toes and wishing I could find some shoes as well. But at least I was in fresh clothes that didn't reek of other people's blood. Be thankful for small mercies, as my gran had always said.

"You look like a carrot that's having a bad hair day," Simon commented.

"Thanks," I replied, leading the way back out of the shop.

"Or a leprechaun on growth hormones."

"Okay, I get it, enough."

"Whose clothes were designed by a Muppet and sewn together by a blind monkey."

I shot him a look and he lifted his arms in surrender, grinning like a lunatic. Outside, Zee had managed to get the car started and was siphoning fuel from the van parked next to it. Lucy was sitting in the passenger seat playing with the radio. They both smirked when they saw my new outfit, but neither of them said anything. I climbed into the back, trying to get my arm inside without killing anybody. Eventually I had to lay it across my lap, the blade taking up the entire seat. Luckily there was another row behind me, and Simon eased himself into it. Static filled the car.

"There's nothing on the radio," said Lucy. "Not even an emergency broadcast or anything. Just dead air, everywhere."

We sat there and listened, the white noise like the whisper of a million dead. Every now and then I thought I made out a word in the relentless hiss, but it was always swallowed up before it could make any sense. It seemed to be growing louder, though, as if the dead knew we were listening, like they wanted to shiver through our radio back into the real world. I was glad when Lucy finally switched it off. There was a series of clanks from outside as Zee poured the stolen fuel into the car, then he was in the driver's seat telling us all to buckle up.

"Stay on the highway?" he asked.

"Yeah, stay on the highway," I replied. But it wouldn't be for much longer. I could feel that hook inside the flesh of my thoughts, the pain more intense now, and I knew it was because we were closer. Another hour, maybe two or three, and we'd be there.

WE DROVE IN SILENCE for a while. The landscape outside the car seemed to demand it.

I thought once we were out of the city the smoke would begin to clear, but it hung like a filthy blanket over the whole world. There weren't many towns and villages along the way but even so there were countless reminders of the apocalypse. Literally thousands of cars lay abandoned on the tarmac, some smoking, others with luggage and bodies spilling out of them. A few had messages painted on the windshields or roofs, all saying roughly the same thing:

Still alive. Help us.

But although we slowed down every time we saw one, those messages all turned out to be wrong. There was nobody left breathing.

At one point we passed a sign for the War Museum, another place I remembered loving when I was a kid. I remembered the tanks and the planes, the weapon displays inside, the guns and bazookas and grenades. We all looked at each other, thinking the same thing but knowing the same truth: weapons, no matter how many we had and how big they were, wouldn't help us. Not where we were going.

About half an hour later I felt the needles in my brain move, the headache sliding from the front of my skull to the left-hand side.

"Time to get off the highway," I said. "Take the next exit, we're getting closer."

Zee followed my directions, speeding down the next exit ramp, following the signs for the port. We passed through half a dozen more villages, all deserted.

"I don't understand," said Lucy. "They can't have killed everyone. How is that possible?"

Nobody answered, even though we all knew. The nectar. It had torn through these communities like the plague. I tried to imagine what it had been like for the people here, seeing the monsters, the berserkers, outside on the street, watching them attack, turning the kids into bloodthirsty, feral beasts. I had seen friends morphed into mindless killers by Furnace's poison, but I couldn't imagine what it would be like to be set upon by your own children, the horror of attempting to comfort your kids even as they tried to kill you, and that impossible choice: do you let them devour you, or do you kill them first? It was unthinkable.

The worst thing we saw, by far, was when we drove past a school. We could see movement through the gates, Zee slowing down for a closer look.

"There are kids in there," he said. "See them?"

I saw them. They weren't kids. They were all wearing uniforms, but their faces were twisted into grimaces, their mouths ringed with blood, their eyes gaping black pits. There were too many to count, all of them throwing themselves at the locked gates, stretching torn fingers out toward our car. A few tried to scrabble up the enormous fences but they just didn't have the strength, dropping down onto their backs and squirming in the wet earth. They looked weak—ferocious, yes, but half-starved. I remembered what Sam had said, that the nectar kept the rats alive for only so long. That was another small mercy, I guess, that those rats, those children, wouldn't have to suffer their nightmare for much longer.

"What do we do with them?" Lucy asked from the passenger seat.

"What *can* we do?" Simon replied. "Let them out?"

I looked at their faces, saw the children there beneath the masks of nectar. It seemed like that would be the kindest thing to do, the humane thing. At least then they wouldn't die like animals in a cage. But it would be too dangerous. The moment that chain around the gates was broken they'd be upon us, not caring that we were their liberators. They only wanted to spread the nectar, spread their disease, and they'd overwhelm us in seconds.

"If we leave them there then *she* will get them," spat Lucy. "That woman. She'll put them all under the knife, the poor things."

"Come on," I said. "The sooner we get to Furnace, the sooner we can make the world normal again."

There was no conviction in my voice, though. It didn't matter what happened when we got to the island. There would be no saving these kids, or the millions who had already been slaughtered. Things would never be normal again. We drove off, Lucy's hand pressed against the glass so hard that her knuckles were white, her sobs concealing the dead and the dying behind a veil of condensation.

THREE MORE TOWNS, another fifty-eight miles on the clock, and then the sea pulled itself up over the rooftops. The effect was so dramatic that at first I thought it really was rising, that slate-colored ocean ready to churn across the land, wipe all this madness from sight. I would have welcomed it, even if it meant being dragged to the depths along with everything else.

Zee followed the main road to the harbor. There were hardly any boats here and I saw that as a good sign—it meant that some people might have escaped. The compass of pain in my head had shifted again, and I told Zee to head down the coast. He did so, all of us gazing at the ocean, all of us thinking the same thing—that we could just go, that we'd be safer on the other side of that horizon. But none of us said it aloud.

Fifteen minutes outside the harbor town the pain detonated, the sensation like a stun grenade going off inside my head. I screwed my eyes shut, seeing the island emerge out of the infinite brightness of my mind.

"Stop the car," I yelled when I could remember how to speak. I blinked the spot of light from my vision as Zee pulled over to the side of the road. "I think this is it."

"No kidding," Simon replied, peering between the seats. I followed his gaze to see two blacksuits, sitting on a bench by the cliff like a couple of tourists. They stood when they saw us approach, their silver eyes brighter than the shrouded sun. One of them carried something in his right hand.

"I don't see any island," said Zee.

Through the side window I could make out nothing except water. But there was no denying it, there was no escaping the fact that we had arrived. Because I could hear Furnace's laughter in my head, louder than the idling engine, louder than the explosion of the waves as they struck the cliff below, louder than the pounding of my heart.

We were here.

THE ISLAND

BY THE TIME ZEE had switched off the engine the blacksuits were striding toward us. They were both wearing red armbands, the Furnace logo—three circles joined by a triangle of lines—emblazoned on them like a swastika. Neither of them looked armed.

I opened the door, struggling out and extending myself to my full height. I was so much taller than the suits now. I thought back to the night I'd first met them, inside the house where Toby was shot, how they'd seemed like giants. Funny how your perspective can change.

I let my bladed hand drop to my side, the black obsidian skin seeming to reflect the clouds overhead. Both the blacksuits hesitated when they saw how big I was, their pace slowing.

"Alex Sawyer," said one, and compared to the echo of Furnace's laughter his voice was little more than a whisper. Unlike the other suits, these two didn't look at me with scorn and disrespect. If anything, their faces were shaped by awe. "It's good to meet you at last, sir. This is for you."

He held out the bundle he was carrying, letting it unfurl from his scarred fist. It was a suit, a black one, and it had obviously been made specially for me because it looked like it was big enough for a polar bear.

"No way," I spat as everybody else clambered out of the car behind me. "You seriously want me to wear *that*? No way."

"You won't get to see him without it," the blacksuit said. "You may be his new general, but even you've got to follow his rules."

I thought about arguing some more, then decided it would be pointless. It was just a suit, after all. It didn't have to mean anything. Besides, it had to be better than what I was already wearing. I didn't really want to face Furnace in orange leggings and a lime green poncho. I grabbed it, carrying it to the far side of the car, beckoning Simon for help.

"Again?" he asked incredulously, but he trotted over. It took us a few minutes, but together we managed to get me dressed. All the while gulls swooped overhead, their cries reminding me of the river back in the city, that tide of corpses.

"There," I said to the blacksuits, feeling their eyes on me, approving. The suit did feel good, despite the fact it was a gift from the man I was about to kill. It was soft against my skin, the material cut to exactly the right size for my new body—although I had no idea how they'd managed to make it. The blade of my right hand jutted out, the same shade of black as the cloth. "Happy? Now take me to Furnace."

"That's why we're here," said the other one. "You ready?"

No, I said, but the word didn't make it out of my head. The blacksuits weren't waiting for an answer anyway, turning and walking across a small swath of grass toward the edge of the cliff. There was a railing there, and what looked like a cast-iron staircase leading down.

"My friends are coming too," I said.

The blacksuits shrugged. "Their funeral."

I looked at Zee, then at Simon, and finally at Lucy.

"You guys don't have to do this," I said. "I don't know what's out there, I don't know what will happen. Once we're on that island the chances of any of us getting off it again are pretty slim."

"Don't you mean nonexistent?" Simon said.

"A billion to one," added Zee.

"So, about the same as the odds of us surviving if you leave us on this cliff," said Lucy. I nodded, looking around. On the other side of the road was a gift shop and a fish-and-chip restaurant, and farther down was a pub. It looked quiet here, but there was no guarantee it would stay that way. It could have been any seaside town across the country, and the thought reminded me of the day at the beach I'd spent with my mom and dad, the one in the photo they'd left for me. I wondered if they were watching me now, wherever they were.

"Yeah, about the same," I said after a moment, turning back to them. The blacksuits were waiting by the stairs, showing no sign that they wanted us to hurry.

"Besides, you can't really be expected to take on Furnace without the big guns," said Zee, flexing those sticklike arms of his. I snorted out a laugh, another one. I don't know why but I must have laughed more in the last twenty-four hours than I had in years. I guess if you lose your sense of humor then you might as well hand yourself over to the grim reaper and be done with it. And the bigger the nightmare, the louder the laughs need to be to keep yourself alive.

"Well, what are we waiting for?" said Simon. "Group hug?"

I waved the suggestion away with a smile, walking toward the blacksuits. They stood to either side of the narrow staircase, letting me past. As soon as I reached the edge of the cliff the sheer drop beyond made my stomach lurch and my head spin. Although farther out the sea looked calm, below me it thrashed and tore against the rock with a ferocity that reminded me of the rats. Each wave detonated with the sound of a bomb going off, a shrapnel of surf reaching twenty meters into the air, beads of saltwater pearling on my new suit.

The staircase cut diagonally down the cliff face, bolted into the rock, looking too much like the staircases back in the prison for my liking. I could see that it led to a small bay. There was a boat there, rocking in the tide. I looked at the blacksuits, thought of the pain they had put me through, the night they had shot Toby, and how they'd treated us back inside Furnace Penitentiary. I didn't hate them, though. They had been turned, like me. They were victims too. I'd meant what I had said to Zee back at the hospital. I wasn't on the same side as Furnace's soldiers, but we weren't enemies anymore either.

"One of you saved us," I told them as I walked onto the first step, the metal creaking. I held on to the railing with my good hand, the chipped iron cold to the touch. "Back at the hospital. His name was Sam. You know him?"

"If he had a name, then he wasn't one of us anymore," replied the suit.

I set off down the steps, taking it slowly, knowing that one slip could send me over the edge. And I wouldn't be the first, I realized. The areas of beach that the sea hadn't covered were littered with corpses, people who couldn't handle the horror, people who had taken the easy way out. They hung over the shingle like seaweed. I tried to ignore them, focusing on my own feet as I descended toward the beach.

"So where is the island?" I heard Zee asking behind me, the wind tugging at his words.

"About five miles out," one of the blacksuits replied. "It won't take long."

I stepped onto the stony beach, walking over to the small motorboat that was bobbing up and down in the surf. A third blacksuit was sitting inside it, and he frowned when he saw us all approach.

"Gonna be a squeeze," he said. I waded into the freezing water, the waves here smaller but no less aggressive, pulling on my ankles, trying to drag me out to sea. It was up to my knees by the time I reached the boat, the blacksuit grabbing my left hand and helping me on board. It rocked alarmingly and I sat down on the small seat at the bow before I could fall back out.

"Welcome aboard, sir," said the pilot, adjusting his red armband so that it sat proudly on his arm. "We've been waiting for you."

I wanted to tell him that I wasn't his general, but it didn't seem worth it. Besides, I couldn't deny that hearing those words, being called "sir," sparked something in my gut, a rush of excitement. I'd been there before, standing in front of the warden back in the prison, dressed in another brand-new black suit. It had been one of the only times in my life when I'd felt I really belonged, when I'd felt I was part of something. It had been truly wonderful and truly awful at the same time.

"Could have parked this thing a little closer to the beach," said Zee, the water up past his waist. The blacksuit pulled him on board, doing the same for Lucy and Simon. The three of them squeezed together on the middle seat, shivering. The other two suits stood on the beach watching us go.

"They not coming?" I asked, tasting salt on my tongue.

"Got reports that the army is heading this way," the blacksuit replied. "Furnace has ordered all units to slow them down, to let you get to the island."

"So where are they all?" Simon asked. "You need more than two guys if that psycho Panettierre is coming after you."

This time the blacksuit did scowl, using his massive arms to pull the starter cord. The engine came to life with a nasal whine, pumping thick black smoke into the air. I looked at the beach, at the cliffs, wondered if I'd ever see the mainland again, asking myself if I'd really miss it. With my parents gone, my old life all but forgotten, the only people who meant anything to me were on this boat. Zee and Simon—Lucy too, I guess—they were what truly mattered. So long as they were with me, I didn't care where I was.

And Donovan too, of course. When I closed my eyes I could see him here, that blazing smile of his bringing light and life back to the world.

The blacksuit pressed the throttle, the boat accelerating out into the open ocean. I could have looked back, one last glimpse at the country where I had spent every single second of my life. But I didn't. I stared ahead, waiting for the island to appear, the place where this would all end, one way or another.

THE BLACKSUIT HAD BEEN RIGHT. It didn't take us long to reach it.

Zee spotted it first, pointing his hand toward a dark smudge against the horizon. The ocean and the sky were almost the same color, looking like two slabs of slate with the island trapped between them. It felt like we were traveling into a tomb.

We sped closer, the boat bouncing on the rolling waves, the island like a tumor on the ocean. It seemed to grow and swell, its knotted black surface expanding until it dominated the skyline. It was just like in my dream, its cancerous cliffs of dark rock rising from the water like the walls of some ancient castle. And perched on top was that Gothic mansion, its bent turrets raised like broken fingers to the sky. There were shapes moving up there, peering over the edge and watching us approach. They were too far away to make any sense of, but I had seen those creatures in my dreams, the very worst of Furnace's creations.

He could see us too. Furnace. I could feel his thoughts inside my head, a wordless welcome that made my ears ring.

"Jesus," said Zee. "It's huge."

It was, and still growing, until it seemed so vast that it sucked the last of the light from the world, plunging us into dusk. The blacksuit steered us closer, heading down one side of the hulking behemoth. The cliffs here were even taller than those at the front, so sheer that when I gazed up at them they seemed to bend out over the water, ready to slam down on top of us like an executioner's blade. I had to look away or risk spewing my guts over the side.

"I didn't think there were any islands out here," Simon said, his face so pale it was almost green.

"You kidding?" replied Zee. "There are thousands. Most are too small to live on, but there are plenty like this one. I saw it on a documentary." He seemed to disappear into himself for a moment, then his face brightened like he'd just had the best idea ever. "Hey, you think they'll ever make a documentary about *us*?"

We laughed, quietly. I think we all knew that this one would be our last.

The side of the island seemed to go on and on, an endless fortress of obsidian stone rising from the depths. I peered over the side of the boat, catching sight of shapes beneath the surface, creatures that moved alongside us, their spidery limbs entwined in some horrific underwater ballet. One rose up, nudging a skeletal head against the hull, making us all lurch. I caught a glimpse of its face, like a corpse whose mouth was open in a permanent rictus of terror. Only bubbles emerged from its toothless maw, but I imagined that if I stuck my head beneath the waves I'd hear it scream. I'd hear them all scream.

"Ignore them," said the blacksuit. "They won't hurt us, not unless Furnace wants them to."

"What are they?" Simon asked.

"He calls them leviathans," the man answered. "Don't get too close, though, and don't look them in the eye. They take it as a sign of aggression. Believe me, you don't want to annoy one of these babies."

The creature beneath us vanished into the murky water, reappearing up ahead. One spindly, bone-thin arm rose up, too-long fingers sweeping through the salt-spray air as if beckoning us on. I could see the end of the island up ahead and the blacksuit throttled down, the boat slowing. The cliffs here sloped right to sea level, but there were man-made stone walls in their place, slick with algae, cannons mounted on top.

"It's an old naval outpost," Zee said. "From centuries ago, right? From the wars."

"This used to be one of the main shipping lanes in and out of the country," the blacksuit said, nodding. "Not anymore, though. Nobody comes out here now, not since Furnace bought the island."

There was a massive archway in the walls, and the blacksuit piloted us through it into a small stone dock. He steered the boat with practiced familiarity to the low mooring, throwing a rope around the rusted metal cleat. We bobbed lazily up and down, the sound of wood scraping against stone seemingly the loudest thing in the world. Each time we rose I could see the narrow path that led from the dock up through the fractured cliffs, the black stone carved by the elements into snaking towers, like we were in some ancient cathedral. There were shadows moving there, fluttering between the pillars, a constellation of silver eyes lighting up the gloom. A cry rose up, as forlorn as it was terrifying, and I wasn't sure whether the flurry of calls that followed was an echo or a chorus.

Either way, it made me wish we'd stayed on the beach.

"Any time you like," said the blacksuit, waiting expectantly.

"You're not coming?" I asked. He shook his head, and I thought I could see the emotion coiling in the molten silver of his eyes. He was scared.

"We're not allowed on the island," he said. "None of the black-suits are. This place is only for Furnace and his pets." He looked at me, at all of us. "And now you."

"Great," I muttered. I grabbed the cleat with my left hand, struggling up onto the stone. The moment I set foot on it a wave crashed against the rocks outside the bay, seeming to rock the entire island, the explosion deafening. I don't know why, but the sound made me think of a coffin nail being hammered in. I reached out and grabbed Lucy's hand, hauling her up, doing the same with Simon and then Zee.

"Good luck," said the blacksuit, wasting no time in revving the engine and steering the boat out through the archway. He didn't look back.

For a moment, the four of us stood and stared at the ocean visible through the gap, at the distant horizon. I could feel the island behind me, its vast bulk like some hideous spider waiting to sink its venom into us. I didn't want to turn around, I wanted to throw myself back into the water, swim for shore. But I couldn't, not with those things out there, the leviathans, the thought of their witches' fingers wrapping around me, pulling me into the depths.

No, we were trapped. There was only one way for us to go.

I turned, looking up at the path that snaked toward the top of the island. Then I started walking, speaking as I went.

"Let's do this."

A ROCK AND
A HARD PLACE

"SO," SAID ZEE AS WE CLIMBED. "YOU'VE GOT A PLAN, RIGHT?"

The path was steep, and in places steps had been cut into the stone. We passed only one building: a crumbling ruin that Zee informed us had probably once been used to store gunpowder. It was empty now, which was a shame. Gunpowder might have come in useful. All around us rose those spires of black rock, eroded by centuries of wind and wave. It was impossible not to think of them as fingers, some subterranean giant ready to crush us in its grip. Or bars; the one time I looked back down toward the dock those towering columns blocked the view, like I was back inside my cell in the prison. Either way, they made it perfectly clear that there would be no getting out of here.

Not until my job was done. Not until my promise was kept.

"Alex?" Zee said. "I don't like it when you go quiet like that. Please tell me you know what you're doing."

"Nope," I replied. "No plan."

Zee's face fell, as he looked nervously up the slope. Shapes danced between the rock up there, moving in time with us, keeping their distance. All I could make out of them was their undulating limbs, too long, too thin, and those unblinking eyes.

"You know this could be a trap, right?" said Simon. "Maybe Furnace isn't even here."

Furnace hadn't spoken to me since we arrived, but I knew he was on the island. This wasn't like back in the tower, in the city, when I thought I was facing him. Back then I hadn't felt his fingers in my skull, pawing my thoughts. But now I could sense him as if he was standing right next to us. It wasn't so much pain—the compass in my skull had faded—I just knew.

"Oh God," said Lucy, clinging on to Zee's arm. "I knew it, he's just brought us here so he can kill us."

"If he wanted to kill us he would have done it back on the mainland," I said. "Or in the water."

"So tell me again why he's asked you around for tea?" Simon asked.

I didn't answer. I didn't know. But it wouldn't be long before I found out.

"You think Panettierre is still following us?" Zee said, changing the subject.

"She doesn't strike me as the sort of person who gives up easily," Lucy replied. "She's coming, no doubt about it."

We walked the rest of the way in silence, eventually reaching the top of the slope. Another castellated wall had been built here, the gate rusted into broken teeth. I could hear those same cries from beyond, half human, half beast, setting my nerves on edge.

"Doctor Moreau, anyone?" asked Zee.

I had no idea what he was talking about.

"H. G. Wells? *The Island of Doc*— Oh, never mind; forget it," said Zee, obviously disgusted to be in such badly read company.

I peered through the mouth-shaped archway, seeing a forest ahead. The trees were thick and short, barely twice my height, and they all looked close to death. It wasn't surprising, there was barely any soil up here, and the permanent cloak of mist that hung in the air tasted like pure salt.

As soon as I stepped through the iron teeth into the forest the cacophony of screeches and moans intensified. My pulse quickened, my heart a motor that drummed the nectar around my body. I held my right hand up, ready to defend myself if anything attacked, but other than the sounds and the distant, unformed shadows there was no sign of danger.

We set off into the trees, the branches knitting overhead, blocking out what little light was left. My silver eyes picked open the gloom, making sense of the knotted trunks and writhing limbs. The ground was thick with undergrowth, centuries' worth of untrimmed roots and weeds doing their best to trip us up, turn us back. Although I knew this wasn't the orchard from my dreams—from Furnace's memories—it looked a little too much like it for my taste.

"This place is majorly creepy," said Lucy. "I don't—" but she was cut off by the sound of footsteps, running hard, the crack of wood as something forced itself through the trees.

Something big, getting closer.

We drew ranks, our backs together, feeling the ground shake beneath us. Then we saw it, a shape in the forest, too big to be human, bigger even than the berserkers. It pushed its way through the thick trunks like it was running through cocktail sticks, splintering the wood, heading right for us.

"Down," I said, pushing the others to the ground and throwing myself on top of them, praying that we wouldn't all be trampled to death. But when it reached us the creature skidded to a halt, demolishing one last tree with its immense bulk.

I stared at it, unable to believe what I was seeing. The beast *was* human, or at least it had been. It stood four meters high, its body proportionately wide, formed of fleshy folds of gray skin. Its head was like a fist of countless knuckles. Two of those knuckles opened and closed, black eyes blinking down at us. Then its head seemed to split in two, a roar escaping its gaping mouth, spraying us with nectar-flecked spit.

But that wasn't the worst of it.

I thought at first that there were people riding this beast, their forms strapped to its side with some kind of harness. When I looked more closely, however, I realized that those figures were *part* of it. Limbs grew from its flesh like buds on a plant, dozens of deformed arms and legs bristling on all sides. And there were faces too, beneath its skin. I could see them pressing outward, their mouths opening and closing as if they were calling to us, pleading to let them out.

I heard a low, desperate moan, a cry of utter terror, and it didn't take me long to realize that it was coming from me.

The creature stomped forward, sniffing the air, snorting from the twin scars of its nostrils. Then it reared, ready to bring its huge legs down on us—no, not legs, I realized, but hands—ready to pound us into the forest floor. I forced myself to concentrate, to close my eyes. I had been able to control the other berserkers, maybe I could give this freak orders too. It was a long shot, but what else could I do? Even stabbing my bladed hand into that thing would have been like trying to bring down a rhinoceros with a butter knife.

I blasted out a message, picturing the monster retreating into the forest, leaving us alone. In those few seconds I must have imagined it a dozen times, silently screaming my commands at it.

I felt the ground shake as it slammed its fists down, opening my eyes to see it backing clumsily away. It shook its head, as if trying to dislodge a fly from inside its skull, never taking its eyes off me. The forms beneath its skin writhed.

I got to my feet, the nectar a storm, making every cell sing.

Lead us to him, I growled inside my head. *Take us to Furnace.*

I pictured the mansion, the beast showing us the way. It opened its mouth again, its bellow like that of a cow being led to slaughter. But it had no choice in the matter. I was its general, and it would obey. With another shake of its head, one that knocked man-sized branches to the ground, it set off along the path.

"What the hell is that thing?" asked Lucy as we set off after it. "It had . . . people in it."

"Just another monster, forget it," said Zee. He turned to me. "What did you say to it? Is it going to lead us to Furnace?"

"I guess we're about to find out," I said.

After a couple of minutes the berserker burst out of the forest, shedding leaves and twigs behind it. We followed the trail into a vast, open clearing, the size of a soccer field. The ground here was rocky and uneven, full of craters and crevices. It could have been the surface of the moon if it wasn't for the mansion that sat at the other end of it. It rose from the island as if it had grown here, built from the same dark stone, its walls and its towers so random that they looked organic. The berserker was charging toward it with purpose, its folds of fat and its surplus limbs bouncing up and down as it negotiated the rough terrain.

And it wasn't alone.

There were other creatures out here, dozens of them, teeming from the crevices in the rock like ants. Some actually resembled giant insects, their bodies hardened by the nectar, their skin the color and texture of a beetle's carapace, their lips twisted into crude mandibles. Others were closer to the children they had once been, still made of flesh. Their faces were broken but they were unmistakably human. That was where the resemblance ended, though. Their bodies were a cruel joke, as if they had been molded from plasticine by a bored child, then left to wilt in the sun.

Each one was unique, and they scuttled and bounded and limped over the rock to get a better look at us. They called out to each other as they moved, some sounding like toddlers wailing, others like pigs squealing. There were words in there too, but nothing that made any sense. These berserkers were too far gone to remember how to speak.

I realized that some of the freaks were closing in, their faces warped by curiosity, or maybe anger. Near the cliff edge two were fighting, their massive arms taking chunks out of each other until one backed away with a whimper.

"Come on," I said. "We should keep moving."

"Can't you control them?" Lucy asked.

This close to Furnace, I doubted it. Two or three of them, maybe, but thirty, forty, maybe even fifty all at once with their master's voice coming from the mansion? There was no way. We started moving again, slowly, afraid that any sudden movements might start a stampede. It was tough going. Some of the cracks in the rock must have cut right through the heart of the island because I could hear the sea down there, pummeling the rock. The sound reminded me of being back inside the prison, inside the chipping room after we'd blown the floor, about to jump into the river.

"You thinking what I'm thinking?" Zee asked, and I could see by the look on his face that I was. "At least we've got an escape route if those things decide they don't like us."

I vaulted a narrow crevice, hearing the sonic boom of the waves down below. We wouldn't last a second down there if we jumped. The river beneath the prison had nearly killed us, and the ocean was a million times more powerful.

The closer we got to the mansion, the weirder it seemed. Two wide, three-story wings sat on either side of a central tower, with a number of smaller turrets and spires reaching up from various other parts. I counted seven in all, each more elaborate than the last. At least twenty dark windows watched us approach. The berserker from the woods was trying to squeeze into the open front door, its bulk preventing it from entering. It heard us coming, pulling its head free and looking at me sadly.

"This place must have been the barracks or something," said Zee as the mansion loomed over us. "They probably stationed a whole naval division out here, to keep a lookout for—"

"You hear that?" interrupted Lucy. I cocked my head, trying to hear anything over the roar of the ocean. And sure enough, there it was, that faint pulse of a helicopter. Simon bolted along the front of the building to the edge of the cliff fifty meters away, peering over, his hand shielding his eyes even though the sun was still masked by clouds. He turned, cupping his mouth and yelling through the wind.

"Boats!"

"Panettierre," I said. I ran to Simon, careful not to get too close to the cliff edge. Sure enough maybe two dozen navy ships of different shapes and sizes were heading this way, churning the ocean into a rage. Maybe half as many helicopters mirrored them in the sky.

"How'd they get here so quickly?" asked Lucy, who had run to my side, clinging on to my elbow to stop her blowing off the edge.

"Must have been ready to roll," Zee answered as he arrived, panting. "They were probably just waiting for coordinates from Panettierre. There's a base up the coast from here, right? Sutter-mouth. No, Colvermouth, that's it. They would have bypassed Furnace's troops if they'd come from there. It's like Normandy or something. There are loads of them."

There were, all packed with troops. They weren't having a free ride, though. One boat was already sinking, smoke billowing from its engine. Two more had collided with each other and I saw a shape through a windshield, a corpse-faced beast that was going to work on the crew. The leviathans were doing their job well, but they wouldn't be able to stop them all.

"Jesus," muttered Zee. "The army out here, Furnace in there, talk about being between a rock and a hard place."

I jogged back to the mansion door, everybody else following. The berserker towered over us, watching curiously. It leaned down as I passed, trying to push itself through, the way I had com-manded it to. I sent out a message for it to stand back and it did so. It kept its head level with mine, bracing its weight on its immense fists. Its knuckled eyes blinked at me, and it uttered gentle whim-pers from its throat. I reached out with my good hand, resting my fingers on its cheek. It seemed to relish the touch, pushing against it. It could have been a massive dog if it wasn't for those extra heads that stretched its skin, opening and closing their mouths in silent screams; if its face, as gnarled and deformed as it was, didn't so clearly belong to a child.

"Thank you," I said to it.

Then I stepped through the door into the cool, dark interior of the mansion. My eyes barely had time to adjust to the dark—seeing a large reception room, decked in old furniture and paintings, grand staircases mirroring each other on both sides—before I heard the berserker utter a deafening howl behind me. I spun around to see that it had positioned itself outside the door, its corpulent body cutting out all but a trickle of light.

"Hey!" I shouted.

"Alex?" yelled Zee from the other side, his voice muted. "Make it move, we can't get in."

I tried to concentrate, ordering the creature to get out of the way, picturing it standing clear of the door. Nothing happened, even when I tried again, mentally screaming at it to obey.

"Move!" I shouted, slapping the berserker with my left hand. It bent its head and glared in at me, another banshee wail blasting from its gaping jaw, but still it didn't unblock the door. I went to slap it again but before I could I heard Furnace's voice erupt inside my head, loud enough to shatter my thoughts to splinters.

You must make this final journey alone, Alex.

I realized that the words had knocked me to my knees, stealing my breath and my voice. I struggled up, feeling like I'd been hit by a freight train. Nectar trickled from my nose, its foul taste in my mouth, and I spat it out.

"Wait for me here," I wheezed to the others, the words nothing more than a whisper. I clawed in a breath, said it again.

"Alex, you can't go by yourself, he'll kill you!" I couldn't tell who had spoken: the berserker's body muffled the sound and the ringing in my ears was just too loud. I put my left hand against the doorframe, saying a silent goodbye to my friends, praying for them to stay safe, praying that I'd live to see them again. Then I made my way into the building.

From now on there was only me.

Me and Alfred Furnace.

THE CALM BEFORE THE STORM

THE MANSION WAS A WARREN of rooms and corridors, but I knew exactly where to go.

I walked through the reception hall, between the staircases and through a set of double doors. It looked as if nobody had been here in years, decades even, everything covered in a layer of dust. The paintings on the walls were all of military leaders through the centuries, their medals muted by grime, their eyes following me. A massive chandelier swung from the ceiling as if something had just disturbed it, but mine were the only footprints on the filthy floor.

A long corridor stretched out from the lobby, doors on either side standing open. I peered into a couple of the rooms but they were mostly empty, a few containing just scraps of old machinery and the occasional desk. One was packed with bunk beds, the same kind as had been used in Furnace, the sheets fluttering in the breeze from a broken window.

I thought about going back to the front door, telling Zee, Simon, and Lucy that there was another way in. But what was the point? If Furnace wanted me here alone then that's what was going to happen. There would be no arguing with him, not in his own house.

I reached the end of the corridor, pushing through another pair of doors to find myself at the rear of the mansion. A staircase led down to the basement, the tiles cracked and stained. There was a window beside them, and through the crusted glass I could see the ocean far below and the battle taking place in it. Once the soldiers got past the leviathans then it wouldn't take them long to find their way onto the island. If I wanted to keep Panettierre's filthy hands off my friends then I was going to have to be quick.

My footsteps rang hollow as I ran down the steps, the echoes seeming to last for far longer than they had any right to—as if the house had been quiet for so many years it didn't quite know how to handle noise. At the foot of the staircase was another corridor, lit only by the sickly glow that seeped down from above. There were no rooms here, but halfway along the passageway was an alcove with a wooden bench. Propped up against the cracked white tiles was a plastic doll wearing a floral dress, one set of eyelashes missing. Next to it was a gas mask, covered in filth, its tube draped over the doll's legs.

I moved on, reaching another set of stairs leading down, these ones narrower. They led deep into the heart of the island, plunging me into such depths of gloom that even my silver eyes struggled to work out where they came to an end. Eventually I saw the outline of another double door, the light through the cracks so bright after the darkness that it was as if a fire raged beyond them.

I hesitated, my bladed hand ready. I didn't know what Alfred Furnace was now, what kind of powers he possessed. He had been alive for so long that he couldn't still be human. I thought about the warden, when I had fought him in the tower. I thought about what he had become when he had drunk the new nectar—a being that lived right on the edge of reality, half real and half dream, something that could bend physics to its own will.

But I had defeated the warden, I had brought him to his knees then let the wheezers slaughter him. And if he could die, then so could his boss. There weren't many creatures that could survive being stabbed through the heart. No matter what Furnace said, what kind of twisted lies he would attempt to tell me, what offers of power he made, I *would* kill him.

Or die trying.

The heavy doors opened without a sound, revealing a world that was the complete opposite of the derelict mansion above. A plush red carpet ran the length of the corridor, the wood-paneled walls gleaming. The ceiling was made of vaulted brick arches and in each one was a spotless crystal chandelier. The light they cast was golden, banishing every shadow.

There were noises here, and I followed them to the nearest door, my heart pounding so far up in my throat that I could taste nectar on my tongue.

Inside the large room were seven rows of wooden cots. Two of them were occupied. In one was a baby, swaddled in cloth and evidently fast asleep. In the other, on the far side of the room, was a boy about two years old. He clung to the wooden bars of his cot, grinning, bouncing up and down on his mattress. When he saw me in the doorway he stopped, his smile vanishing, his brow creasing.

I was so shocked by the sight of him that I almost didn't see the wheezer in the room. Only, it *wasn't* a wheezer. It wore the same clothes, that long trench coat, a bandolier of syringes around its chest. It had the same face too, pasty flesh, its eyes like blocks of coal.

But it wasn't wearing a gas mask.

It stared at me, its lipless mouth peeling back into some hideous parody of a smile, its black tongue flopping around inside like an eel. It twitched, the same way the wheezers in the prison had, its head snapping then its whole body juddering. The toddler watched it, starting to laugh, clapping its chubby hands together. I turned away, back into the corridor. I had to; the sight inside the room was almost enough to obliterate the last of my sanity.

I carried on along the corridor, past a dozen more rooms like that one. I tried not to look but I couldn't help myself, catching glimpses of more children, older now, strapped to machines or lying on operating tables. Some weren't human anymore, I realized, their bodies so bent and broken that they could only be called berserkers. The wheezers watched me pass with their dead men's grins, uttering those same nightmare purrs and ear-piercing shrieks that I knew so well.

I wanted to run in and kill them all, but there wasn't time. For all I knew Panettierre was already on the island, rounding up Zee and killing the others. Besides, my fear of being caught by the wheezers, of ending up once more under their knives, was overpowering. The thought of looking up into those piggy eyes while they smiled down at me made me nostalgic for the old wheezers, the familiar ones in gas masks.

I walked on, feeling the nectar rage only for its fire to be dulled by fear, each cycle leaving me more exhausted. It was okay, though. I wouldn't need my strength for much longer. There was just one more job to do, one more promise to keep, then I could rest for all eternity.

The corridor ended up ahead in yet another double door. On one door was painted a coat of arms—a red and white shield, two apple trees growing on either side and an animal in the center. I wasn't quite sure what the beast was—a jackal, maybe?—but I recognized its silver eyes. They seemed to sparkle in the light from the corridor, as if the creature was ready to spring from the painting and devour me. On the other door was the Furnace logo I was more familiar with, emblazoned on a red flag.

Even without the markings I would have known that these were Furnace's quarters. I could feel him there, his presence an endless pulse that seemed to reverberate through my body. I paused, offering a prayer to anything that was listening. Then I reached out my hand, turned the handle, and pushed open the door.

ALFRED FURNACE

I HONESTLY DON'T KNOW what I'd been expecting. But it wasn't what lay before me.

I stood at the entrance to a large chamber, the ceiling draped in shadows. Columns of crumbling brick seemed to grow from the floor, and although they weren't carved like trees—the same way as the ones back in the tower had been—they still resembled them, their vaulted branches interwoven overhead. A handful of flickering lamps were embedded in the walls, their nervous light doing little to illuminate their surroundings.

A berserker was perched on either side of the room, basking in the darkness. I couldn't get a good look at them behind the pillars, but I could make out bladed limbs of obsidian, jaws that dripped dirty saliva, and piggy eyes watching me warily. One of them growled when I entered, but neither seemed to see me as a threat.

It wasn't them that both fascinated and terrified me, though. It was the machine. It dominated the entire room, a monstrous engine of copper, glass, and steel. Countless moving parts danced back and forth, producing a quiet pulse that made my bones shake. And yet it seemed organic too, as if it had sprouted from the damp stone, endless pipes like the thorny tendrils of a plant. It was enormous, stretching from one end of the room to the other and lost in the dark pools of the ceiling. Its design was so complex, and its movement so mesmerizing, that it took me a while to notice the figure that was strapped to it, almost as if he had been crucified there.

It was Alfred Furnace.

He was human, and yet at the same time he wasn't. His body had been ravaged by age, his skin so rotten that in places it hung off him in strips, like old jerky. Parts of him weren't there at all—the upper half of his right arm, and the whole left side of his throat—and in those places sat a network of tubes and pipes, carrying the nectar around his body. He was so emaciated that he could have been a corpse, his skeletal ribs pulled open to reveal the organs beneath. Most seemed to have been replaced by pieces of machinery, yet his heart remained, as shriveled and as black as a decayed fig, but still beating.

It was his face, though, that almost sent me tumbling back through the door, that made a scream vomit up from my stomach, held in check only by the fact that there was no air in my lungs to fuel it.

It was as if Furnace was three different people at the same time. I could see the child there, the one from my visions, a kid no older than me. And yet he was also an old man, his face as withered as his body, his skin the color and texture of decomposed apples. The two faces seemed to strobe back and forth, so fast that they almost merged.

But there was something else there too, a figure laid over Furnace's head and body like a photographic negative, one that couldn't seem to stay still long enough for me to focus on it. I knew what it was, though. I had seen this thing before.

The stranger, the creature from the orchard.

It was as if Furnace's skin was radiating a living darkness, an impossible silhouette that thrashed and pulled and fought like a prisoner trying to escape his chains. I recognized his face, or the void where his face should have been, opening and closing as if formed of a million moving parts. The stranger's eyes—no, the place where his eyes should have been—watched me, two gaping, boundless portals in his head that were infinitely darker than the shadows around them, like holes burned through the skin of reality. They seemed to suck in all the light and warmth from the room, devouring it, throwing out only cold night. I knew that to stare into those eyes for too long wouldn't just erode my sanity, it would kill me.

I collapsed to my knees, the pillar beside me the only thing stopping me from falling flat on my face. The same fear that had gripped me in my dream of the orchard had found me again, that unspeakable, unthinkable, unbearable terror. Everything in the room seemed to be unraveling, as if the surface of the world was peeling away to reveal the abyss beneath. That endless void was infinitely quiet, and yet at the same time it was deafening. I could feel drops of nectar drip from my ears, squeezed from my tear ducts, from my nose. I was unraveling too, every cell in my body withering into a dust that defied gravity, rising toward the ceiling.

Alex, said Furnace, and his words ended the chaos, rooting me back inside the room. His voice was the sound of continents shifting, and yet within it I could also hear the husky, gentle tones of an old man and the higher pitch of a boy, each speaking the same words and yet ever so slightly out of sync. *There is no reason to fear me.*

"What are you?" I asked. I wasn't sure if the words left my

mouth, but it didn't matter. He could see inside my mind as if it were his own.

I am old, he said.

He was, not just years, not just decades, but centuries. That knowledge lay in my head, impossible but undeniable. The nectar had kept death at bay while generations of people had lived and died, while billions turned to dust and ash around him.

Not nectar, Furnace corrected, reading my mind. *What runs through my veins is something far more powerful.*

I remembered my visions, the stranger in the orchard, the one who had forced Furnace to drink his blood. What was it if it wasn't nectar?

In your soul, you already know, he replied. *This blood is eternity, immortality. It has existed since before mankind stepped onto the earth, and it will exist long after the last of us has rotted back into the dirt. It is the very essence from which the nectar is made. I died, and behold I am alive forevermore, and I hold the keys of death and the grave.*

My thoughts were a storm and I fought to remember why I had come here. But all that existed were questions. Questions, and the unrelenting terror.

"What was that thing? The creature in the orchard?"

The two faces—the old man and the boy—seemed to howl in silent agony at the question, their mouths open too wide as their heads writhed back and forth. But the being that overshadowed them smiled without smiling, the place where his eyes should have been seeming to grow brighter and darker at the same time.

He has no name, and yet he has many, said Furnace. *He saved me, and now he will do the same for you.*

Furnace's hands moved as he talked. The two smallest fingers were missing on the left, the thumb absent from the right. His remaining digits were slender and too long, three or four knuckles on each one. They unfolded with a sound like popping joints until both his palms were facing me. Pipes and valves punctured his ancient flesh, imprisoning him within the machine. I doubted he could move even if he wanted to, and surely even if he did break free then he would just fall apart.

The thought brought me back, quenching some of the fear, reminding me why I was here. I attempted to get up, ready to attack. Furnace was so withered, so broken, that killing him would be no different than smothering an old man in his bed. I was so much stronger than him. I called out to the berserkers in the room, imagining them reaching out for Furnace, ripping him from his contraption, tearing him limb from limb.

"Kill him," I wheezed at them. "Do it!"

The berserkers didn't move, blinking their oil-well eyes at me. One shifted its position like a restless cat and I could see the immense bulk of its body, endless clusters of muscles barely held by a patchwork of skin. It settled on its haunches, its face the most human thing in the room.

"Kill him," I commanded, but those few words had used up all but the last of my strength. Furnace began to laugh, a sound that I felt rather than heard. It seemed to sit on my spine, gripping my vertebrae like a dirty fist. I tried to get back to my feet, ready to run my bladed hand through Furnace's open chest, but my body wouldn't obey.

Did you really think it would be that easy? Furnace asked, his eyes blazing black light, roaring like blowtorches. *Did you honestly believe you could control them?*

I *had* been controlling them, the berserkers. Ever since the hospital I'd been able to tell them what to do, hadn't I? Once again Furnace plucked my question from my skull.

You did not have the power, he said, his voice like liquid thunder. *I read your mind, Alex, and I relayed your commands to my children. It was not you who gave them orders, but I.*

I didn't want to believe him, except I knew it was the truth. I felt panic once again claw through my body, dousing the nectar like a blanket over a fire. What the hell was I doing? Did I honestly think I could just walk into Furnace's own house and kill him? I was going to die here, I was going to be executed.

No, said Furnace, his tone surprisingly calm. *It is I who will not live to see tomorrow.*

I lifted my head, feeling like the weight of the world was pressing down on it. For a second the blurred, flickering silhouette of the stranger faded and I could see the two other people beneath, the boy and the man. Both looked utterly exhausted, especially the kid. His thin face reminded me of the inmates inside the prison, the ones who looked like they would never be able to get through another day behind bars. The face vanished once again behind the invisible grin of the stranger.

"What do you mean?" I said.

Why do you think I brought you here, Alex? said Furnace.

I opened my mouth to give an answer, realizing that I didn't have one. I thought I had known. There had been a reason I had come here, a reason I had thought it would be so easy. I had come to kill Furnace. My thoughts were disintegrating, collapsing in on each other. I saw one in the confusion, grasping for it before it could disappear.

"You didn't bring me here," I said, faltering. "I . . . I came for you."

Did you? More laughter, insects scuttling on the underside of my skin. *Are you sure about that, Alex?*

I wasn't sure about anything anymore. The weight on my head grew too much and I let it drop, collapsing onto my elbows, looking like I was praying in front of an altar.

Why do you think I showed you everything I did? Furnace went on. *Why do you think I let you escape from the prison?*

"You didn't," I spat. Furnace laughed, gesturing to his side where an old-fashioned telephone nestled in an alcove within the machine. It reminded me of the one in the warden's office, back in the prison, and I knew instantly that they had once been connected. I wasn't sure why he'd needed one, given that he could talk to the warden through the nectar, but the sight of it there brought back the memory of when I'd first heard Furnace, the way his voice through that phone had made my ears bleed. He had known everything that we were doing, he had seen it all, and he had let it happen.

Didn't I? he went on. *Why didn't I stop you, Alex? Why didn't I send a hundred berserkers, a thousand? Why didn't I turn your friend Simon against you?* He laughed, the sound making the blood boil in my head. *Why did I lead you to the tower, and give you the strength to defeat my old general, Cross? Why did I grant you the power to fight the human army? And why did I show you the path here, to my kingdom?*

"You didn't!"

Except he *had* done all of those things. Everything that had happened had been orchestrated by the creature that hung before me, this madness of man, machine, and monster. I shook my head, unable to accept it, coughing out the same denial again and again and again.

That is part of the nectar's beauty. It makes puppets of mortals. This is something that you will soon discover for yourself, if you are willing.

"Willing?" I managed, a ribbon of black blood oozing out with the word.

You have to be willing, said Furnace. *It can work no other way. But you will be. I am old, Alex, so very old, and even he cannot keep me alive forever. By doing this you will keep your promise. The only way to kill me is to take my place. I need an heir, but such a gift cannot be given lightly.*

I shook my head again, fury detonating inside me. There was no way I would do what he asked. I was here to kill him, to stop him, not to *replace* him.

"Why me?" I asked.

Save your breath, Alex, he said. *It will become clear. Let me show you something.*

The room came apart, the columns and the vaulted ceiling spinning away from the floor with such speed that I was gripped by vertigo. I realized I was back outside again, standing on the top of the island, surrounded by berserkers. I tried to look around but I had no control, like in my dream. Then the view swung from side to side and I realized that I was looking at the world through somebody else's eyes.

They are here, Furnace said. *And they come without mercy. Watch.*

I heard the soldiers before I saw them, swarming from the forest in groups, their weapons blazing. Bullets tore through the first berserkers, so much firepower that their immense bodies were pulled into the air and dismembered by the hail of lead. I expected the others to fight back, but they all seemed rooted to the spot, including the one whose head I occupied. I could almost taste its emotions, a mix of anger and panic that sat in my mouth like bile.

"Fight back!" I called to it, to all of them, but it was no use.

A soldier fired a rocket from a bazooka, the missile hitting one of Furnace's freaks and causing a fireball so big that I could feel it down here in the vault. Pink and black rain steamed down onto the island, and yet still none of the berserkers moved.

The creature whose head I occupied looked around, showing me the front of the mansion. I could see the behemoth we had met in the woods, its frame dwarfing the people who cowered by its side—Zee, Lucy, and Simon. At the rate things were going out there it wouldn't be long before they were dead. And even if they survived the firefight I knew that Panettierre was here on the island, leading her troops, wanting to turn us into specimens.

The view of the island vanished with the same gut-wrenching speed it had appeared, sucking me back down into the basement. I retched, a string of black spit hanging from my lips. It felt like the room was still spinning, the confusion causing my vision to darken, my body to shake uncontrollably.

"Why are you showing me this?" I demanded, anger returning some of the strength to my body. I managed to crawl up on my knees, my hand resting against the pillar. "Why aren't you fighting back?"

I am old, Furnace repeated, lifting his mangled hands in surrender. *My time for fighting is at an end. It is your turn to take control, Alex. Only you can save them, only you can win this war. Come to me, child; accept what I have to offer.*

Furnace's hands lifted, gesturing toward part of the machine I hadn't really noticed. There was a human-shaped space there, straps for arms and legs and a metal cradle for a head.

It will be easy, child. And it will be quick.

I knew that even now I was following Furnace's plan, just a marionette dancing along to the movement of his fingers. But what could I do? If I stayed here, on my knees, then the army would win. Panettierre would have her victory, she would create monsters of her own, and the world would be buried beneath a tide of nectar. Zee would be dead, Simon and Lucy too, probably. And what of me? There was little doubt about my fate either. They would cart me back to the hospital, run more of their tests until I took my last breath. Either that or they would execute me in this very room.

At least if I obeyed Furnace, if I accepted his offer, I would stand a chance. If nothing else, at least I would be in control. If I accepted, *I* would become the executioner. And isn't it always better to be the one who kills than the one who dies? A seed of doubt wormed up from the anger, from the fear, but it was too slow. I had made my decision.

"What do I do?" I asked, pushing myself up, my legs almost too weak to hold me. I staggered over to Furnace, trying not to look at his tattered flesh, at the glass pipes that ran through his body.

Will you accept my gift? he asked. It was the same question that had been asked of him, centuries ago, in the orchard. And I knew I would give the same answer. I saw the blood that pumped through Furnace, the pure, undiluted power from which nectar had been distilled, and the truth was that I wanted it more than anything else in my life.

"I accept," I said. The stranger's face unfolded, shadowed petals blossoming, contracting, blossoming again.

I knew you would, Furnace said.

He reached out to me, his fingers on my head, pushing the hair back from my brow. His flesh was as cold as ice.

Thank you.

LIFE

THE MOMENT I MADE CONTACT with the machine it seemed to know what to do. The pulse inside it grew in pace and in volume, vibrating so much that it made my bones rattle. Two figures walked through the chamber door, the maskless wheezers, their corpse grins so wide that it looked as though somebody had sliced them open from ear to ear. They staggered toward me, the needles around their chests clinking, and the sight of them made me feel like I was back inside the prison, watching the blood watch stalk the cells. I panicked, every muscle in my body tensing, my lungs unable to draw air.

What the hell was I doing?

Do not be afraid, said Furnace, and his voice—half whisper, half thunder—was impossible to disobey. It chased the fear away. *They will not hurt you.*

He was right. The wheezers were gentle, and they were kind. One slotted my hands into the straps before buckling my legs in place. The other held my head tenderly in its creased, leathery hands, pulling the cradle down over my scalp and fastening it under my chin. They worked together to clip a massive belt around my chest, leaving it loose enough for me to be able to breathe.

When they stood back, their bodies spasming, their fat, black tongues thrashing in the wet pools of their mouths, I was held fast. But there was no pain.

When I was turned, all I had to do was drink, Furnace said. I remembered the vision, the boy who had been nailed to the tree drinking the blood of the stranger. *But we are a more civilized people now. We trust in science as well as magic.*

I angled my head so I could see him, both of us strapped side by side, like we were on the fields of Golgotha. His head swiveled around, those three faces still fighting for superiority, their movement so fast now that it made my head hurt to look at them. I didn't turn away, though.

Begin, said Furnace. The wheezers separated, walking to the sides of the machine where they busied themselves with wheels and levers. I didn't care. The method of what was happening wasn't important, only the result.

Something slid from the framework around me, half a dozen needles connected to plastic tubing. They sank deep into the flesh of my upper arm but there was still no pain, only a slight discomfort. With a stomach-turning noise three of the needles began to pump, and I watched as the red-flecked nectar was sucked out of my body.

That nectar, the new nectar, is the most powerful we have ever managed to create, Furnace explained as he watched the flow. *But even its power dims in comparison to the blood. We must drain you of it before I pass on my gift.*

I could feel my body growing weaker as the nectar flowed out of it, the same way it had back in the hospital. Unlike then, though, I was about to be given something far better, something that would turn me into a being of unthinkable power.

A being? Furnace said, once again reading my thoughts. *You will become nothing less than a god.*

I looked at the figure beside me, a boy who should have died hundreds of years ago, a man who built an empire and who lived to see it change the world, and a creature that was older than time. I smiled, knowing that I too would experience the same gift.

The smile was short-lived. The chamber was growing dark as the last drops of nectar were cleansed from my body. A sense of dread began to rise in me, like I was sinking into cold water. Without the nectar, I would die. Was this just another of Furnace's cruel tricks, to lure me to my death with the promise of eternal life? There was another noise, the gurgle of a straw in an empty cup, the red-flecked fluid in the tubes disappearing. My vision had now faded completely and my hearing was following fast. Furnace said something to me but his words were no more than an incomprehensible noise, as if my ears were stuffed with cotton wool.

Then, for what felt like an eternity, there was nothing.

Distantly, I sensed the machine change pitch, its growling pulse softening. Immediately my body began to burn, an onslaught of fire and ice in every single cell of my being. Even the rush of the nectar was nothing compared to this. It was as if the very fabric of the universe was a plaything that I could use—or destroy—any way I wished. I was instantly alert, more alive than I had ever been. My eyes snapped open and I saw that the other three tubes had turned black as the stranger's blood was pumped from Furnace into me. I heard myself laugh, and that laughter was as loud as Furnace's had once been, an explosion that rocked the chamber and flooded into the world beyond, to be felt in the soul of every living thing on earth.

The thought of it made me cry out with joy. I felt my mutated body slough away, felt myself rise up out of my scarred, twisted flesh, felt the fear and the anger wash out of me, knowing that I would never again be punished by the weakest of human emotions.

I kept on cackling like a lunatic, even though some last part of me, of the boy I had once been, realized the horror of what was happening. There was almost enough of him left to make sense of the nightmare that was unfolding, to know that of all the fates I could have prayed for, this was by far the worst. But that part of me was almost completely lost now, a lone voice whispering in the middle of a hurricane.

And then it was gone. There was only the stranger's blood.

"Why me?" I asked again, each word a sonic boom.

It is you because you are here, Furnace said, his voice muted, more human. I saw his body begin to fall apart as the blood left him, his skin cracking into dust, his bones breaking, his limbs folding into crooked spirals. The figure of the stranger was fading, and I knew why. It was leaving Furnace, deserting its old host. It was moving into me. For a second there were only the two human faces, then in a blink of an eye the boy's alone remained. He inhaled, as if it was the first breath he had ever taken, and his pale eyes were filled with sorrow. But whether it was for me or for himself I couldn't tell.

It is you because you remembered, he said.

Then, with an almighty crack, his head crumbled into itself, his face breaking into a hundred pieces, drifting to the stone like snow and ash. And with his final words I saw the rest of his story, his memories now mine, flooding into me with the last few drops of blood.

In that second I lived an entire life, Alfred Furnace's life.

* * *

I WAS BACK in the orchard, feeling what the young Furnace felt as he drank the blood of the stranger, filled with a power he was barely old enough to comprehend. I charged with him through the trees, back toward his village, with the mind of an animal and the strength of a god. That cloud of dark energy surrounded him, the stranger somehow superimposed over Furnace's body, looking like he was hemorrhaging black mist into the air. He tore through his own people with such ferocity that I could feel the bile rise in my throat. His viciousness left nothing behind but an island of severed limbs in an ocean of blood.

It was only when he finally found the corpse of his brother, József, that he seemed to emerge from his bloodlust. I watched him drop down onto his knees beside the boy, felt his horror, his shock as he realized that his veins now ran with the blood of his sibling's murderer. He reached out, cradling the dead body, rocking back and forth and howling so loud that his breath threatened to extinguish the fires that had started in the village.

It does not want anger, I heard Furnace's voice in my head, the boy's voice, as if he were here too watching a replay of his life. *It is not enough for it to possess a mindless creature bent on destruction. It needs somebody who can remember, somebody who will never forget the child they once were. It needs you to be able to keep control.*

"*I don't understand,*" I said.

The moment I saw József I remembered, Furnace said. *I remembered who I was. József would never have wanted me to be like this; it was the memory of him that stopped me from becoming a berserker, or worse. The stranger's blood gave me power, but it was the memories of József, of my old life, that let me control it for so long, and to make it even stronger over the centuries. You are the same, are you not?*

"*What do you mean?*"

Furnace's lifeline sped up, so fast I could barely follow it—I saw him hiding out in a forest, years spent by himself as he tried to understand what was happening to him; I saw him spurned and cast out by the people he encountered, the men and women who attacked him without question, sensing the evil inside him, then the armies who declared war on what they saw as a devil. The battle I had seen before, in my dreams, was but one of many, I realized. Tens of thousands had tried to kill Furnace, and they had all paid with their lives.

I saw the barn, the boy who was being kicked to death by the posse of howling adults. I watched again as Furnace shared his blood with the kid, the boy taking his revenge on his attackers. This was the first of Furnace's children, those few droplets from his master's vein multiplying the boy's strength a hundredfold. I watched as, only two days later, the same kid died, the undiluted poison wreaking havoc on his flesh.

Most people cannot handle the blood, Furnace said. *It is too much for them, it breaks them. I survived because it was not just some of the stranger's blood inside me, but all of it—the stranger himself dwelling in my body, in my mind. And it was because I remembered my life, my name, because I had kept my mind, that he could use me. You, like me, still remember. That is what it wants, Alex, because if the host remembers nothing of the world it came from it is no more use to the stranger than a dog.*

More flash-forwards, Furnace older now, trying to find a way to share his blood with other children without killing them. I saw countless victims become rats. Furnace commanded them as his personal army, their deformed bodies hidden beneath chain mail and armor, unstoppable in battle but never living much more than a week. A few survived, still growing, starting to change into berserkers, but even these would eventually fall apart before the process could complete, their bodies swelling uncontrollably until they simply burst.

Decades passed, Furnace growing richer as he conquered his enemies, reducing entire cities to dust. Then the scene changed and I was in an old-fashioned laboratory, watching a bearded man working with beakers full of black blood. The stranger was still there, part of Furnace, his featureless face smiling and yet not smiling, watching intently as the man worked.

It was in Vienna, more than a century ago, that I created the nectar, Furnace said. *I found a way to dilute the blood, to replicate its effects without causing certain death.*

I watched as the man in my vision pricked his finger with a needle, a tiny bead of blood dropping into a container of clear liquid. Instantly the fluid began to cloud, until it looked like a vat of oil filled with tiny golden flecks. I recognized it, the nectar that the warden and his wheezers had used back inside the prison.

He filled a syringe from the container and injected it into a child. The kid, the guinea pig, bucked and thrashed as the poison entered his veins, but he remained human. Days passed, the boy growing stronger, bigger. When his expanding body threatened to split his skin, Furnace performed surgery, patching him up with grafts and muscles salvaged from a fresh corpse until, maybe a week later, I recognized him as a blacksuit. A Soldier of Furnace.

This was the first time I managed to harness the nectar's power successfully, I heard Furnace say. *My soldiers were strong, yes, and fast, able to heal themselves of most injuries. But they only had the nectar, they only had a fraction of the power of the stranger's blood. Any more and they would simply become monsters. They would lose their minds. They were good soldiers, yes, but none could become my heir. The blood would kill them.*

Another gut-churning leap forward in time, Furnace much older now, his face so gaunt beneath his beard that he could have been a walking corpse. He was standing inside a bunker, surrounded by young men, teenagers. They were all dressed in long black coats, red swastikas emblazoned on their armbands, a bandolier of needles strapped to their chests, gas masks concealing their faces. I could see their eyes, though, as black as coal. Whoever these men were, they had consumed the nectar, and it had already kept them alive far longer than they deserved.

As my experiments progressed I found that some were immune to the nectar, he said. *Or nearly so. Their new blood processed the atmosphere differently, the air they breathed setting off a chemical reaction that proved fatal. Many died before I discovered the cause, and the solution—to filter out nearly all of the oxygen using modified gas masks. I made them my scientists. They grew old with me, so old, forgetting everything but the desire to experiment, to create. I have heard you call them "wheezers." Your friend Zee would make a suitable candidate . . .*

The room was full of cages, and I realized that I had been here before, in my dreams back inside the prison. Kids crouched in the shadows inside each container, their sad eyes fixed on the men around them, and on the pile of corpses in the corner.

The problem was that I only had a limited supply of blood inside me, so could make only a small quantity of nectar. One or two soldiers a week. We almost developed a new nectar under Hitler, but he failed before we could finish. Hitler wanted to use it on himself, but of course it would have killed him, he was too old. Besides, he was a weak man, Alex. Far weaker than you.

Another scene I recognized: gas-masked men struggling through the mud carrying a stretcher, looking for the wounded, the nearly dead. I saw them carry off dozens of men, all of them screaming to be let back onto the battlefield, crying out to die. I saw Furnace himself, pulling a teenage boy from the blood and filth. I recognized the warden.

He was to be my heir, he said, and I saw them working together, Furnace feeding Cross nectar until the warden's eyes became a mirror image of his own twin vortexes. *He drank of the nectar, consumed more of it than I believed possible, and yet he still remembered who he was, who he had been and where he had come from. I knew that one day I would pass my gift, my blood, to him.*

More images, changing too fast to make sense of, time peeling away. I saw the construction of the tower in the city, then the prison being built, its purpose to create an endless supply of test subjects, the warden inside continuing the same experiments, all under his master's supervision. By now Furnace was trapped here on the island, fixed into his infernal machine, his body wasted, decayed, but his mind as sharp as ever. I witnessed him and his wheezers creating the new breed of nectar, the one that could pass from mortal to mortal with just a bite, the one with the power to create the berserkers outside, the leviathans in the water.

But, alas, Cross disappointed me. He could not keep his house in order. Where one failed, however, another succeeded. I found somebody else, somebody more deserving. Somebody who, like Cross, had consumed far more nectar than I thought possible, and yet who still remembered who he was.

I saw myself, the boy I had once been—so human he was almost unrecognizable—the day I traveled down to Furnace in the elevator. I saw those doors opening to reveal the hell where I thought I would spend the rest of my life, the place in which I thought I would die. Donovan was there, leading me up the stairs, scowling. Then inside my cell, when his face had opened up and suddenly the prison hadn't seemed so dark, so far underground. I saw it all, everything that happened, our attempts to escape, the day we made it back onto the streets, my fight with the warden in the tower, everything right up to this one ageless, endless second.

We are the same, you and I, said Furnace. *We were both accused of a murder we didn't commit, we were both sentenced to death for that crime, and we were both given a chance to right that wrong, to take revenge on the world that had condemned us. It was necessary for your friend Toby to die so that you might share those emotions with me. It is these similarities that led us to each other. Given a choice, of course, I would never hand over the gift. But I do not know how much longer I have—it may be another hundred years, it may be another hour—and if I die without passing on the blood then everything will have been for nothing.*

I had a vision of myself as I was right now, strapped to the machine, the stranger's blood pumping through me. My entire body seemed to radiate darkness, waves of absence ebbing from my pores. And my eyes were vast portals, black holes of infinite nothingness.

I wasn't scared, though. I wasn't excited either. There were no emotions, only the feeling that this was right, that I belonged. Another kid had been here, Alfred Furnace, a *good* kid, an innocent kid, and I was to replace him. Nothing in my life had ever seemed more logical, or made more sense.

I wanted to make a world where there is no more weakness, Furnace said. *I still do. A world where a boy like me can never be nailed to a tree and slaughtered, where a boy like you can fight back against those who attack him. A place where there is only strength, where all are equal, where all fight on the same side. Do that for me, Alex. Finish this.*

The boy I had once been, the boy Furnace had once been,

would both have seen the twisted logic of that argument for what it was, would have understood that what really drove Furnace was the stranger in his veins, a creature of evil that wanted only to wreak destruction upon humanity, to turn life to rot. But the stranger's blood was too powerful, its cry for power too loud, and that understanding was obliterated from my mind.

"*I will*," I said. "*I promise*."

And even as I made one promise, I honored another. I could sense Alfred Furnace hanging on somewhere inside me, a trace of him left in the blood he had given me—just a boy terrified of the end, of what might come next. Then I felt him leave, my body shuddering as the last of his consciousness fled. I had seen his whole life, centuries of it, flash by in an instant, and it ended just as quickly.

Furnace was dead. I had killed him.

And I had taken his place.

THE GIFT

FURNACE WAS GONE, leaving me alone with the creature from the orchard.

I could feel him there, like a weight inside my head, his blood in my veins like puppet strings, as though he could make me do anything he wanted. Furnace had argued against injustice, but the stranger did not care about right or wrong. He told me so without words. All he wanted was to watch the world burn.

AND YOU WILL TOO, he said.

I concentrated on the power of the stranger's blood. It surged inside me, setting every nerve ending alight, making me feel like I could snap my fingers and stop time, cut the stars from the heavens. I was still strapped to the machine inside the chamber, I knew that much, but I was also in countless other places. I could see a thousand different sights, smell so many different scents, could hear all the world at once and make sense of everything.

I knew what was happening. I was inside the head of every single being with nectar in its veins, from the wheezers who stood in this very room to the blacksuits who waged war on the mainland, from the berserkers on the island above me to the leviathans in the ocean, even the rats, so many of them. I could sense

Simon there too, his fear, his hysteria, as the army continued their attack.

This was the true gift, I realized. I couldn't just see these things—the blacksuits, the berserkers, the wheezers—I *was* them. The stranger's blood, *my* blood now, flowed inside them. They were mine to do with as I pleased.

"It's okay," I said, directing the message to Simon. I could feel the shift in his emotions when he heard me, first disbelief, then hope breaking through the despair like a starburst. He replied, but I had already moved on. I could see the island from dozens of different viewpoints at once, the effect dizzying, like looking into a kaleidoscope. The soldiers had broken out of the trees, still mowing down the motionless berserkers with their weapons. I felt those bullets as if it were me who was being shot, the sudden flash of pain cutting through the numbness inside my mind, filling me with rage.

They would pay for that.

I ordered the berserkers to attack, feeling the nectar begin to pound in their hearts, their thoughts turning to murder as their paralysis was broken. I followed one, watching from inside its head as it bounded over the fractured rock toward two marines in camouflage. They saw it coming, firing their weapons, but it was too late. I could feel its strength as it lashed out, its claws spearing one of the soldiers through his torso, wrapping its jaws around the other man's arm, the sensation making me feel like I was crunching ice cubes.

At the same time I directed six more berserkers toward the tree line, seeing through all their eyes at once, feeling as though their feet were my own as they stampeded. One fell, caught by a mortar blast, the sudden darkness of its vision, the gaping emptiness of its thoughts, throwing me for a second. But the others made up for their fallen brother, laying into their enemies with a ferocity that made the ground tremble.

The soldiers were panicking at this sudden onslaught, falling back, their faces warped by fear. I scanned the retreating crowds, looking for Panettierre, but I couldn't see her anywhere. It didn't matter. She could wait. There was no place for her to hide, not now.

A jet roared overhead and suddenly the island turned to flame as its missile struck, the effect like a volcano erupting. The inferno blazed over the rock between the trees and the mansion, eradicating everything that stood there. I heard the berserkers scream inside my head, their voices those of the children they had once been. I could feel the heat, its touch unbearable.

"Don't be afraid," I commanded, trying to wipe the fear from their minds, trying to absorb the pain as the life ebbed from them. I talked to them as they died, telling them that they were going to a good place, that they would be safe there, and free. I don't think they understood my words, but I could feel their relief at the sound of my voice, sensing that they weren't alone, and that there was something better than this. I experienced their agony as if it were my own, but I accepted it, knowing that even though it felt as if I was dying over and over again I was safe inside the chamber.

I retaliated instantly, commanding the rest of the berserkers into the trees, telling them to show no mercy. Blood flew, limbs lopped off like felled branches, skulls broken, chests and stomachs pierced, throats chewed out. It was a sight from the very inner circle of hell, one that would have driven a mortal insane. But I was no longer mortal. I heard myself laugh grimly as I watched the carnage, the sound silent and yet deafening, those impossible howls a perfect soundtrack to the madness.

Some of the soldiers had bolted, tripping down the steps back toward the dock. There were boats there, rising and falling in the tide, filling fast. But they wouldn't provide a safe haven. I entered the head of a leviathan, feeling the cold water flow against its skin as it dived and somersaulted below the waves. It welcomed me with joy, relishing the chance to attack, and I watched through its dark eyes as it surged upward, gaining speed, ramming the boat so hard that it cracked the hull with its skull.

I saw the bodies falling overboard like I was watching from the bottom of a swimming pool, their thrashing forms silhouetted against the sky, their screams muted by the water. It all seemed to be happening in slow motion. The leviathan unfurled its spider-like arms, wrapping them around the flailing figures, pulling them into the depths where they would spend all eternity.

More troops were moving in, two Chinook helicopters dropping toward the mansion side of the island, an Apache alongside them, its cannons tearing up anything that moved. I was running out of berserkers, the army's firepower just too much.

I remembered that the big one, the one we had encountered in the forest, was still stationed by the front door and I told it to attack. I watched through its eyes as it ran toward where the helicopters were landing, bullets thudding into its flesh, no more painful than mosquito bites. One of the choppers saw it coming, tried to take off, but the berserker was too quick. It threw itself at the open loading ramp as it left the ground, the soldiers there still fighting to free their weapons. In seconds it had slaughtered them all, squeezing through to the cockpit, leaving it looking like a butcher's shop. The chopper spun, dropping like a stone, the berserker leaping out moments before the Chinook vanished over the edge. The beast didn't even pause for breath, bounding toward the second helicopter as a plume of fire rose up behind it, the explosion causing a section of the cliff to crumble loose.

It didn't make it far, a missile from the Apache reducing it to chunks of wet flesh. I called out to it, remembering the way it had nuzzled against my hand, just a child desperate for contact. But there was no response, all it was now was a gaping absence in my head.

There was another bone-jarring eruption of fire as a jet screamed overhead, but this time the air strike missed its target. If anything it seemed to confuse the army, the troops splitting up in all directions, trying to find cover in the super-heated smoke. Picking them off was easy, like shooting fish in a barrel.

Chaos gripped the island in a fist of fear and flame. Through every set of eyes I saw death and murder, claws and bullets flying. One of the berserkers took a round in its eye, dying instantly. Another saw what had happened and I could feel its pain and its fury at the loss of one of its brothers. I didn't need to tell it what to do, it sought instant revenge, dashing the murderous soldier against the rock.

Things were no better in the water, four more leviathans joining the first. They had scuppered most of the smaller boats and I ordered them to attack the ships. They looked like vast, spindly crabs as they scaled the sides of the battle cruisers, ripping the soldiers from the decks. The ocean around the island churned red. Some of the boats were turning, heading back to the mainland, but I was determined to make sure that none of them made it, directing my soldiers after them.

And all the while I could feel the stranger whose blood flowed in my veins, the one who had made all of this possible. He didn't speak, didn't make a sound, and yet I could sense his rancid glee in every fiber of my body. He was delighted with me, his new host. Never had I felt such malevolent joy, such cruel, sadistic happiness.

I was distracted by Simon's thoughts, and I observed through his eyes as he, Zee, and Lucy ran through the unguarded front door of the mansion.

"I'm downstairs," I said, showing Simon a mental image of the chamber. *"It's safe here."*

I heard him repeat the message to the others, his voice sounding strange as it echoed inside his own head. He led the way across the hall and down the corridor. Both Zee and Lucy were bombarding him with questions but I didn't stop to listen, returning my attention to my troops as the island came under yet another assault.

The second Chinook had managed to land, masked soldiers pouring out into the smoke. Half set up suppressing fire, a wave of bullets that cut down another two berserkers. The rest used the cover to clamber into the house, some through the door and others throwing themselves at the windows. Once they had set up position they started shooting out across the island, allowing the rest of the soldiers to enter.

It was impossible to identify the men and women behind the masks, but somehow I knew she was one of them, Panettierre. I felt my pulse quicken, pumping the stranger's blood around my system, the noise so loud that it was as if the very earth had a heartbeat. I called on the remaining berserkers, telling them to return to the mansion, to find her.

There were still two berserkers here in the chamber and I ordered them to intercept her. Panettierre and her army would be pinned between two unstoppable waves. The creatures bounded past me, giving me a glimpse of myself—a demon crucified to a machine. In seconds they had reached the top of the steps and were running down the corridor on all fours. There was a weird moment when they passed Simon, the same event seen from two different angles. My friends fell back against the wall, Lucy knocking a painting loose, but of course the berserkers weren't interested in them and kept running.

I saw what happened next through six sets of eyes, three creatures from outside leaping through the windows onto the soldiers. A fourth tried to get in through the door but somebody had rigged up an explosive, the blast sending it flying back out, dead before it hit the rock.

Even so, what followed next was a massacre, the five surviving berserkers attacking from all angles, giving the army no chance. The soldiers didn't know which way to turn, some of them firing in wild circles, killing their own friends. They scattered, a few vanishing through doors or throwing themselves back outside. Most were too slow, though, screaming for mercy.

They received none.

"Nobody survives," I told the berserkers, relishing their excitement. They were an extension of my own body—when they tasted blood so did I, the warmth gushing down my throat; when they lashed out with their monstrous limbs my own arms twitched, my new fingers gouging at the air, my blade slicing. Never had I felt power like this. I truly was a god. My delight echoed that of the stranger, our strength unmatched, unsurpassable.

There were only a handful of men and women left, both inside and outside the mansion. All but a couple of the boats had been destroyed as well, the rest already out of sight over the horizon. There were still helicopters in the air, the jet a gleaming sliver of light in the distance, but other than that the only evidence that the army had been here were the corpses that carpeted the smoking ground.

I watched as the berserkers inside the house chased down the last few survivors, killing them in ways that I never could have imagined possible. I saw one approach a woman. My heart drummed, thinking it was Panettierre, but when she pulled off her gas mask in an act of defiance I saw it wasn't. This was a girl, barely older than Lucy, her features gray with terror.

The berserkers moved in for the kill but I held them back, my bloodlust fading. This soldier wasn't Panettierre, she wasn't evil. She was just following orders. Her eyes were so wide that the whites seemed like glowing rings, the pupils dilated by terror. They flicked between the berserkers as they surrounded her, but each time it seemed as though she was staring right at me.

"Go to hell," she said, tears streaming down her cheeks. "All of you."

Too late I realized she was holding a satchel in one hand, her other reaching inside. I drove the berserkers forward, but even these goliaths of muscle and nectar couldn't get to the girl fast enough. She closed her eyes and flicked a switch, the C4 detonating loud enough to rain dust down on me from the ceiling of the chamber.

The senses of those creatures were ripped away from my own so fast that it felt as if part of my soul had been torn out. The darkness that flooded into the vacuum where those living, breathing things had been was so overpowering that I thought for an instant

I'd gone blind and deaf, my entire body numb. Gradually, however, the light and the noise crept back. I let my mind fly out to find the remaining berserkers. There were only three of them left on the whole island, two of them fatally wounded. I did my best to mute their pain, but their bodies were broken beyond repair and they seemed to know it.

I felt my anger grow, seeming to make the new blood inside me boil. It wasn't right that the berserkers had to die, they were just children. Panettierre would pay for this. They would *all* pay for this.

I cast my mind out wider, over the ocean to the mainland. There were a small number of blacksuits left on the coast, the seaside town where we had caught the boat, and they were fighting with more soldiers. I sensed berserkers nearby, directing them to the battle, unleashing them on the men and women in camouflage. I could feel them all, thousands of berserkers and blacksuits across the country, each of them unique, each of them mine to control. I could even get inside the minds of the rats, although there was so little there—nothing but a tornado of violence that shook them to their core—that all I could do was point them in the right direction.

I sent out a message, a clarion call to arms. And I heard their answer, a battle cry that rose up from every last one of my soldiers. They would never stop fighting, and neither would I.

I had made a promise to Furnace. I would see his creations win this war, eradicate every inferior being so that we could start again, so that we could create a world of equals; a world populated only by the children of the nectar; a world where the wickedness of human nature would be no more. It would be our planet, for us alone, a Fatherland for the Soldiers of Furnace.

It would be a paradise.

CONTROL

I DON'T KNOW HOW MANY PEOPLE I saw die, how many I killed. Thousands? Tens of thousands? A million?

The parade of slaughter was endless, waves of berserkers working together under my command, unleashing the full force of their fury against my enemies. It was as if I were watching countless television screens at once, hundreds of acts of violence packed into every second, each one as personal as if I had committed it myself—which, in a way, I had.

More than anything else it reminded me of the screening room in the prison, watching reel after reel of film showing humankind's worst sins against its own species. Only instead of having to spend days tied to that chair, my eyelids pinned, I was seeing it all in an instant, every beat of my heart containing enough horror for a hundred hours of film.

And the truth was, I was enjoying it.

My anger was so overwhelming that I almost lost myself to it completely. Every time I felt a berserker or a blacksuit or even a rat die, my thirst for revenge became more insatiable. These were my children, and seeing the darkness, the abyss inside my head where they had once been was unbearable. Every time a soldier was torn apart, though, I howled with laughter, delighted that there would be one less human to stand in our way.

Even though my mind existed in my troops there must still have been a part of me inside the chamber back on the island, because I realized that I wasn't alone. My friends had arrived, and I saw myself through Simon's eyes—an impossible creature whose gaze blazed down on them. If it wasn't for the fact that one of my arms was a blade, and that Lucy's silver necklace glittered past the collar of my shirt, I wouldn't have recognized myself.

"Alex?" said Zee, stepping forward, his face warped by sadness, tears rolling down his cheeks. The wheezers in the room moved to intercept them but I held them back. "What have they done to you? Where's Furnace?"

I looked at the bundle of desiccated flesh and broken bone to my side that had once been Alfred Furnace. Without the stranger's blood inside him time had quickly caught up with his corpse, reducing it to little more than ash. Clumps of it crumbled from the straps that had held him, drifting lazily to the floor. Only where his body had been plugged with tubes and wires, anchoring his flesh in place, did it still resemble anything human.

"He is dead," I said, and my voice didn't seem to come from my throat, but from all around me, as if the entire room was speaking. My friends took a step back, their jaws dropping. *"I killed him."*

Even as I spoke I was still fighting, commanding the berserkers and the blacksuits in battle. It felt as though I was living a thousand lives at the same time. I was still hunting for Panettierre, but with only a single set of eyes left on the island I wasn't having any luck. Hopefully she was already dead, killed during the massacre in the mansion.

"But what happened to you?" Zee asked. A wave of annoyance

passed over me at the sound of his voice, the whine of a fly. There was no time for this. I wanted to order the wheezers to attack, to take care of Zee and Lucy. They were enemies, after all. Humans. Or maybe I could delve into Simon's thoughts, force him to kill his own friends. Manipulating him would be as easy as breathing.

Something held me back, the knowledge that I had shared a life with these people. But the memories of them were leaking from me, driven out by the stranger's blood. That life seemed like an age ago, so distant now that I couldn't believe it had actually happened. The past was no longer important.

"It was the only way," I answered, the walls and the floor trembling at the sound of my voice. *"To kill him I had to take his blood."*

Zee shook his head, swallowing his fear and walking closer. He stopped right in front of me.

"You're not him, Alex," he said. "It doesn't have to be like this."

"We need to get out of here, before those things find out where we are," said Lucy.

"I wouldn't worry about that," replied Simon, looking nervously at the wheezers. "Alex is controlling them all."

"Is that true?" Zee asked. "Are you doing this?"

My remaining berserker on the island was hunting down the last of the soldiers, a few of the survivors trying to hide in the forest. One threw himself over the cliff, preferring to die by his own hand than be killed by his enemies. Another used his final breaths to fire a rocket, the missile missing the berserker and hitting the east wing of the mansion. We could all feel the explosion down in the chamber, the impact causing Furnace's remains to disintegrate further. Brick dust rained down from the vaulted ceiling and Zee wiped it from his eyes.

"His powers are now my powers," I replied. *"His war is now my war."*

Zee looked at the others, appalled, but they had no help to give him.

"You have to stop this," Zee said, turning back to face me. "This isn't right. Furnace was the enemy, his creatures, the wheezers, the suits, they said they were on your side but they're not. Think about it, Alex. Remember the prison, remember your old life. If you do this then there's no going back, not for any of us. We'll all die."

"*I cannot die,*" I said, feeling the stranger's blood surge through me. It would keep me alive for centuries, long after the last human had been devoured by worms. The thought of it made my pulse quicken, but there was something else, something bad at the back of my head, something that the blood wouldn't let me make any sense of.

"You *can* die," said Lucy, walking to Zee's side. "Maybe not your body, but the real you can die." She stood on her tiptoes, placing her hand on my chest, over my heart. "*This* can die."

I tried to ignore her words, my mind back inside my creatures, urging them to destroy.

"Alex?" Zee again, pulling me back into the chamber. "Please, make it stop."

"*Why?*" I demanded. "*Why let the humans live? You know as well as I do that they will use the nectar, they will create demons of their own. Sooner or later this world will end; there is too much evil in humanity for it to survive. It is better for their occupation to finish now, with us as the victors. That way, when the new dawn breaks, when the new Fatherland rises, there will be no more war. When only the strong exist, when we are all Soldiers of Furnace, who will be left to fight?*"

"That isn't you talking," Zee said. "It's Furnace. He's still there, somewhere inside you. He's making you say this."

"No," I replied. *"Furnace is dead. There is only me."*

Furnace *was* dead, there was no doubt about that. These were my words, my thoughts, weren't they? I struggled to put them into some kind of order, but the thunder of the stranger's blood was just too loud.

"You remember the prison?" Zee went on.

His words sparked memories, him and me inside an elevator being carried to the bowels of the earth, making a promise to each other that we would find a way out.

"You remember Donovan?"

Of course, how could I forget him? I could see him now, sitting beside me on my bunk, his laughter echoing out over the yard, making me feel like maybe I could survive inside, that this didn't have to be the end. I could hear it, that laughter, infinitely different from my own, because it had been so human.

"You remember our jobs, the chipping, the laundry?" Zee said.

"The stink," Simon added. And I could see myself, Donovan, and Zee sitting in the canteen, Zee's face a portrait of utter disgust as he described having to clean the toilets—*well next time you do it can you try to miss the seat*. I shook my head, attempting to chase the images away. They weren't important, none of it was important. How could it be? I wasn't even that kid anymore, I wasn't Alex Sawyer, I was a god laying the foundations for a new race.

"You remember slop?" Zee went on, his voice cutting through the storm. "The leftovers we had to eat. And Monty's meal, that time he cooked for me and you and D in the kitchen?"

I could see it as if I were back there, scoffing down that heavenly stew of beef and peppers and tomatoes, the best meal I think I had ever had. I remembered how Donovan had cried, because it had been so long since he'd last tasted real food. The memory bled into another, me and D standing in the kitchen having an argument, him stuffing a glove full of rancid chicken and throwing it at me. That's what had given me the inspiration to get out, the idea of filling the gloves with gas and using them to blow the floor in the chipping room.

"And Toby," Zee said. "You saved him from killing himself."

He had been going to jump, and I had stopped him by telling him about the plan. In the end he had died during the escape, the heat of the explosion ravaging his body and the merciless cold of the river finishing him off. But he had still been free. Each memory seemed to multiply, other thoughts blossoming from them like a flower in bloom. I saw us standing on the lip of the hole, the rock still smoking, the river raging beneath us, our own personal expressway out of Furnace. I saw myself smiling as I jumped, not caring if I died, only that I had beaten the prison.

Zee was looking at Simon, urging him to help.

"Solitary," the bigger boy said. "You remember the first time I pulled you out of your cell, you broke my nose?"

With a head-butt, because I had thought he was a rat.

"When we talked to each other by banging our toilets," Zee added, and incredibly he was grinning. "That time we played I Spy, even though we couldn't see anything."

Donkeys, I had guessed, and dog crap.

"Playing paper-scissors-stone to see who'd be bait for the rats," said Simon, snorting a laugh. "And stealing all that equipment. Like we really thought we'd be able to use scalpels as climbing gear. We almost made it, though, didn't we, climbing the chimney. If that bastard Cross hadn't lit the incinerator then we'd have been home free."

"Yeah, Cross," spat Zee, his grin vanishing. "The warden, don't forget about him, Alex."

I couldn't, even if I'd tried, his devil's face appearing before me now. I remembered the first time I'd seen him, walking out of the vault door with his sick entourage of blacksuits, skinless dogs, and wheezers. I couldn't meet his eyes, nobody could. Every time I tried it was as if I had been plunged into a pool of black water, all the joy and happiness in the world stripped away. I knew now why those eyes had seemed like vortexes in his head, why none of us could meet them. He'd consumed so much nectar that he had the stranger's blood inside him—not much, just enough to make him far older than he had any right to be, enough to strip away all but the semblance of humanity.

He had been chosen to become Furnace's heir. It might have been him here instead of me, hooked up to this machine, commanding his troops to kill. The thought of us as brothers, joined by the same blood, by the same murderous desire, made me sick.

"You know how much we hated him," said Zee. "Everything he did to us—the blood watch, the wheezers. Think about what happened to Monty, turned into a freak, then into a blacksuit. Think about what happened to Donovan."

I saw myself in the infirmary, holding a pillow over the face of the thing that had once been Donovan, putting him out of his misery before he could become another of the warden's soulless guards. I felt a pressure in my chest, one that rose into my throat and sat there like an iron ball.

"Think about what happened to *you*," Zee went on, touching my arm, the blade. "The warden, Furnace, they tore you apart and tried to make you a monster. Think how hard you fought it back then. You wouldn't let them take you. You got us out of there, you saved us all."

I didn't want to see the memories but there was no stopping them. I *had* hated the warden, more than anything else on earth. I hated what he had done to me, to my friends. I had hated Alfred Furnace too, the man who sat in the shadows, who orchestrated the madness. That's why I had vowed to kill him, wasn't it? So that this would all end. Not so that I could take over. It was all too confusing, I couldn't make sense of any of it while the stranger's blood still churned.

"Think back, think about when we were inside the prison," said Zee, relentless. "You wouldn't have wanted this, you would have killed yourself rather than become like him."

And I *was* like him. I was the force behind the darkness, the mind behind the chaos. I was the very thing that I had despised so passionately. *I was Alfred Furnace.*

The thought filled me with such complete and utter horror that I screamed, a noise so loud it caused more dust to rain down from the arches above, a howling that pierced the heart of every single creature with nectar in its blood.

"I know you're still in there, Alex," said Zee, holding his hands to his ears as my howl died away. "You're my best friend. Don't give yourself to him, not without a fight."

I looked at Zee, at the tiny kid who stood before me. It would be so easy to kill him, kill them all, and yet just like me they could never truly die. They would live on inside my head, inside my memories, they would never let me go—Zee, Simon, Lucy, Donovan, and Alex too, the kid I had once been, the kid I *still was*. I saw him now, his body so different from mine, his scarless face almost unrecognizable, his eyes blue instead of silver. He stood there, in my mind, dressed in prison overalls and smiling sadly.

"*Alex?*" I said. "*Tell me what to do.*"

"You know what to do," he replied. "You always have."

Then he was gone, just another fading memory. The others stood in his place. There was nothing more they could do. They could only wait and see what my next move would be.

I thought of the creatures under my control, kids just like me. They had been created for one reason, to be soldiers in an army of hate, to turn the world upside down. Like me they had been forced into war for far too long. I wouldn't make them fight, not anymore. I would give them peace.

"*I know what to do,*" I said, feeling the stranger's blood rage like a hurricane inside me, furious at the thought of what was to come. "*I'm going to end this.*"

POWER

I HAD MADE MY DECISION, but the creature whose blood flowed inside my arteries had yet to do the same.

He could sense what I was about to do, and he called to me, demanding to be heard. His power sluiced through my brain like a million voices, all wordless, all somehow saying the same thing.

YOU WOULD NEVER DARE TO DEFY ME.

Zee was pulling at the straps that held me, trying to cut me loose, but I shook my head. There was no time. I let my mind out, once again occupying the countless nectar-filled monsters that roamed the land. I could read their thoughts, see what they were seeing, feel their emotions as they fought. Hundreds of them—blacksuits, rats, and berserkers—all with the same blood-drenched goal. They waited for my orders and I prepared to give them, one last command that would end this war once and for all.

Before I could, however, I felt something take hold of me. It wasn't a physical sensation but something much, much worse—as though a fist had wrapped itself around my soul, wrenching it out of this world, out of reality. The chamber vanished, replaced by a void, as though I had been dragged to the bottom of a vast, light-less ocean. It was the same sensation I'd had back in the hospital, on the operating table, when I had died. Only this time I wasn't alone.

Of course I wasn't. How could I be? There were two of us in this body now, me and something ageless, something infinitely wicked, something that never had been, and never could be, human.

Shapes began to form in the darkness, pillars of burned wood. It didn't take me long to realize that they were trees. Gradually the scenery settled around me, a ceiling of branches cutting out the sunlight, plunging the carpet of rotten fruit into shadow. Crows danced out of my way, flapping their wings as they feasted on decay.

I was back in the orchard.

There was no sign of Furnace now, the boy. But the stranger was here. He stood in the shadows between the trees, the same way he had back in my dream. And I knew that this was a dream too, a vision, even though I could smell the decomposing apples beneath me, feel their mush between my toes, hear the whistle of the wind and the forlorn creaking of the skeletal trees.

"Why have you brought me here?" I asked, my voice weak, once again that of a boy. The stranger didn't speak, but I heard his reply.

I WILL NOT LET YOU UNDO MY WORK.

"Your work?" I asked, trying to take a step forward. I should have known not to bother, I was always a prisoner in my dreams. I realized that he was talking about the nectar, the blacksuits and the berserkers and the rats—the end of the world. He showed me these things with a pride that emanated from his invisible form.

"That wasn't your work," I spat back. "That was Furnace."

He pushed himself from the trees, his face a nightmare collection of indiscernible parts that folded and unfolded into infinity. Just seeing him there made me want to run, to hand my body and my mind over to him and never look back. This thing, whatever he was, was something that never should have existed, something left over from the darkest moments of creation. He was the opposite of all that was good, of all that was life. Once again he spoke to me without speaking.

I WORKED WITH FURNACE, WORKED *THROUGH* HIM. AND NOW I WILL DO THE SAME THROUGH YOU. THAT IS OUR AGREEMENT—I WILL GRANT YOU POWER, AGELESS LIFE, AND IN RETURN YOU WILL OBEY, YOU WILL SPREAD MY GIFT TO THE CHILDREN OF THE WORLD.

"Why?" I asked.

BECAUSE THIS IS WHAT I HAVE ALWAYS DONE, EVER SINCE YOUR SPECIES TOOK ITS FIRST STEPS. THIS IS WHAT I HAVE ALWAYS WANTED. ONCE UPON A TIME, SO LONG AGO, IT WAS JUST ME AND MY APPETITE FOR BLOOD. BUT YOUR KIND, YOUR SCIENCE, HAVE MADE IT SO MUCH EASIER, AND SO MUCH MORE FUN.

"What if I say no?" I asked.

He lifted his hand, the limb sweeping over the orchard ground like an evening shadow. Even if I could have moved I wouldn't have been able to outrun it, the stranger's long fingers wrapping themselves around my throat. His grip tightened, crushing my windpipe, and when I tried to breathe my lungs stayed empty.

FURNACE TRIED TO SAY NO AS WELL, IN THE BEGINNING. BUT THERE CAN BE NO REFUSAL. AND WHY WOULD YOU WANT TO? I HAVE ALREADY MADE YOU A GOD, AND THERE WILL BE MORE TO COME, SO MUCH MORE.

My guts twisted, the excitement of having the whole world at my mercy, but it was short-lived. All I could feel was the cold flesh of the stranger's fingers around my throat, the panic as I tried and failed to breathe, the knowledge that I might die here, in this orchard.

It isn't real, I told myself. *None of this is real.*

I struggled, managing to wrench a hand loose from the chains of the dream. I gripped the stranger's fingers, pulling them back, away from my windpipe. Although he had no face, no expression, I could sense his shock. He seemed to glide forward without walking, looming up before me. The way his body moved, like some monstrous engine of blades, was terrifying. I knew that if that face touched me, even in the dream, my soul would be shredded.

I ALREADY OWN YOU. YOU ARE ALREADY A MONSTER. LOOK . . .

More figures began to appear between the trees, hundreds of them, shuffling into the orchard. Most were wearing camouflage, the material burned and torn, a few were dressed in Furnace overalls. Some were missing limbs, others had gaping wounds in their chests and stomachs.

All of them were dead.

They marched toward me, their hands held out, and I could feel their corpses' eyes crawling over me like insects.

THESE ARE YOUR DEAD, THE ONES THAT YOU HAVE KILLED.

I shook my head, trying to deny it, but this was the truth: every single one of the men and women—children too—that staggered across the broken ground was dead because of me. I hadn't killed them myself—not all of them, anyway—but I had caused their murders at the hands of the freaks. The first of their ranks reached me, pawing my skin with their rotting hands.

THEY SEEK REVENGE, the stranger said. SHOULD I GIVE YOU TO THEM?

"No," I grunted, feeling the weight of the fallen, knowing that they would trample me into the dirt, thousands of them piling on top of me, pinning me, burying me alive beneath a mountain of squirming decay.

ONLY I CAN KEEP YOU ALIVE. ONLY I CAN KEEP THE DEAD AWAY.

That's a lie, somebody from the crowd shouted. I knew the voice, scanning the faces until I saw him there. It was Donovan, the way he had been back in the prison before the wheezers had put their scalpels to his flesh, to his eyes, before I had smothered him with a pillow to put him out of his misery. The vast wave of corpses moved, pressing against me, and I lost sight of him for a moment. But then there he was again, his smile blasting light through the darkness. *It's a lie,* he said. *He can't hurt you because you're not really here.*

He was right. This felt more real than anything I had ever experienced—the cold flesh of the dead against my skin, the smell of their rotting bodies, the sound of the crows as they feasted on eyeballs and organs—but it was an illusion. I pictured myself, strapped to the machine back in the chamber on the island. I was safe there, my friends were there. This was all in my mind.

Your head, your rules, kiddo, Donovan said. It was just like when I'd been back in solitary. Donovan had been there too, nothing more than a figment of my imagination, I knew that, but it had been enough. He had saved my life back then, and he was saving my life now.

"My head, my rules," I said, and his smile widened.

You got it, Alex. Now for God's sake finish this and get us out of here. I never want to see another apple again.

I laughed, and the sound of it seemed to push the stranger back, as if he didn't know what the noise was. The movement of his face grew more agitated, his body flickering like a broken light.

YOU WILL NOT DEFY ME. IT IS NOT POSSIBLE.

"My head, my rules," I repeated. This time when I tried to move, the dream let me. I wrenched my arms up from my sides. I looked at my hands. They were normal again. I bunched them into fists, then, with a scream of defiance, I lashed out, catching the stranger in his temple. There was no pain, my soul wasn't shredded. All that happened was the beast staggered backward, his distended hands shrinking, sweeping up to his head. He roared, the noise deafening, full of rage. But it was nothing. I snatched in another breath, unleashing a howl of my own, one so powerful that it blasted the legions of the dead away, bodies exploding into dust as they disappeared between the trees. I saw Donovan there among them, his smile the last thing to go, hanging over the ground like a crescent moon.

"Thank you," I said when my voice had returned. And he answered me with laughter.

The stranger looked like he was about to attack again but I moved first. My body seemed to expand, growing as big as the trees, far bigger than the creature. I wrapped a fist of my own around his scrawny neck, his skin as wet and cold as an eel, and I lifted him from the ground. I could almost see his outrage emanating from his body like a dark mist, but what could he do? It may have been his blood pulsing through my body, but it was still my mind controlling it.

I WILL KILL YOU, he screamed wordlessly. I WILL SLAUGHTER YOU A MILLION TIMES OVER.

"No," I said. "You won't. Because if you kill me, then you die too. That's what happens to parasites, they need a living host."

The stranger knew that I spoke the truth, another strangled groan breaking free from him. He struggled against my grip, the same way I had against his own only moments ago. But he had no more power here, no more power over me.

"You're a prisoner," I spat. "Inside my head. I'll never let you out."

I didn't know whether I'd be able to make good on that threat, but the stranger believed me. He seemed to shrink, substance bleeding out of him like ink, pattering on the orchard ground. I let go, disgusted, watching him shrink into what he really was— the dried-up husk that was all that remained after he had poured his blood into the young Alfred Furnace. He had no body in the real world. He could do no harm, not anymore. The roots of the trees coiled up from the earth beneath him, knitting a twisted cage around the stranger. A single spidery finger poked between the bars, one last desperate shriek creeping from the darkness. And then the last of the gaps closed over, encasing his soul—if such a thing as this could ever have one—in a coffin of living wood.

I took one last look at the orchard, knowing I would never return. Then I pushed myself up from the dream, rising from it as if swimming up from a great depth, leaving the stranger far below with only the crows and the maggots for company.

PROMISES

I EMERGED FROM THE DREAM gasping for breath, coughing and wheezing so hard that the entire machine rattled and shook. Simon and Zee and Lucy all fell backward in shock.

"Jesus!" said Zee when he had recovered. "You almost made me cack myself. What the hell was that?"

I clawed in a breath, hacking up a spitball that tasted like dirt and rotten fruit. It took me a while to remember what had happened in the dream. The events in the orchard were fading fast. But I could sense the stranger there, locked inside my thoughts, unable to escape. His blood still pumped through me, but for now his wordless voice had been silenced.

"My head, my rules," I said, my voice a hurricane of sound.

Zee frowned, looking at me like I'd gone mad. It wasn't surprising, really, considering that my eyes were still whirlpools of nothingness in my head.

"All right, there's no need to shout. You okay, though?" he asked.

I nodded, reducing my voice to a whisper.

"Just had to take care of something," I said. "But it's done now."

I could hear the muted bark of gunfire from outside, knowing that I still had a job to do. There were no doubts now, though. The blacksuits and the berserkers were kids, but they had been torn from their world and turned into monsters. Their thoughts were only of rage, of hatred, of murder, utterly relentless, and that was no way to live. At least in death they would be at peace.

"What are we gonna do?" asked Simon.

"The right thing," I said. "It's time for the war to end."

"How?" asked Zee. "You just gonna surrender?"

"I'm going to try."

I closed my eyes, my mind splitting into thousands of pieces as I entered the heads of Furnace's creations. They welcomed me back, and I could feel their fury there, their insatiable hunger for mayhem and murder. The battle on the mainland was still in full swing, the blacksuits and berserkers winning. I could see endless piles of human dead on the streets, slumped like sandbags. The stranger's blood began to boil inside me at the sight, and for a heartbeat I almost succumbed to his call. But it was only a heartbeat, gone as quickly as it had appeared.

I focused my thoughts, trying to make my command as clear as possible. Then I sent out that message, directing it like a blade into the head of every single one of the blacksuits, berserkers, and rats.

Stop fighting.

Their reply echoed back to me, confusion quickly becoming disbelief which in turn led to more anger. Some obeyed, even if they were in mid-battle. They simply froze, and I watched as their consciousnesses went black, substance turned to absence as they died. It was unbearable. I felt as if I experienced every one of their deaths, each more painful than the last.

But the ones who surrendered were the minority, just a hand-ful. Most ignored my order. It was no surprise. I just didn't have the control that Furnace had, the conviction. They didn't obey me because they could sense that I didn't really know what I was doing, that I didn't believe in my abilities. Like a dog discovering that his master is weak. Even with the stranger's blood inside me I had just a fraction of Furnace's authority. He had been able to stop the ones on the island from fighting even when they were being attacked. But their instinct for self-preservation overrode my childish command. That and the fact that these creatures were machines built for war, for destruction. They knew no other way to live.

I opened my eyes, bringing myself back into the chamber. Zee, Lucy, and Simon still stood there, looking up at me expectantly.

"Any luck?" asked Lucy.

"They won't listen to me," I said. "They won't stop fighting."

Zee ran his hands through his hair, deep in thought.

"If they won't give up . . ." he said, leaving the end of the sentence hanging. He didn't finish, he didn't need to. I knew what he meant.

I thought back to the berserker from the city, the fleshy one that Panettierre had tortured and shot after we'd fled from my house. Trapped, scared, alone. I had put it out of its misery, ushered it out of life. And it had welcomed it, for a fleeting second it had remembered who it had once been, it had sloughed off the horrific shell that Furnace had given it and it had been free. It had died a child instead of a monster. That kid had died as *himself.* I hoped that was better than never remembering. It had to be better.

Zee seemed to read my mind, because he nodded.

"Can you do that?" he asked. "Can you do that for them all?"

I didn't know. Last time it had been one berserker, on the very edge of death. But thousands of them, blacksuits and wheezers and rats too? Surrender may have been impossible for these soldiers, but the thought of freedom was a far more powerful thing.

I was about to answer, but a sad, quiet laugh cut me off. I looked at Simon, leaning against a pillar, and suddenly I realized what would happen if I went ahead with my plan. Zee did too, because I heard him curse.

"It's different with you, though, isn't it?" he asked Simon. "You're too . . . human."

Simon shrugged.

"I don't think it works that way," he said, looking up at me. "Right, Alex?"

"I don't know. I mean, Furnace never managed to control you while we were in the prison, or after we escaped, did he?"

Simon looked uncertain, lost in his memories.

"I . . . I'm not sure," he stuttered. "I don't think so. But . . ."

"But what?" asked Zee. Simon glanced at him, almost ashamed.

"Something told me you guys were locked in solitary," he confessed. "It wasn't that we'd seen you being taken there. I just *knew* it. I was never really sure how, but I guess it makes sense. I guess *he* was telling me."

"Why?" I asked.

"Because he wanted you to escape," Simon went on. "And he wanted you alive. And that's what I've been doing, Alex, helping you escape and keeping you alive."

There was no point in arguing. Simon had been Furnace's puppet the same way I was. He'd come here thinking he was acting under his own free will, but the truth of it was we'd been controlled and manipulated in exactly the same way.

"It doesn't mean you'll die," I said, grasping at straws. "You're not that far gone."

I tried to sound convincing, but in my heart I knew that if I sent out a command for Furnace's creations to let go of life then the sheer scale of what would happen would affect every living thing with nectar inside it—the blacksuits, the berserkers, the rats, and in all probability Simon too. It was a risk I wasn't willing to take.

"We find another way," I said. "There must be something else we can do to end this."

But the silence that followed revealed my statement as false. Simon laughed again, shaking his head.

"There is no other way," he said. "You know that, I know that. Furnace knew it too, remember?"

"What do you mean?" Lucy asked, wiping a tear from her cheek. Simon glanced at me again, his eyes unable to hold my own blazing portals for longer than a second.

"The vision," he said. "Back in the underground station in the city, when that berserker grabbed us."

I had seen the tower, Furnace calling to me, asking me to be his soldier in the new world. It was weird, thinking that he had been speaking from this very room, the same way I now communicated with his creations.

Simon hadn't received that message, though. His had been different.

"Furnace told me that I had no place in the future. You remember? He told me that if I helped you, then I'd die. He told me that if I helped you, then sooner or later it would be *you* that killed me."

I shook my head, my thoughts reeling. Furnace had obviously

assumed that by the time we'd gotten to the tower in the city Simon's role in his plan would be over. Furnace had wanted me to fight the warden alone—even though in the end I'd needed Simon's help after all. Had Furnace changed his mind when he saw me losing the fight? Had he guided Simon to me, made him shove a grenade into the warden's mouth in order to save my life? It was impossible to know.

I guess Furnace had also believed that once I was here, once I'd seen his grand design, his vision of the world where only his children could survive, I would not tolerate a half-breed like Simon. It didn't matter now, all that mattered was that Furnace's prophecy looked like it was coming true.

"For real?" asked Zee, his face a mask of shock. "Furnace really said that to you?"

Simon nodded, the room plunged into silence once again, only the two wheezers in the corner showing any sign of life, twitching gently.

"He was wrong, though," I said eventually. "Because it doesn't have to happen this way. We'll think of another plan."

"What other plan?" Simon spat back. "Go out there and kill all those things by hand? Hope that Panettierre wins the war and doesn't start another one? This ain't never gonna end by itself, Alex. Those freaks are still out there, and they're winning. The rats are still infecting people, Furnace's army just keeps getting bigger, stronger." He paused, taking a deep, ragged breath. "And what about when it starts to spread? What about when the black-suits cross the border, cross the oceans? It might already have happened. This isn't just about the country, it's about the whole human race." He shook his head. Nobody else dared to speak. "You've got a chance to end this right now. If you take it then I might die, and that sucks. But if you don't, you're signing a death warrant for everybody else."

"Simon . . ." Zee said, his eyes filling. "There's no way, I won't let you." He looked at me. "Right, Alex? We can think of something else. Right?"

"That's your problem, Zee," Simon said, smiling gently. "You always think too much."

Zee was sobbing now, looking back and forth between Simon and me. Lucy was crying too, her sleeves in constant motion as they wiped her eyes. I would have burst into tears myself, if the stranger's blood had let me. It didn't mean I couldn't feel it, though, the sadness clawing up from my gut, nesting in my throat.

Zee ran to Simon, wrapping his skinny arms around the bigger boy, his face buried in his neck. Simon hugged him back, so hard that I heard something pop, the two of them holding each other, the tears flowing freely now, as if by never letting go they would never have to say goodbye.

I just let my head hang, desperately trying to think of another plan. My thoughts wheeled around each other like birds in a flock, too many, moving too quickly, for me to catch them.

Simon shrugged Zee away, both boys patting each other awkwardly on the back. Zee's tears had left a patch on Simon's shoulder, on the hoodie he'd gotten back in the mall, the morning we escaped, when we thought that everything just might be okay. Lucy walked over, gave the bigger kid a hug. It was short, but she meant it.

"Stay with us," she said. "We can make sure nothing happens to you."

"We can chain you to one of these pillars," said Zee. "That way you won't do anything stupid."

Simon shook his head.

"Whatever happens next, I don't want you guys to see it," he said. "I don't want you to remember me that way."

"Simon . . ." I started, unsure what else to say. He looked up at me, that lopsided grin never leaving his face. It made me think of being back in solitary confinement, his goofy smile the one good sight that lay in wait for us when the hatches opened. Down there, at the very bottom of the world, it had been the only thing that kept me going. The lump in my throat seemed to expand, as if something in there was about to burst free.

"Thank you," Simon said. "Thanks for getting us out of there. Death, it doesn't seem so scary, y'know? Not when you've got the sky over you and the wind on your face. Rather die a million times out here than once inside Furnace."

"You don't have to die," I said, my voice cracking. "It might be okay."

"Then why's everyone blubbing?" he said.

"It *will* be okay," I said again, although it was more to try to convince myself than him.

Simon turned, as if to leave the room, then thought better of it and loped over to me.

"I'm not gonna blow up or anything if I touch you, am I?" he asked.

I shook my head, and he reached his arms around me as best he could, squeezing me once. I wished I could pull myself from this infernal machine, return the gesture. I may have been able to share my mind with a thousand creatures, but the only people I was truly part of were in this room. We had shared so much, the good and the bad and everything in between, that we were linked by a far stronger bond than the nectar. To lose either Zee or Simon would be like losing a piece of myself.

He broke the contact and stood back, his cheeks wet with tears.

"Now you've got me started too," he said, wiping them away. "We sure had some adventures, eh?" He grinned.

"And there will be more," Zee said. "I promise."

Simon nodded, his next breath a shuddering sigh. He ran his sleeve over his nose, sniffing, then he began to walk.

"See you on the other side," he said. This time, nobody corrected him.

"I promise!" Zee called out. But it was one that I knew he wouldn't—couldn't—keep.

Simon paused as he went through the door, looking back at us, his eyes like diamonds. He winked, smiled, then disappeared out of sight just like he'd done back in solitary when he needed to lock us into our cells. I pictured him scampering along the corridors beneath the prison, evading the blacksuits and the rats, staying alive. He'd never abandoned us. He had always come back.

Not this time, though.

We never saw Simon again.

FREEDOM

THE ONLY SOUND INSIDE THE CHAMBER, other than the deep,
endless pulse of the machine, was a symphony of sadness. Zee
and Lucy stood before me, wrapped in each other's arms, their
sobs almost perfectly in tune. Behind it all were the last echoed steps from the corridor outside, then a final click of a door
closing.

I don't know how much later it was that Zee lifted his head off
Lucy's shoulder, his eyes red raw.

"Are we going to lose you too?" he asked, his voice hoarse.

I didn't know what would happen to me. I was just another one
of Furnace's creations after all. There was no nectar inside me, not
anymore, but my body was full of the stranger's blood. If I sent out
a command for my soldiers to take their own lives then would I
fall victim to it as well?

And would it really matter if I did? I mean, if I died then surely
the last vestiges of the stranger would die with me, die inside me.
No parasite can live long without a host. Maybe this was the only
way of making sure it never infected another kid again. Maybe
this was the only way of truly killing it.

"Alex?" said Zee.

"It will be okay," I lied. "Come on. Let's do this, before it's too late."

"Good luck," said Lucy. "Be strong, okay?"

"And don't you dare not come back," Zee added. "Or I'm gonna seriously kick your ass."

I smiled, my lips lifting for a fraction of a second before falling again. Then I closed my eyes, inhaled deeply, and reached out with my mind.

THERE WERE NO WORDS THIS TIME. WHAT COULD I SAY?

I occupied their heads like a phantom, my thoughts becoming their thoughts. Once again they welcomed me back because they saw me as their father, as their creator. And I was. I had the stranger's blood inside me, keeping me alive, giving me my powers. Right now the blacksuits and the berserkers and the rats were my offspring. They were my children.

Guilt burned through me, the knowledge of what I was about to do. My heart pounded, every beat seemingly hard enough to fire it right out of my chest. And I could sense the stranger there, as though each pulse was him banging on the bars of his prison cell, his fury seemingly enough to shake the universe to dust. The chains inside my head held, though. He couldn't escape, not in time to stop me.

Out in the world the war was raging, the tide of blood never ending. From every single pair of eyes—fewer now, but still thousands of them—I saw nothing but carnage and chaos. The land had been painted with ruined flesh, mountains of broken bones rising from the wet earth, smoke the color of rock overhead. It was a tapestry of murder and destruction the likes of which had never been seen. We truly were in hell.

I didn't know how there could be people out there left to kill, and yet the resistance kept fighting. Soldiers in camouflage took cover behind their dead friends, firing off the last of their ammunition. Others charged with bayonets, screaming in defiance, refusing to surrender even though death was inevitable. There were civilians out there as well, joining the ranks of the army, throwing themselves into battle armed with hammers and kitchen knives and pool cues. They had no hope, and yet I could see it in their faces—they were fighting for their very existence, they would never stop.

I saw them on the oceans too, berserkers and rats on boats, being pulled along by the leviathans, spreading their plague to foreign shores.

I turned my focus to Furnace's children—my children. Their minds boiled, ravaged beyond repair, each thought screamed *kill*, over and over again, a ceaseless command that came from their very blood, that would not let them rest.

And yet beneath their fury, in a part of their minds buried so deep that even they no longer knew it existed, I could see the children they had once been, before Furnace had gotten to them, before they had been turned. Those kids had been drowned beneath a lake of nectar, too far gone now to remember their names, to remember their old lives, and yet somehow still holding on. They all called for the same thing. They all called for peace.

Simon was there too, still walking, sunlight on his face and the wind in his hair. There was fear there, yes, but there was something else too, something I couldn't quite identify, something good.

No, there were no words now. I called out to my children not with language but with feeling. I thought back to my own history, those few positive memories that remained, those rare gems that sparkled in the dirt. I saw my life as it once had been—soccer at lunchtimes, the joy of celebrating a goal with my mates, in the garden with my mom, building models with my dad, blowing out the candles on my birthday cakes, bike rides in the rain, Christmas and playing with new toys in the flickering light of the fire. And I thought about that day on the beach, the one with my mom and dad, both of them laughing their heads off when the ice cream from Dad's cone fell over the edge of the pier. It had been so good to hear them laugh.

I thought about that sound now, that twin giggle cutting through the screams, through the growls, through the horror of rending flesh. I amplified it, projecting it into the minds of my children. They hesitated, all of them, thrown by the noise. They must have recognized it, though. They might not have been able to laugh themselves anymore, but no matter how much nectar you've got inside you, the sound of laughter—genuine, beautiful, human laughter—is unforgettable.

It wasn't enough. The beasts were distracted, but not for long, their rampage continuing.

I concentrated, shutting out everything except for the positive memories. I thought about Furnace Penitentiary, about the friends I had met there. I thought about the times inside the prison that we hadn't been able to stop laughing, even though we were trapped inside a nightmare. I thought about Zee and his endless documentaries, about Simon and his lopsided grin.

And I thought about Donovan.

Donovan, that smile like the sun, blasting away the darkness until all that was left was goodness and light. Donovan, his own laughter rising up alongside that of my mom and dad, unstoppable, unforgettable, until that deep, tuneful bass was the only sound in the world. Donovan. He had been there for me always, even after he had been taken by the blood watch. He had been there for me in solitary confinement, nothing more than a memory and yet somehow keeping me alive. He had been there for me even after he died, refusing to let me go, keeping the nectar at bay, helping me to remember, stopping me from losing my mind.

And he was there now, his skin glowing the way it had when I had imagined him back in the cells beneath Furnace, like some corny Christmas angel, so bright that even in my head I had to squint. His smile still radiated light, pulsing through my thoughts into the minds of the berserkers and the blacksuits and the rats, pushing the nectar aside, clearing away the darkness. It was only for a second, but a second was enough.

It doesn't have to be this way. There is more than just anger, more than hatred. This is not your life, you do not have to live it. No words, just those thoughts. Just Donovan, a shepherd of lost souls, proof that there was a way out, that there was a way to escape. He ushered them on, pulling them out from the nectar, drawing them into the light.

The berserkers were the first, their minds cracking open, memories spilling out. I could feel the rush of a thousand kids remembering, the surge of their thoughts overpowering. It was too much, my own mind sparking like it had been short-circuited, like it was about to blow. I didn't stop, though, focusing on Donovan, transmitting the image to my children, showing them the path out of their prison, the way to freedom. I could sense the blacksuits laying down their weapons, sloughing off their mutilated flesh and moving into the light. Happy, so happy, to be reunited with themselves, with the kids they thought they had lost forever. My head was ringing now, like glass about to shatter, but there was no stopping it. I sensed the wheezers, their complete and utter relief as they shed their twisted forms after so many decades trapped inside. The rats held on for longer, their personalities so ravaged that I wasn't sure if there could be anything else left. But eventually they too succumbed, falling hard as the souls inside their broken bodies soared. I watched them go, holding on for as long as I could, feeling my own mind begin to peel away from the real world, caught by the tide. The light was everywhere now, so bright, so warm. It pulled us in, Donovan at its heart, welcoming us all. And I went to him, my smile echoing his smile, his arms around me, holding me, keeping me from falling.

There was only light, only silence, only him.

We were free.

END

AT SOME POINT, THE LIGHT BEGAN TO FADE.

My head was ringing, a constant whine as if I had been standing too close to an explosion. My entire body was numb, so much so that I wondered if I had stepped right out of it, if maybe, somehow, I had gone with Donovan. The light had been so tempting—promising peace, rest, freedom—that the thought of not being there, of finding myself back inside my ravaged flesh, was terrifying. I prayed that the light would let me stay, that I wouldn't be thrown back into the darkness, into life.

Yet still it continued to fade, ebbing away like the last desperate gasps of twilight until all that remained was night. A noise began to emerge from the ringing, a faint pulse. It took me a while to recognize it as my own heart, and when I did I felt that heart sink. I was still alive, still wrapped in old muscle, gristle, and skin. And the stranger's blood still pumped through me.

My eyelids were so heavy I didn't think I would be able to open them, but after a few attempts I managed it, staring out of the crack in the shadows to find Zee and Lucy there. When they saw that I was still alive they broke into identical grins.

"Jesus, Alex," said Zee. "Welcome back. We weren't sure if you were gonna make it."

"We thought you were dead," said Lucy. "You weren't breathing for, like, minutes, and you were freezing."

"What happened?" I said. Zee nodded to the corner of the room and I followed his gaze to see the two wheezers slumped there, their limbs entwined like suicidal lovers. "Are they dead?"

"They just collapsed," said Zee. "We haven't checked for a pulse or anything, but they look pretty dead to me."

They were. I wasn't sure exactly what had happened but it was clear that the spark of life no longer existed inside those motionless bodies. I concentrated, trying to extend my thoughts into the minds of the blacksuits, the berserkers, the rats, but there was nothing there anymore, as if they had all simultaneously been switched off. I might have simply lost my powers, but deep down I knew it wasn't that. There was nobody left to communicate with. All of my children were dead.

"What happened to Simon?" asked Zee. I just stared at the floor. I couldn't meet his eyes. Simon was gone. I had killed him. The same way I had just killed hundreds, no *thousands*, of living, breathing things.

"You did the right thing," said Lucy, obviously reading the grief in my expression. She looked at my neck, at the silver St. Christopher medallion that hung there. "It was the only way."

"And he might be okay," said Zee. "He might still be okay."

I didn't reply. The sensation was gradually returning to my body, the straps cutting into my skin, my muscles stiff from being so long in the same position. I looked down at my left hand, realized that it had completely changed. Those three fingers were now long and thin, too many knuckles and joints there, reminding me of Furnace's hands. It made my flesh crawl just to look at it. I lifted the blade of my other arm, wondering whether I should try to cut myself down. But there were still needles and tubes lodged in my flesh and I didn't know what would happen when they were taken out. The last thing I wanted after everything was to bleed out on the chamber floor.

Or was it? Those same thoughts circled my head—Furnace's creations might be dead, but the stranger was still imprisoned in my mind. It wouldn't be long before he found a way to escape back into my thoughts, and then what would happen? I couldn't keep him at bay forever. It might take years, decades, maybe even centuries, but eventually I'd give in to him. He would force me to create another army, to declare war on the world once again. I knew this the same way I knew that my plan had worked, that my children were dead. The truth of it was undeniable.

"What happens now?" Lucy asked. "I don't hear any gunfire or anything. You think it's safe up there?"

She was right. The muted roar from overhead had faded, the room eerily quiet.

"You should go," I said. "Get off the island. It should be okay on the mainland now, just stay clear of the army. I bet they still want you."

"What about you?" Zee asked. "You know I'm not leaving you here."

"I can't go," I replied. "For all I know, this machine is what's keeping me alive."

I could have told them about the stranger's blood, the thing that lived inside me, but I chose not to. I didn't even understand it myself.

"I'm not leaving you," Zee said, firmer this time. And I could tell he meant every word of it. "You either let me cut you down, and you take your chances, or I'm moving in right here."

"Make that two of us," said Lucy.

"Yeah, we'll put some paintings up, get a nice sofa or something, there's room for a bed."

"Two beds," she added, raising a stern eyebrow. Zee blushed.

"Two beds," he said. "Three beds, really, when Simon turns up again. Either way, make your choice. We stay together, or we leave together, it's up to you."

"How about you die together?"

The voice came from the door, startling all of us. I looked up, seeing the figure silhouetted in the light from the corridor outside, the military cap, the camouflage, the emblem on her uniform reflecting the light with the same fierce glint as her eyes.

Colonel Alice Panettierre.

SHE LOOKED POSSESSED. That was the first thing I noticed when she finally stepped into the chamber. Her eyes were wide and wild, never blinking. It seemed like she'd lost half her body weight since last time I'd seen her. Her face was gaunt, her cheekbones almost piercing her skin. And her thin lips were peeled back into a parody of a smile, one that seemed like it had been fixed there with pins.

She was holding a pistol, and even from here I could see that it was cocked and ready to fire. Two more figures appeared in her wake, young men in camouflage and combat helmets. One looked like he'd been shot or clawed in the arm, his clothes drenched with blood, his face warped by pain. They were both carrying machine guns, and they lifted them toward me.

"Did you think we wouldn't find you?" Panettierre said, strolling into the middle of the chamber. Zee and Lucy scampered out of her way but she didn't spare them a glance, her gaze never leaving me. I knew that my eyes still resembled Furnace's, those blazing pools of darkness, enough to strip the sanity from the sanest of people. But she didn't flinch, she didn't look away. She had lost her mind a long time ago.

"Ma'am," said one of the men, the one without the injury, touching a radio receiver lodged in his ear. He couldn't bring himself to look at me, his whole body trembling. "We're getting more reports that the enemy has been neutralized."

Panettierre ignored him, taking step after step until she was standing right in front of me. I lifted my right arm, sweeping the blade toward her, but it didn't quite reach. The straps of the machine held me tight, stopping me from launching another attack.

"I thought you were dead," I said, my raised voice seeming to emanate from every stone in the room. She fixed me with that frozen smile.

"You thought wrong," she said, still not blinking. Her eyes bulged, lined with so many veins that they seemed to be filled with blood. "It was close, up there in the house, but three of us managed to hide from your pets. Did you honestly think you'd get away with this, Alex?"

"It's over," hissed Lucy. "He killed them all, those monsters. He saved us, all of us."

Panettierre's head didn't move but her swollen eyes swiveled slowly in their sockets like some grotesque puppet, peering at Lucy and Zee as if it was the first time she had noticed them.

"It's true," said Zee, pointing at the wheezers. "See? Take a look outside too, they're all dead. It's finished."

The colonel lifted her pistol, pointing it at Zee. Her arm was rock steady, not the slightest tremor, and her finger was tight against the trigger.

"Don't," I said. Panettierre looked back at me but the gun didn't move.

"You know how many soldiers I've lost?" she asked, her voice strangely emotionless. "How many of my brave men and women have died? Thousands. Tens of thousands. You think I care about your little friends here? You think I won't kill them right where they stand just to see the look on your face?"

"Ma'am," the soldier repeated. "They're right, there's word coming in from every division, the enemy is falling, dying for no reason. I think it's over."

"It's not over," Panettierre spat back, and I could see the emotion now, bubbling fiercely beneath her masklike expression. Her eyes seemed to have grown even bigger, her pupils little more than pinpricks in an ocean of fire. "Not until I say it is."

She turned her attention to the machine, to the remains of Alfred Furnace beside me. Forgotten for now, her gun arm dropped to her side.

"What is this thing?" she asked. "Is this how you get your powers? How you control the nectar?"

I kept my mouth shut. Even if I knew what the machine was and how it worked I wouldn't have answered. She tilted her head back, talking to one of the soldiers.

"Get over here, Bates; find out how this thing works."

"Ma'am," the wounded man replied. "Our orders were to leave it—"

"The hell with our orders," she barked back. "Get over here, Sergeant, and do as I say."

The two men looked at each other, unsure, but they weren't about to disobey. Bates walked nervously to the machine, giving my arm a wide berth, and began examining it. Blood from his wound pattered to the stone floor, making a sound like a ticking clock. I didn't protest. An idea was starting to form in the back of my mind, something I couldn't quite put my finger on. I struggled to find it but the roar of the stranger's blood in my veins kept it hidden.

"You know you've lost," said Panettierre. "But I can make you a deal. Tell me how it works, this machine, and I'll let your friends live. That sound fair to you?"

I turned to Zee and Lucy. Both of them were shaking their heads. They knew as well as I did that no good could come from Panettierre learning how to use the machine. As far as I knew, it had only been designed to keep Alfred Furnace alive when his body started to fall apart, piping the stranger's blood through the areas where there were no more veins, no more flesh. That and the blood swap, the mechanism that drained my body of nectar before transferring Furnace's blood—the stranger's blood—to me.

There was that idea again, a flash of light submerged beneath the ocean of darkness, gone as quickly as it appeared. Panettierre was talking again before I could make any sense of it.

"I can make their deaths very painful. I can make it last for days, weeks. I can keep them alive just to feel pain, just to suffer. We have people for that, and they're very, very good at what they do."

"Don't listen to her, Alex," said Zee. He and Lucy clung to each other, afraid but defiant. They would choose to die here rather than give Panettierre what she wanted. I hoped they wouldn't have to.

"*You're right,*" I said, not sure if I was lying or not. "*This is the machine that lets you control the nectar.*"

"And that's Furnace?" she asked, nodding at the husk of desiccated skin and powdered bone hanging next to me.

"*The machine let him pass his powers to me,*" I said. She glanced at Bates, the soldier on his knees now, using a combat knife to pry at the exposed gears and pipes. He sensed her gaze, looking up.

"Never seen anything like this before," he said. "But it looks like a giant pump, designed to keep something circulating." He paused, shrugging. "Could be a transfusion machine too. There's bits and pieces here I recognize from the OR."

"Transfusion?" Panettierre asked. Her eyes seemed to light up, and that did it, the idea emerging from the dark surface of my blood like a whale breaching the ocean. I knew what Panettierre wanted. It was the only thing she had ever wanted, even right back at the beginning when I'd first met her in the hospital. She wanted control.

"*The blood is power,*" I said. "*It is blood, not the machine, that lets you manipulate the nectar and everything it touches.*"

"Alex, what are you doing?" Zee said. "Don't tell her anything."

But neither Panettierre nor I was listening. Our eyes were locked, both of us refusing to look away.

"Your blood?" she asked, her small tongue flicking over her lips, lizardlike.

"*It isn't my blood,*" I replied. "*It belongs to something else, something older than time, something evil.*"

"And you expect me to believe that?" she said, her painted grin never slipping.

"*I don't care if you believe it or not,*" I said, my voice pulsating. "*It is the truth.*"

How could she deny it, after everything she'd seen? The entity she looked at now, that she talked to, was no boy, it was a god whose eyes were spinning portals, black holes in the fabric of space and time, whose voice echoed from every cell, every particle in the room. I could see the desire burning through her, her hunger for power.

"It will kill you," I said, guessing the thoughts that ran through her mind. *"The blood cannot survive in everyone, only in children."*

I wasn't sure if that was true or not, but the nectar worked only with kids, and the stranger had chosen Alfred Furnace—and me—when we were young. Panettierre shook her head, uttering a snort of laughter that sounded more animal than human.

"Can you work it?" It took me a moment to realize she was talking to the soldiers.

"Colonel," said the one who wasn't wounded. "This is a bad idea."

"Can you work it?" she said again.

"Ma'am, please—" started Bates.

Panettierre walked to him, punching the barrel of her pistol into his mouth. I heard the crack of broken teeth as his head crunched against the machine. Her finger tightened, and for a second I thought she was actually going to shoot him. Then she bent down and whispered into his ear.

"Do as I say, soldier, or I will kill you. We're at war, and dis-obeying a direct order is punishable by death, do you understand?"

He nodded, his teeth clacking against the weapon.

"Can you make it work?" she asked, and he tilted his head for-ward then back again, as gently as possible. She paused a moment more, then pulled the gun free, wiping the blood and spit off on her trousers. Bates spun around, his face gray. He beckoned for the other man to help him, both soldiers looking like frightened children as they inspected the levers and dials built into the machine. Panettierre was back in front of me, her face so twisted by excitement and insanity that she reminded me of a lunatic Punch doll.

"What are you doing?" Zee asked, even though he must have already known.

"I'm ending this war," Panettierre replied. "I'm taking control of enemy troops. Once I can command them, it will all be over."

"But they're already—" Lucy said. I flashed them a look, shaking my head, and Zee must have recognized it because he put a hand on Lucy's arm, stopping her from finishing. Panettierre didn't see the exchange, her attention on the straps beside me, the ones that held the remains of Furnace. She reached up, pulling chunks of him away, his body crumbling at the slightest touch, filling the air with powdered flesh.

"It will kill you," I said again. But there was no stopping her. Every last shred of sanity that remained had been obliterated. There was only hunger.

"It will kill you too," Zee said to me. I didn't answer.

Panettierre had pushed herself into the slot where Furnace had once been suspended, calling on one of the soldiers to fix her into place. The man didn't argue, tightening the straps across her arms and legs, looping the belt around her waist and easing the cradle down over her head. The pulse of the machine seemed to speed up, as if it could sense a fresh body in its grip.

"Is it ready?" she asked. Bates nodded, but his expression told a different story.

"I think it's just a case of pulling these levers," he said. "There's a pretty simple transfusion system in place. But I don't know what's going to happen."

"I do," Panettierre said, her face wild.

I could feel my blood begin to race, the stranger's excitement at the possibility of a new host. I had failed him, I had refused to give in to his requests, I had imprisoned him inside my own thoughts. Now he faced his freedom, and the possibility of revenge. I thought about what had happened to Furnace when the blood had gone, his body turned to dust. I tried not to picture the same thing happening to me. If I had to risk sacrificing myself to kill the stranger, though, then I was willing to do it. It wasn't like I had a lot to live for.

I turned to Zee. I looked like a monster, and I didn't want him to remember me this way, but the least I could give him after everything we'd been through was a smile.

"Alex," he said, reaching out for me. But it was too late for goodbyes.

"Do it," ordered Panettierre.

Bates pulled the first lever, the mechanisms inside the machine powering up. It knew what to do, those needles sliding from the frame and piercing the colonel's skin. She grimaced, her eyes burning, seemingly the brightest things in the half-light of the room. There was a sucking sound, then the tubes ran red as her blood spurted into them.

"Oh Christ," said the other soldier, staggering back. Panettierre was turning white, her skin wrinkling like empty sausage casings as the blood drained away. I could see the panic there, her hands straining against the straps, but she was too weak to resist. Bates swore, waiting for the pipes to start gurgling before wrestling with the second lever.

The machine changed pitch, a needle sliding into my spine, so deep that I could feel the pain even past the storm of the stranger's blood. There was an ice-cold rush inside me as the poison began to flow from my arteries. I could see it inside the tube, pumped toward Panettierre. She was out cold, totally drained, but as it passed through the needles into her arm she was reborn, throwing her head back and howling with delight. I knew that feeling, the blood awakening every cell, exploding inside her mind, promises of power the likes of which she could never imagine. The stranger's response was the same, I could feel his euphoria as he took control of his new host.

Both reactions lasted for no longer than an instant.

Panettierre's face warped from joy to terror. She looked at me, her eyes already black, as if they had simply disappeared from her skull. But her expression was now one of dawning horror. I could sense it from the stranger too, the realization that his blood wasn't pouring into a child but an adult. There was a moment of silence, then both of them began to scream.

It was a noise like no other I had ever heard, one that could have been the universe ending. It grew louder and louder, inside my head and out of it, promising to turn my ears to mush, to demolish every last sane thought in my mind. It went on and on and on, for so long that I thought it would never stop, that this was my hell and it was eternal.

I heard the stranger, felt him try to reverse the flow, to hang on inside me. But there was nothing he could do. The machine was designed for a single task, and it performed it well, sucking every last drop of blood from my body and pumping it into Panettierre's.

The world was going dark but I didn't panic. I'd been here before, so many times, drained and then refilled. Only this time there would be no saving me. There was nothing left, nothing to put back. My vision sparked, as if there were a fireworks show in the chamber. I peered past those slivers of stardust to see Zee, tears like jewels in his eyes. Lucy was on her knees by one of the dead wheezers, rummaging in its coat. My head swung back around, the world seeming to dissolve like paper in water, separating, disappearing. But I could still make out Panettierre, hung up beside me, her mouth so wide as she screamed that it was as if her face was unraveling.

No, it *was* unraveling. Her jaw sagged, the bones beneath the skin seeming to bend as though they were rubber, her teeth dropping out, clattering to the floor like beads. Something was bubbling through her cheek, as if she had acid in her veins, her flesh fizzing as it fell away. Dark patches were appearing beneath her uniform, the blood seeping through ragged holes in her stomach, in her arms and legs. Her throat had begun to dissolve, her shriek dying out into a wet, gargled moan.

The stranger's cry was louder now, though, a roar of undiluted rage powerful enough to crack open the earth. But it was a song of desperation, and it was futile. He knew that his time had come.

The two soldiers were freeing Panettierre as fast as they could, cutting the straps and pulling her out of the machine. They lowered her to the floor, one of her arms breaking off and sliding from her sleeve, exploding as it hit the stone. A leg followed, severed at the knee, the skin pocked with blisters. The men dropped her in disgust, and she hit the ground like a sack full of wet flesh, a butcher's trash bag, a lake of black liquid spreading out beneath her. She somehow found the strength to look up at me, those depthless eyes flickering in a face that had melted almost to the bone. She began to spasm, a jet of oil-colored blood spewing up from her ravaged windpipe. Then the darkness in her eyes faded, leaving two bags of bubbling pus embedded in her skull.

Panettierre was dead. The stranger was too. They lay together in silence.

I had time to understand this, before the darkness came to collect me. I had time to understand that I had won, that even though this was the end it had ended well.

One last breath. We all have to take one eventually.

It was over.

BEGINNINGS

IF I WAS DEAD, THEN WHY COULD I STILL HEAR ZEE?

His voice seemed to be coming from a million miles away, muffled as though I was underwater, but it was definitely him. Nobody could manage that panicked squeak quite like Zee.

I couldn't work out what he was saying. I was stranded in a void of absolute nothingness, not dark, not light, just absence. I struggled to remember why I was here, what had just happened. The memories had all but faded, their detail gone but their essence remaining as a single, wonderful thought:

It was over.

Was this death, then? I had imagined it so many times, tried to picture what it would be like. But never like this, a consciousness trapped and paralyzed as the aeons passed, a prisoner until the very end of time.

An eternity listening to Zee prattling? I think I'd rather have woken up in hell.

I felt something sharp pierce the skin of my arm, even though I couldn't tell if I still had limbs. Zee was shouting now, and with his words came a familiar rush. It was nectar. Only it was different somehow. I could feel it flood into my parched arteries, coursing through my system, repairing damaged flesh. But there was none of the rage that normally went with Furnace's poison, none of the anger. I don't think I had ever felt so calm, so at peace.

Another jab, another rush of nectar. This one made the noises around me much clearer, as if my ears had been unblocked.

"Find some more," yelled Zee, his voice an octave higher than it should be.

"This is the last one," came the reply. It was Lucy, and I could hear the slap of her shoes as she ran across the chamber. A third mild pain, like an insect bite, more nectar surging into me, firing up the parts of my brain I thought had been switched off forever. My sight flickered on like a computer monitor, seeming to wobble for a bit, everything too bright to make sense of. Then it settled, two faces looming over me, their expressions of concern so extreme that the first noise I made was a laugh. It spluttered out of me, unrecognizable, sounding more like an engine trying to start on a cold morning. I realized I was lying on the floor.

"He's coming out of it," said Zee, his eyes lighting up. "Alex? That you?"

Who else is it going to be? I tried to say it out loud but the words seemed to jumble up inside my mouth, emerging as one long groan. I saw Lucy pull something out of my arm, the empty syringe glinting. She threw it to the floor, gently pressing a scrap of cloth against the needle hole. Her other hand rested against my forehead, brushing the hair out of my eyes.

"We need to find some more," Zee said. "There must be some out in the corridor, in those rooms we passed."

He shot up but I grabbed him with my left hand before he

could go. He crouched down again, gripping my new fingers so hard it hurt. I didn't mind, though. The pain was good, anchoring me inside my body, keeping me from drifting away.

"Don't move," said Lucy. "Don't speak, just rest. Those soldiers have gone to get help. You'll be fine, okay?"

"But what if that isn't enough?" Zee asked. "What if it doesn't keep him alive? He might die if we don't find some more."

His agitated tone made me laugh again, and this time it must have been clearer because his frown deepened.

"What?" he asked.

"You," I replied, managing to get most of the word out. I coughed, my throat feeling like it was lined with sandpaper. At least my voice was back to normal, though. "Yabbering on. I was dead and I could still hear you."

Lucy laughed, the sound like chiming crystal. Zee scowled at her, then at me, folding his hands against his chest.

"Charming," he said. "We save your ass and all you can do is insult me."

His pout only made me laugh harder, until I was racked with coughs. Lucy was giggling too, and it must have been contagious because after a moment Zee's face opened up.

"It's just good to see you," he said, his hand squeezing my shoulder.

My strength was returning, my pulse steadying as it distributed the nectar around my body. I squirmed, managing to prop myself up on my elbows.

"Easy there," said Lucy. "Don't overdo it."

"I'll be okay."

I looked around the room until I saw the mess, the lake of

oil-black blood that lay congealing in the middle of the chamber. There was nothing left of Panettierre now but a few scraps of clothing and what looked like a half-dissolved jawbone jutting up from the surface. The stranger too was no more. He and Panetti-erre had been so consumed by their desire for power that they had killed each other. The thought of that just made me laugh harder.

"How did you bring me back?" I asked when I had recovered my breath.

Zee nodded over at the wheezers, their coats open and the syringe bandoliers visible beneath. There must have been a dozen empty needles scattered around me.

"Lucy's idea. Wasn't sure if it would work. But we had to try something. You feeling all right?"

"I've never felt better," I said. And it was the truth. I may still have had nectar inside me, but it was no longer channeling the stranger's evil. Without its master, the nectar seemed to function just like regular blood. I looked at Lucy. "Thank you."

"Thank *you*," she replied, stroking my brow.

"How come you didn't explode, y'know, like Furnace?" Zee asked.

I didn't know the answer to that. Furnace was so old when he had finally died, he had existed for centuries. Without the blood, his flesh was nothing but dust. I'd only had it in my veins for a short time. I was still a kid.

"Just lucky, I guess," I said.

"At least your eyes are back to normal," said Zee. "If you can call silver normal."

I heard footsteps from the corridor outside, shadows blossoming on the stone walls. Zee and Lucy whirled around just as

Sergeant Bates and his partner barged back into the chamber. They stood to attention as a third man followed, dressed in beige combats, silver stars gleaming from his collar. He was much older than the others, his hair a gray fuzz and his face lined with wrinkles. When he saw me his hand strayed to the pistol holstered at his waist, but it only hovered there for a second before he let it fall.

"Here they are, sir," said the wounded soldier, Bates.

I sat up, ready to defend myself. The stranger may have been dead but that wouldn't stop the army from trying to harness his powers, from cutting me up to learn the secrets of my mutations. The older man raised a hand, his face creasing. It wasn't quite a smile—he didn't seem like the kind of man who would know how—but there was kindness in his eyes.

"It's okay," he said. "I'm not here to hurt you. My name is General Hamilton, I want to help."

I'd heard that before, but this time I could sense it was the truth. The man scanned the room, his eyes falling on the puddle of black blood.

"Was that Colonel Panettierre?" he asked. Bates nodded, his face blanching as he studied her remains. Hamilton nodded too, wiping a hand over his mouth. "Good riddance," he muttered before turning back to me. "I don't know what's going on, but my men here tell me you had something to do with killing off those monsters."

"He did," blurted out Zee. "He was the one—"

"I don't need to know now," the general interrupted, raising his hand again. "Save your strength, kids. Tell me everything when we get back to base." He must have seen the panic in our faces as we remembered the hospital, because he clamped his hand against his chest. "Listen, I know you had a rough ride with Panettierre, but we're not all like her. I swear before God and my country that it won't happen again. You're safe with me. Can you walk?"

"I can try," I replied.

The general nodded at the two soldiers and they laid down their guns, running over and helping me struggle to my feet. It took a while for me to get vertical—I was still the tallest person in the room by a meter or so—but they stayed by my side, holding me up. I draped my hands over their shoulders, careful not to skewer anyone with my blade. Zee squeezed in between me and the man to my right, his hands around my waist, doing his bit to stop me falling over. Lucy reached up, taking my left hand and holding it gently.

"We've got a chopper outside," the general said. "It'll fly us back to HQ. Then, if you don't mind, I'd really like to ask you a few questions."

"Sure thing," I said, limping slowly across the chamber. The general walked through the door, leading the way. The rest of us struggled after him, resembling some weird spider as we did our best not to trip each other up. I looked back just once, saw the machine against the far wall, still humming gently, its pulse felt in every stone beneath my feet. I saw the space where Alfred Furnace had been, his body crucified there the same way it had been hundreds of years ago in the orchard.

"Forget it," said Zee, peering up at me. "It's finished."

"I know," I said. "But what happens now?"

Zee laughed, shifting his arms to better hold me up.

"All for one," he said.

That brought back so many memories, some happy, some sad, a bittersweet mixture that made the smile on my face almost painful. I knew that this would be another one, a memory that would accompany me to my dying days. I realized that Zee was waiting for me to finish and I didn't disappoint him, the words tumbling out through my growing smile:

"And let's get the hell out of here."

WE HEARD THE HELICOPTERS before we saw them, their thunder audible from the top of the stairs. The inside of the mansion was a mess, the walls blown to pieces, the ceilings drooping, barely able to hold their own weight. Dead bodies covered the floor, but we steered around them, clambering over the wreckage of the front entrance until we were clear. There were two choppers in the sky, a third on the ground fifty meters or so away. Soldiers clustered around it, and as soon as they saw us they ran over, two of them holding a stretcher. They offered to carry me but I shook my head. The way my body was now they'd probably need the whole army to hold my weight.

The sun hung low on the horizon, blindingly bright. Its fierce light threw everything into relief, revealing each burned corpse, each severed limb, each lifeless face in hideous detail. But only the human dead seemed to have resented their passing. I saw a berserker—recognized it as the only one that had still been fighting—and it wore an expression of calm, as if the end had been a relief. I honestly didn't know what had happened to it, to its brothers, where they were now. I hoped they had gone somewhere good. And if they hadn't gone anywhere at all, if they had simply stopped living, I hoped at least that they had *believed* they were going somewhere good. I hoped I had given them that.

"You ready?" asked General Hamilton. I nodded, but didn't move, squinting into the brilliance of the setting sun. There were two figures standing on the cliff edge, nothing but blurred silhouettes yet somehow familiar. I put my hand up to shield the glare, trying to work out who they were. One had a huge arm, a body that seemed to be melted out of shape, and he wore a lop-sided grin. Before my excitement had a chance to rise I recognized the other kid, somebody I knew just as well, and somebody who was just as dead.

Donovan slung his arm around Simon, both of them waving at me.

"Thank you," I said, waving back.

"For what?" asked Zee, thinking that I was talking to him.

We started for the chopper again, and I watched the figures fade into the sunlight, nothing more than the heat haze rising from the scorched earth.

"For everything."

THE GENERAL HADN'T BEEN LYING. WE WERE SAFE.

The chopper flew us to a small military base hidden in the mountains halfway across the country, one that hadn't been hit by the berserkers and the blacksuits. It was pretty much deserted when we landed, a handful of personnel welcoming us from the helipad. This time there was a trolley waiting, one used for carrying heavy equipment, and the soldiers helped me, Lucy, and then Zee onto it. We traveled in silence, all of us noticing how peaceful the air was—no explosions, no gunfire, no screams. Even the birds had started singing again, their quiet evening chirps cautious but beautiful.

We were taken into the main building, a squat concrete bunker embedded into the hillside. A bed had been prepared for me, so big it took up almost the entire room. There were doctors here, dressed in the same white overalls as Panettierre, but they wore genuine smiles instead of gas masks and held stethoscopes instead of needles. They helped me lie down, plumping the pillows beneath my head and pulling a sheet up to my chin.

"First things first," said General Hamilton from the door. "They're going to make sure you're healthy, that you're not going to die on us. Okay?"

I nodded, watching him stand to one side as Zee and Lucy walked in.

"You two can come with me if you like," he said to them. "Get cleaned up, get some hot food. We might even be able to rustle up a cup of tea."

"No thanks," said Zee, walking to the far side of the room. There was a sofa there, beneath a wide window, and he collapsed into it, Lucy sliding next to him and resting her head on his shoulder.

"We stay together," she said.

"I understand," said the general. "I'll have somebody bring some grub up to you from the mess." He walked to my bedside, smoothing down the sheet. "Far as we can tell, every single enemy combatant is down, dead. You think there will be more of them, another attack?"

I shook my head and I could see the relief in the man's expression.

"That's good," he went on. "Then there's no hurry. You can talk to us about this just as soon as you're ready. As soon as you've had some rest."

I tried to think back, tried to remember everything that had happened to me. It seemed as though I had lived a million lives, the days countless, and already I could feel those memories disappearing like sand sculptures before a rising tide. If I didn't catch them now then they'd be gone forever.

"I'm ready to talk," I said. "Just give us a few minutes."

"No problem," said the general. He stood straight, then he saluted me, not waiting for a response before striding out of the room. The doctors left with him, closing the door behind them. The silence that followed was so immense that it didn't seem real.

Zee's eyes were already closing and I knew he'd be out cold in a matter of minutes. Lucy sat beside him, her fingers curled around his sleeve. I called to her quietly, beckoning her to the bed. She sat on the edge of the mattress, watching curiously as I lifted my left hand and rested those weird, elongated fingers on the pendant that hung around my neck, the St. Christopher.

"I promised to give this back to you when things were normal," I said. "I don't think I can keep that promise. I don't think things will be normal again, not after this."

"You kept your promise," said Lucy, placing her hand on top of mine, squeezing gently. "You did good."

I reached around the back of my head, trying to find the clasp, but Lucy pulled my arm down.

"Keep it for another day or two," she said. "I think you've earned it."

She stood, then leaned over and kissed me on the forehead, the heat of her lips remaining there even as she sat back down on the sofa. The movement stirred Zee, his eyes blinking in shock.

"It's really over?" he asked when he remembered where he was, his voice slurred.

"It's really over," I said.

He was quiet for a full minute. I thought that he'd dozed off again and I realized I was about to do the same, the silence and stillness of the room ushering in a wave of tiredness that almost carried me away. I fought the current, keeping my eyes open.

"You remember that first day?" Zee asked, his eyes still closed. "The day we arrived in Furnace, in the prison."

"Yeah, of course," I said, picturing the bus ride, the elevator doors opening onto a nightmare.

"Feels like a billion years ago." He opened one eye in time to see me nodding. "I'm glad I was there," he said, his words almost unintelligible now.

"Seriously?" I asked.

"I'm glad I was there. With you." And then he was gone, snoring gently, his head lolling against Lucy's.

"Me too," I said. And I knew that if it hadn't been for Zee then I would be a long time dead. He'd saved my life, but it was more than that, I think. He'd given me something to live for.

I had almost drifted off again when I heard a gentle knock on the door. It opened a crack, the general's friendly face appearing. He must have seen how exhausted I looked because he started to retreat, but I waved him on with my bladed hand.

"We have surgeons here who can do something about that," he said, gesturing toward my mutated limb. "And your other injuries too, we'll do our best to sort them."

"Thanks," I said, looking down at my distorted body and wondering whether I'd ever be able to shop for clothes at the mall again.

"Have faith," he said, smiling with his eyes. "Anyway, down to business. Sure you're up for this? It's got to be a long story."

It was, but I needed to tell it. I needed to remember everything. I'd been through so much that I barely even knew who I was anymore, but telling my story, reliving it all, would heal me. It would let the boy back in, it would let me be Alex Sawyer again. More than that, though, telling my story was the only way of keeping them all alive—Donovan, Simon, and the others too. They may have died, but this way they would live on. The whole world would know who they were, and what they had done.

The general sat down on the edge of my bed, placing a digital recorder between us.

"Ready when you are, son," he said. "You know where to begin?"

I thought back to before the island, before the city, before the breakout, before solitary confinement, before the prison, before the night that Toby had been murdered, before I had started breaking into houses. And I saw the instant where everything had changed, where this had all begun—a normal day in a normal school, me stealing twenty quid from a kid called Daniel Richards.

I looked at Zee and Lucy, asleep on the sofa, then past them, through the window, where the last of the sunlight rested over the world. We were safe. We were free. I could feel my story rushing up from my stomach, a tide that would not stop until every last word had been spoken, a tide that would bring me home.

"Yeah, I know where to begin," I said.

I turned back to the general, waited for him to switch on the recorder. Then I took a deep breath. I was going to need it.

"I can tell you the exact moment that my life went to hell."

EPILOGUE

IT TOOK ME FIVE DAYS TO TELL MY STORY.

Well, it took five days for my story to tell *itself.* I lay there, in that oversize bed inside the army base up in the mountains, and the words just came. They boiled up from my stomach like a geyser; I couldn't have stopped them even if I wanted to. I was so exhausted that I'm not sure I was even aware of what I was saying. I think I could have fallen asleep right there and that story would have kept on coming. Those words, they were like breaths. After everything I'd been through, everything that had happened, I needed to keep talking or I'd just slip away into the night. My story, it kept me alive.

General Hamilton didn't say more than a handful of words during those five days. He sat beside the bed, his digital recorder perched between us on the soft, lavender-scented sheets. His expression barely changed, although there were times when his mouth dropped open, his eyes widened and a sheen of sweat broke out on his sunburnt forehead. Once or twice, when I faltered, he would reach out and lay his hand on my arm, squeezing gently until I found my way again.

Zee and Lucy listened in silence as well, drifting in and out of sleep on the sofa next to the window. Both of them had nightmares;

I could see it in the way their faces creased, their bodies twitched. But every time they woke, and remembered where they were, they smiled at me. It was those smiles, more than anything else I think, that kept me going.

I dozed off too, on that first night, although I didn't dream. I don't think so, anyway. I woke to pitch-black, thinking that I was back in Furnace, the day I first arrived, pressed against the bars as the symphony of cries and screams rose up all around me. And for a second I thought I saw a wheezer there, its wrinkled face twitching, its piggy eyes devouring me. I lurched so hard I pulled the IV out of my arm, and even when the lights blinked on and the doctors ran in it took me a while to calm down.

"You sure you're up for this?" General Hamilton asked. "None of us will blame you if you just want to forget."

I didn't want to forget. Forgetting was the easy way out. And if I forgot about the wheezers, the warden, Alfred Furnace, and the stranger, then I'd forget about Donovan, Simon, and all the others too. That wasn't a trade I was willing to make. I just opened my mouth and started where I'd left off—as soon as I'd made it clear that I never wanted the lights switched off.

To be honest, I haven't slept in the dark since.

I don't think I ever will again.

EACH OF THOSE FIVE DAYS seemed to be brighter than the last, the sunlight like honey dripping through the room's only window. Each day was louder too, as the birds continued to find their voice, singing like this was the first week there had ever been. I guess, in a way, it was.

People were the same. They stopped speaking in hushed, frightened whispers as the news they talked about got better and better.

They would burst in with announcements like "We've heard from second platoon" and "The government is on the com, more of them survived than we thought." By the end of the fifth day they were singing too.

I didn't really take it in. I was lost in my own world, my own story. And it felt so good to be telling it. I didn't miss a thing— every last event, every single emotion, every word and every action. I told it all to Hamilton. Only, I wasn't really talking to him. I was telling this story because I had to, because it was the only way to find myself again. My body was bent and broken out of shape, covered in a Kevlar-hard suit of nectar. And my mind too felt like it was entombed in darkness, buried deep beneath the residue of everything that had happened. But each word I spoke worked away at that filth, chipped off a little more of the nightmare. By telling my story, I was escaping from it. I knew that when I got to the end, I'd be me again.

It wasn't all easy. It didn't all want to be told. There were moments—when Donovan died, and Simon too; no, let's be honest, when I *killed* them—that I couldn't speak. The words locked themselves in my throat, they just wouldn't come. On both of those occasions Lucy climbed onto the bed with me, holding my head in her hands and stroking what was left of my hair. I don't think I'd have gotten through it without her.

Remembering the good times was almost as bad. It was heartbreaking. It still is. That's the one wish I have. Not that none of this ever happened, not that my parents were still alive, or my old friends from before the prison. It's that Donovan and Simon had made it, that they were here with me now. I miss them so much. I thought that maybe I'd still see them, the way I had on the island, just before we left, the way I'd seen D back when I was locked up in solitary. But they're gone. They're somewhere else now. I hope it's somewhere good.

God knows they deserve it.

THE ONLY THING that really stopped me talking during those five days was when the doctors came to check on me. They would barge in, shunting General Hamilton out of the way and pulling back the sheets to get a good look at me. I hated those moments, because I couldn't help but look too. My body was a wreck, every inch covered in scars and black scabs of nectar. My right arm was an obsidian blade that I didn't dare move for fear of skewering somebody in the small room. My left arm was distorted as well, the fingers too long, too many joints, like fat spider legs. They reminded me of the stranger's fingers, and every time they twitched I wanted to scream.

For the first few days those doctors didn't say much. They barely even spoke to me except to ask me to move this or flex that. They took photos and X-rays and scans with the big shiny machines they wheeled in and out. They drew on me with felt tips like they were playing join-the-dots between the various grotesque injuries. Some even peeled pieces of me away with glinting scalpels, making me think of Colonel Panettierre, the butcher that she was. But none of them had the same sickening glint of excitement in their eyes. They looked at me with compassion, and with gratitude too, I think.

It was on the fourth day, as I was telling Hamilton about the burger we'd eaten in the City after we'd escaped from the blacksuits, that one of the doctors came in and sat next to me on the bed. She was old and frail and her gray hair was pulled back into a ponytail, but her face was creased into a gentle smile. She told me her name was Lorna.

"We think we can fix you," she said. "Not everything, of course, but enough."

I already felt like I was lighter, like I was floating out of this bent and broken body, laughing so much that I thought they would have to pull me down from the ceiling.

"Thank you," I said. She took my hand, the one with fingers, and held it.

"You're welcome, Alex. It's the least we can do, all things considered. You saved us all."

AND MY STORY kept on coming, unstoppable. When I woke up on the fifth day, after another dreamless sleep, Hamilton was waiting, pacing back and forth and chewing his nails with impatience. Zee and Lucy had both been given a room, but they still hadn't left me. I think they wanted to wait until I had finished, until every last word had been spoken.

I think that final day was the easiest. I don't really remember talking; I was in a trance, the words burning up my throat by themselves. By the time I'd gotten to the bit where we reached the island, Zee and Lucy were sharing the sofa with half a dozen doctors and at least twice as many more were packed like sardines around the general. They all watched me with open mouths and eyes like pickled eggs, waiting to hear what came next. I ignored them, closing my eyes and reliving everything that had happened with Furnace and the stranger until the last of the story tumbled from my lips and I fell silent.

Only then did it hit me, the sheer impossibility of what had happened. In those few seconds after my final words I felt the darkness slough away, the golden light from outside seeping right into my core, so bright, so warm that I thought I might just melt.

The feeling was incredible, so overwhelming that I was crying before I even realized it—huge, heaving sobs that were half tears and half laughter.

By the time they had faded it was growing dark outside. Zee and Lucy lay either side of me on the bed, but other than them the room was empty.

"Sorry about that," I said sheepishly, wiping my cheeks against my shoulders. "Where'd everybody go?"

"Got embarrassed watching you blub like a baby," said Zee. Lucy reached over and slapped him on the belly.

"Shut it, Zee," she said, beaming. "They wanted to give you some space. You've been through a lot."

"Twice," I said. And it really did feel like I'd lived it all again. In telling my story I had locked myself back in the prison, in solitary, and I had fought on the streets and on the island. I'd felt every blow, every wound, for a second time. I'd experienced the terror and the hatred and the sadness and the desperation and the hope, *everything*, just the same as when it had actually happened. No wonder, then, that at the end of that fifth day I could barely keep my eyes open.

That night is the only one where I remember dreaming. I was inside Furnace Penitentiary, sitting on my bunk with Donovan and Zee and Toby. Simon and Lucy were there too, and Ozzie and Pete and Monty and Jimmy and Bodie and Sam the blacksuit and even the young Alfred Furnace.

"You don't just wanna go now?" Donovan asked, and I knew that we'd put all the gas-filled gloves in place, that we were ready to break out through the crack in the chipping-room floor. Even in my dream I knew that Donovan had asked me this before, for real, the night that he'd been captured by the blood watch. Back then I'd said no, and that decision had ultimately killed him. There was no way I was going to deny him his freedom again.

"All for one," I said.

"Oh God, not this Musketeer crap again," said Simon with a laugh. But it didn't stop him answering along with everybody else:

"And let's get the hell out of here."

The walls began to expand, the red rock peeling away, crumbling until it was no longer a cell but a tunnel. A raging river surged along it, carrying us upward through a mile of solid stone, pushing us out into the moonlight. We stood barefoot on the grass, the wind in our hair, the endless expanse of the stars overhead, and we howled with delight at our freedom.

I slept soundly inside that dream for nearly four days.

IT'S BEEN THREE MONTHS NOW, since the island. Three months since it ended.

It's a mess out there. Nobody is sure how many died, but the whispers that float on the wind say things like "two-thirds" and "tens of millions." Most of those were ordinary people torn apart by the unrelenting fury of the rats and the berserkers and the blacksuits. Others were kids who'd been bitten and infected with the nectar, who had turned. Some of these had been killed by the army, but the rest died at my hand. I had executed them without a trial, without giving them any hope of a cure. And on the bad days I see them everywhere, crowds of angry faces like the ones in the dream of the orchard. *My* dead. Their hate-filled stares are a promise that they will never let me rest.

I'm learning to deal with it, though, the guilt. What else can I do but say sorry? Take a life to save a life. It's not the first time I've done that.

The survivors are learning too, learning a new way of life. Everything has changed. No schools, no hospitals, no police, no television, no shops, no Internet or phones—but slowly, very slowly, we're healing ourselves. There was a radio broadcast from the government the other day, the first one since the war ended. Zee and Lucy and I huddled in my room and listened to them talk about recovery and strength and perseverance. They're doing another one next week and they want me to talk about what happened— not everything, just the good bits. To be honest I'm bricking myself more about speaking to the nation than I ever was fighting Furnace and his freaks.

But if there's one thing I know how to talk about, it's hope.

THERE ARE BAD DAYS, AND THERE ARE GOOD DAYS.

On the good days, I almost manage to forget. I can almost pretend that nothing ever happened.

On the bad days, I can't stop thinking about it.

I can't stop thinking about *him*. The stranger.

I'll never understand what he was. He was a crack in reality, a gaping hole in the world where something ancient and evil seeped through. *He's gone now,* I tell myself. *He's dead.* But on the bad days, the *really* bad days, I wonder if there are more like him, if maybe a different stranger will appear, will plunge his hands into the ground and pull out another piece of hell.

Hamilton tells me there are people studying the stranger's remains, and the nectar, trying to work out what he was. They're looking for the orchard too, the place where it all started. I don't think they'll ever find out the truth, though. There are some things that we just aren't supposed to know.

I'm grateful that I've had a few transfusions. The last trace of the stranger's blood, and the nectar that Zee and Lucy used to bring me back, has gone. What flows through my veins now is one hundred percent human.

Even so, when I have bad days the world feels like it's paper thin, that everything in it—the ground, the sky, the people—is just a brittle skin plastered over a seething, churning, howling mass of darkness. When I have bad days I see that skin peeling away and the madness pouring through like filthy water, drowning us all in chaos and pain. When I have bad days I feel that I'm the only one holding it back, that if I stop thinking about it for a second then everything will be lost. When I have bad days I lie awake and see the end of the world played out again and again and I scream into my pillow. When I have bad days I wonder how life can be worth living when things like the stranger exist, when everything you love can be cut away from you at any moment. What is there to fight for?

But there *is* something to fight for, to hang on for. There are the good days.

And there are more of them all the time.

My parents never showed up. I knew they wouldn't. I miss them, especially after what I found in my bedroom at home, the message they'd left me. One of these days I'll go back to my old house and sort through their stuff, but not yet. I'm not quite ready for that.

I do forgive them, though. I owe them that much.

Lucy was lucky, her mom made it. An army chopper brought her up to the mountains last month from where she'd been hiding—in a church crypt somewhere by the Lakes. I watched the reunion through the window in my room. The first half of it, anyway. My heart was so heavy I had to turn away after a minute or so, tears steaming up the glass. Not that I wasn't pleased for her, I mean I really was. I guess I just wanted to feel the same thing, you know, seeing someone I thought was dead stepping out of the helicopter and into my arms.

Zee's folks showed up about a week later. His dad's pretty badly hurt, lost a leg in the fighting, but they think he'll make it. I've seen less of Zee since they arrived, he spends his time down in the infirmary—no, the *hospital*, I never want to hear the word *infirmary* again—talking about the documentary he wants to make about it all. Zee and his bloody documentaries. He seems really happy, though. He deserves to be happy. More than anyone else Zee was the one who gave me the strength to carry on, who saved me. In truth it wasn't really me at all who ended the war. It was him.

Seeing Zee chatting away at a hundred miles per hour, hearing Lucy's laughter, it makes me think that one day, if we work hard enough at it, things might just be normal again.

They found Simon's parents too, although they didn't come up to the base. From what I heard they decided to stay put, helping to clear the streets and pull survivors out from under the rubble. I'm not sure what they were told about their son, but I hope they know that he was a hero, that without him the war, and the world, would be lost. I hope they understand that his sacrifice was worth it.

The army has been back to the island to look for his body, but they haven't discovered it. I'll go back too, one of these days. There's still a chance we might find him.

But I'm not quite ready for that just now either.

General Hamilton told me that when things were better they would hold a ceremony in honor of the fallen, and that Simon and

Donovan would have their place among the heroic dead. They're going to mark off a square mile of land in the City—an area of remembrance, they call it. Trees and lakes and stuff like that. They won't have much to put in either of their graves, but it feels good to know they won't be forgotten. It feels good to know I'll have a place to go to talk to them.

I hope for Donovan's sake they put a burger van there.

AND ME? They call me a hero too, wherever I go. They want to shake my hand—the one that still has fingers—they hug me and ask me to tell them my story.

I don't feel like a hero. What these people don't know is that I'm a killer, and a coward too. Like I told you, I'm not a good person. I did some awful things before Furnace, and I'm guilty of much, much worse since. But I'm starting to understand that you don't have to be perfect to be good. You can do bad things and still be a good person. And like I've said before, sometimes it's better to do bad things for the right reasons than good things for the wrong ones. Right?

So maybe I am just a little bit hero. I guess a little bit hero is enough. A little bit hero is all anyone really needs to be.

I've had my first surgery. I went in a couple of weeks ago and they took off my right arm, the blade. I can't tell you how good it feels not to have to drag that thing around with me—without nectar in my system it weighed a ton. It's a little weird having an arm that ends at my elbow, but they're going to make me a military-issue prosthetic, which is pretty cool.

"Man, I hope it has laser guns and stuff," Zee said when I told him. "Rockets, like Iron Man."

I'd be happy with enough false fingers to hold a cup of tea.

They asked me if I wanted my other hand taken off but I told them to leave it. As hideous as it is, and as many bad memories as it conjures, it's still pretty useful—especially for scratching my back.

And the best thing about all this? I can eat again. Not much, just baby food really, everything churned into mush. But they tell me that sooner or later I'll be able to tuck into burgers, mac and cheese, chocolate slices, and all the other stuff I thought I'd never get to taste again. Man, I cannot wait. I'm drooling now just thinking about it.

I go under the knife again next Thursday. They're going to try to strip out some of the muscle tissue that got stitched in back inside the prison. It'll be good not having to look like the Incredible Hulk anymore. They're working on a way to put my eyes back to normal as well. It's the one thing I want more than anything else, especially as without nectar they don't even work in the dark anymore. I can't wait to see the world the way it was meant to be seen, not in shades of molten gray. Silver is a bad, bad color for me now.

Piece by piece I'm getting myself back, I'm becoming Alex Sawyer. My body is getting repaired the same way my mind was when I told my story. I was never perfect, I was a hell of a long way from perfect, but it feels good to be me again. I think I can be happy with me now.

And I'm never going to be handsome, not with all the scars. But something good happened the other day. One of the volunteer nurses, her name is Mia and she's maybe a couple of years older than me, came to visit me when I was recovering from surgery. It wasn't even her shift, but she just sat on the edge of my bed and chatted—not about what had happened, but about TV and video games and how the things she missed most were soccer and

Monopoly and her DS. When she left she kissed me on the cheek, and I swear I can still feel her lips there.

Zee and Lucy didn't let up about it when I told them.

"Ooooo Alex and Mia sitting in a tree," Zee sang.

"Getting M-A-R-R-I-E-D," Lucy added.

"That's not what I was going to say," Zee said with a frown.

"I know, your mind is filthy."

"Nothing's gonna happen, guys," I said when they had stopped laughing. And I honestly don't think anything will. But it's nice—it is *so* nice—to know that I have a future, to know that there is somebody out there for me, to know that I don't have to be on my own. It makes the days burn just that little bit brighter.

SOMETIMES I GO for walks. We're in the middle of nowhere here, and I just like to get away, head up into the hills where the air is exactly like we dreamed it would be when we were back in the prison. I remember standing outside the boarded-up entrance to Room Two, feeling that breeze and thinking of mountains and realizing for the first time that there might be a way out. Hope. It is the most important thing in the world. I believe that now more than ever. Hope is what saved my life, hope is what gave me the courage and the strength to carry on. Hope—that unshakable, golden belief that things can get better—is why I'm here talking to you now. Without it, we are nothing.

I have hope. When I sit here on the roof of the world and look down I just know we're going to get through this. There has been so much death, yes, but with hope we can repair ourselves. With hope we can build a better world. How can you sit with the warm touch of the sun on your face and the gentle wind in your hair and not think that things will be okay?

Things *will* be okay.

Back in the prison I had that thread of silver light leading me to freedom. I still see it, you know, but now it seems to lead everywhere. I think that's a good omen. I can follow that thread to any place, and do anything. It makes me feel like I've still got a life to lead.

Oh, and I gave Lucy back her St. Christopher medallion this morning. I thought it was time.

So I guess this is where I leave you. And it's a good place. Zee found a soccer ball in one of the lockers down in the barracks and he's organized a match later on this afternoon. I don't know who's playing, a bunch of soldiers I think, and General Hamilton said he'd get involved if he could sneak out of the command center. Zee wants me at left back, and I know I'll be pretty crap—too big, too lopsided, only one arm—but I don't care. I just want to get out there and mess about with my mates. I have a feeling it will be the best damn kick-around I've ever had.

I've lost a lot. We all have. But I've still got so much to be grateful for. I've got Zee and Lucy. I've got my life, and I've got my future. I've got my heart and my soul and my smile too, and I want to use them all now to say something important, to say *thank you*. Because without you all I don't think I'd have been able to tell my story, let alone live it.

And I've got something else too. I've got my name. It's what kept me human. It's what kept me alive. *Just don't forget your name,* Monty told me, so long ago. And I didn't. I never lost that. Even now, on the bad days, it stops me falling back into the abyss.

So, from up here in the mountains, I say goodbye.

My name is Alex Sawyer.

And I am free.